George W. Hill

Memoir of Sir Brenton Halliburton

Late Chief Justice of the Province of Nova Scotia

George W. Hill

Memoir of Sir Brenton Halliburton
Late Chief Justice of the Province of Nova Scotia

ISBN/EAN: 9783337424145

Printed in Europe, USA, Canada, Australia, Japan

Cover: Foto ©Raphael Reischuk / pixelio.de

More available books at **www.hansebooks.com**

MEMOIR

OF

Sir Brenton Halliburton,

LATE CHIEF JUSTICE

OF THE

PROVINCE OF NOVA SCOTIA.

BY REV. G. W. HILL, M. A.

HALIFAX:
PRINTED BY JAMES BOWES & SONS.
1864.

PREFACE.

THE following Memoir was written several years ago, and was on the eve of being published by the committee of a public institution, in behalf of whose funds a lecture on the "Life and Times of the late Sir Brenton Hallibur-ton" had been delivered by the author. Circumstances delayed the publication of this little work, of which the lecture was an abridgement, and in the end caused it to be abandoned. The manuscript was thrown aside and almost forgotten, when the present publishers — the Messrs. Bowes—after the lapse of two or three years, made a proposal to publish it wholly at their own risk. Their request was acceded to, and the manuscript placed at once in their hands. The author does not wish to disarm criticism by apologies, based on want of time and press of other duties, knowing that however true, they are rarely believed.

With many acknowledged faults, the book is pre-sented to the public as a very small contribution to our provincial literature.

SIR BRENTON HALLIBURTON.

CHAPTER I.

THE history of Sir Brenton Halliburton claims the attention of his countrymen. The prominence of his position, the order of his talents, the excellence of his character, and the extraordinary length of his career as a public man, may give an interest to the following memoir of his busy and useful life, which extended over a period of more than fifty years. His early associates had passed away; of the long list of prominent men, with whom he had mingled in public and private, the name of not more than one still living could be pronounced when his life closed. They had dropped off one by one, while he continued to bear the burden of public affairs. As memory recalled the past, or he gazed upon the present, he stood almost alone—the last of that band with whom he had started on the race.

It cannot be an unprofitable labor to review the part which he took in the affairs of the Province, social, legal, ecclesiastical, or political; to bring back to memory the times in which he lived, and the great share which he had in moulding the most valuable institutions in the colony; to recall the graces and virtues which adorned him in private, and, above all, to observe those

1

principles of religion which increasing in strength with
his advancing years, rendered him in the evening of
life an eminent Christian. In him may be found an
encouraging example of what time well spent, and
talents faithfully occupied, will enable a man to accomplish even within the narrow limits of a colonial
sphere.

The late Chief Justice started upon life on the eve of
troublesome times. The year previous to that which
ushered in the Revolution of the American Colonies, by
the formal Declaration of Independence, was the year of
his birth, which took place in Newport, Rhode Island,
December 3rd, 1775. In his name, *Brenton Halliburton*,
we have those of the united families from which he
sprang. His mother's ancestors had settled in New
England more than two centuries ago,—some fourteen
years after the landing of the Pilgrim Fathers at
Plymouth.

William Brenton, the founder of the family, left
Hammersmith, England, and landed in Boston, in 1634.
He took with him a commission from Charles I., which
bore the date of 1633. It was termed a grant, and gave
him authority to take so many acres to a mile of all the
lands which he should survey in the New England
Colonies. His office gave him a position. Soon after
his arrival he was made a freeman of the colony of
Massachusetts, and the year after, representative or
deputy of the General Court of Boston. In 1638 he
removed with his wife to Newport, Rhode Island, and
took an active and prominent part in forming the
township. Eventually appointed Deputy Governor, and
then (1666) Governor of Rhode Island, he became more

and more settled in the country. In 1665 his son Jahleel was born, who was the father of that Jahleel Brenton who was the head of the family in the middle of the last century. In the lapse of a hundred years the successive generations had accumulated a valuable property, and an influential character. They stood high in the estimation of their fellow-countrymen.

In the year 1750 the town was visited by a frigate commanded by Lord Colville. On board, acting as surgeon of the ship, was Dr. John Halliburton; he was the son of a Presbyterian clergyman, who was in charge of the church at Haddington, Scotland. Whilst the ship rode at anchor in the harbour of Newport, this gentleman became acquainted with the family of the Hon. Jahleel Brenton, whose son was so well known in the British Navy as Admiral Sir J. Brenton. Doctor Halliburton became attached to one of Mr. Brenton's daughters, and, after completing his stipulated term of service as naval surgeon, returned to Rhode Island, and was married to Susannah Brenton, on the 4th of January, in the year 1767. This alliance caused him to adopt the colony of Rhode Island as his home, and follow his profession among his newly-found friends and acquaintances. As a physician he was skillful and attentive, and these qualifications soon produced their most favourable results; his practice was extensive, and he acquired property. Circumstances, however, made his residence in the Island of short duration. Whatever may have been his visions of a permanent abode, and the founding of a comfortable homestead for future generations, they were rudely dispelled by the difficulties which arose, between the Parent Kingdom and the Colonies. From all his earliest associations, the nature of his education, the society with which he had most mingled, the position which he had occupied as the servant of the Government, in one of his Majesty's ships of war — his feelings of loyalty were deeply rooted.

When those unhappy disputes arose, which eventually resulted in sundering from its centre so large a portion of the British empire, as now constitutes the American Republic, Dr. Halliburton, as was most natural, espoused and warmly supported the Royalist party. The consequence of his openly expressed opinions, and unconcealed acts, was soon felt. In the month of July, 1776, he was banished, together with several other loyalists, for refusing to subscribe the test ordered by an act of the Revolutionary Assembly. The place of his banishment was Hopkinton, and there he remained until September of that year, when it was voted that he and Dr. William Hunter, "have leave to return to Newport, until the October session of the Assembly." This privilege was granted, however, not out of consideration to themselves, but because their services as physicians were much needed by the inhabitants. The forbearance thus shown lasted but a short time, and he was finally compelled to sacrifice all the property which ability and application had enabled him to accumulate, and escape from the town. Nor was it, by any means, a trifling surrender which he was compelled to make. The loss incurred by firm adhesion to his political principles was very great. The abandonment of property, the resignation of a lucrative practice, the dismember-

ment of social ties and domestic arrangements, formed,
in their combination, a very serious sacrifice.

His residence was one of the most valuable in the
town of Newport, and furnished with the appliances of
comfort and convenience then at command. For this
reason, doubtless, it was selected as a suitable abode for
the Duc de Lauzun, who accompanied the French army
sent to assist the revolting colonists. Whilst this
nobleman was billeted upon Dr. Halliburton, he manifested great anxiety to relieve his host of all unnecessary trouble and inconvenience. The military necessity
was counterbalanced by sincerity of manner and kindliness of feeling. When, in deference to his rank, and
considerable thoughtfulness of his accustomed comforts
and habits at home, the best rooms in the house were offered to the Duc, for his use, he declined accepting them,
lest he should needlessly disturb the existing arrangements of the family. This freedom from selfishness,
and manifestation of respect, continued to the very close
of his compulsory visit ; and when the friendly, though
uninvited, guest parted with his hospitable entertainer,
he addressed him in these words : " I respect you, sir,
for your fidelity to your Sovereign, under the most
adverse circumstances."

The exciting events which transpired, and their constant discussion in his hearing, made an impression upon
his son Brenton, child as he was. That he understood or appreciated the loyal principles which animated his father, cannot be supposed ; but, placed in the
way of constantly hearing the opinions expressed re-
garding the disaffection which prevailed, it was not
unnatural that he should, at least, have learned to echo

the sentiments which he incessantly heard. His friends were on the king's side, and as his friends *must* be right, so of course was he. On one occasion, he independently gave vent to his patriotism in a manner so conspicuous and unmistakeable that he involved himself in trouble. At the time of the surrender of Lord Cornwallis at Yorktown, in 1781, Brenton Halliburton was about six years of age. He had heard the critical situation of the British army frequently discussed in his father's house, and well knew the anxiety which was felt. Coming out of school one day he heard the people calling through the streets, " Good news !" " Glorious news !" Asking the cause of the cry, he was informed of the surrender of the Royalist troops, whereupon he raised the counter cry, as he ran along, " Bad news !" " Bad news !" An old Quaker, who lived opposite to Dr. Halliburton, and bitterly disliked him for his loyalty, hearing these boyish shouts, bustled out and enquired who cried " Bad news ?" Seeing and hearing the little loyalist in the act, so exasperated were his feelings that he actually gave him in charge to some militia men who were passing at the time, and directed them to carry him to the jail. They obeyed orders, and led off their dangerous prisoner in triumph. He was not, however, long detained within the walls. Whatever fears may have been awakened in his mind as he passed through the prison gate, they were soon allayed. The jailor's wife happened to have been an old servant in his father's family, and entertained for them great respect. Instead, therefore, of consigning her young charge to cell and iron bolts, she patted his brow with motherly tenderness, gave him some tea and cake, and sent him home.

Although the Quaker had permitted his irritable temper to get the better of his judgment, and had acted with such petty and childish haste on this occasion, he liked the little boy for his lively disposition, and not unfrequently called him in from the street, and endeavoured to persuade him by a bribe of cake, to drink the President's health. Brenton, however, having obtained the cake, invariably changed the toast, " to the health of the king," and made the best of his way out, knowing that the old Quaker, though lame and unable to catch him, would, at least, throw his crutch at him.

The time when it became necessary for Dr. Halliburton to leave Newport, arrived, and though that crisis was reached by an interesting circumstance, it need not be related here, as it refers more to the father than the son. It became unsafe for the loyalist to remain any longer, and he, therefore, resolved to leave the township as soon as possible. Upon his return from Hopkinton he had been in the habit of following his profession, as usual, and making visits to his patients at some distance from his home; and, one night determined to take advantage of this self-allowed liberty.

In his latter days Sir Brenton could recall how his father had in the evening put on his hat and coat, to see, as he supposed, some sick patient on the main land; and yet, how strange and unaccountable to him, was the display of feeling manifested by his mother and the older members of the family upon bidding him "good night!" He had been accustomed to the Doctor's leaving the house, and he saw no reason for more than

ordinary regret. The morning, however, to some
extent, revealed the mystery: his father had not
returned.

That night Dr. Halliburton left the town in a barge
from Castle Hill, (the estate of the Hon. J. Brenton,)
and landed safely at Long Island, where the British
army was stationed. On his arrival at Head Quarters
he presented himself to Sir Henry Clinton, who (as
some small recognition of his services) offered him the
headship of the Naval Medical Department in that
city, or in Halifax, the capital of Nova Scotia. After
due deliberation he wisely chose the latter, no doubt
deeming it likely to be a more permanent office than
the other. He sailed in a British ship of war from
New York soon after, and arrived at his destination in
1782 ; his wife and family followed him in the succeeding spring. A brother of Mrs. Halliburton's undertook
the conducting of them to their new home. Having
obtained a white flag, he embarked with his sister and
all her children, consisting of John, who died in youth.
—Mary, who married Captain Beckwith,—Elizabeth,
who married Judge Stewart,—the youngest daughter,
who married Admiral Murray,—and Brenton, who was
the youngest of the family,—and their aunt, Mehitabel
Brenton. During their voyage to Halifax a high wind
compelled them to put into LaHave, a river flowing
through the south-western part of Nova Scotia. Mr.
Brenton went on shore, and took his little nephew with
him. On entering a small dwelling they found a sick
man, who was in great destitution : the sight affected
the child so much, that he pressed his uncle to give him
some assistance. "Brenton, my boy," said he, "I have

but little money with me, I want more myself." "Uncle," he replied, "you are well, and have good clothes, but look, just look at him." Of course his appeal succeeded. Thus early did that prominent feature of his character which distinguished him through a long life manifest its presence and its power. If we are able to follow him to the close of his career, we shall note its permanent continuance and its growth. This little incident occurring on his first touching the soil of Nova Scotia is a type of thousands during almost eighty successive years. "The blessing of the poor rested on him."

In addition to his official duties Dr. Halliburton entered into general practice, and became, as at his former place of residence, a leader in his profession, and an influential member of the community. Some five years after his settling in the town, he was elevated to a seat at the old Council Board: his appointment is dated June 7, 1787. It was in the same year, about two months after (August 11,) that his Majesty, by letters patent, created the Province of Nova Scotia an episcopal See, and appointed as the first Bishop of a British Colony the Reverend Charles Inglis, formerly Rector of Trinity Church, New York, with whose family that of Dr. Halliburton was to be one day closely connected.

It was about this time that the Doctor crossed the Atlantic for the purpose of bringing home his eldest son John, whom he had sent to Scotland for his education. As the means of instruction in the colony were exceedingly poor, he resolved that Brenton should accompany him, and occupy his brother's place. The first part of

2

this resolution he carried into effect; the last he did not. Brenton accompanied his father on the voyage, but when they reached Scotland, the Doctor drew a comparison between that country and England, as a place of education for his younger son, which resulted in favor of the latter. Accordingly, he took his child to England, and selected a school established at Enfield, and conducted by the Rev. Mr. Shaw. There Brenton remained until the death of his brother John, in 1791, when he was brought out to Halifax. During his childhood he was animated and cheerful. Several stories still current among his relatives indicate the buoyancy of his spirit, and the fertility of his imagination in devising for himself amusement. But such anecdotes might be related of thousands of children, and they are only valuable, not because peculiar to the talented, or sure prognostics of future pre-eminence, but simply because they prove the identity of the boy with the man, and, in this case, manifest that the liveliness of disposition and even cheerfulness of temperament which distinguished him through his long life, were innate.

Upon his arrival at Halifax he commenced the study of the Law, in the office of the Hon. James Stewart, who, at that time, was practising at the Bar, but was afterward elevated to the Bench. Whilst he was prosecuting those studies, for the pursuit of which the sequel of his life proved him to be so eminently qualified, a great national event took place, which suddenly brought them to a close.

On the 18th of April, 1793, Governor Wentworth, afterward preferred to the dignity of a Baronet of Nova Scotia, received instructions from Mr. Dundas (Secretary of State) that France had declared war against England the preceding 1st of February, and that his Excellency was authorised to raise a provincial corps, of which he should be Colonel. It was no very difficult task to evoke from the colonists—many of whom were loyalist refugees—a feeling of patriotism sufficiently strong to be manifested in military devotion. Nor was it entirely new to the inhabitants of the Province to be thus enrolled for active service. Some years before, on the outbreak of the revolutionary struggle in America, companies of infantry had been raised from the militia in various parts of the Province, and ordered to be in readiness for duty on the shortest notice. In accordance with this, on the 28th September, 1775, four hundred militia from Lunenburg, two companies from King's county, and one hundred Acadians from Clare and Yarmouth, received a command to march to Halifax, for its protection. So important was an organization of colonial troops then deemed, that a month afterward Lord Suffolk ordered the Governor to raise, in Nova Scotia and Newfoundland, a regiment of one thousand men, with the promise of the same pay and allowance as regulars, but no half-pay upon retirement or in case of being disbanded During the disturbed period which followed, until the peace of 1783, these soldiers were very useful, being constantly sent to such places as were exposed to the attacks of those roving plunderers whom war invariably produces, and who take advantage of excitement to prosecute their own designs.

When the war was brought to a termination the regiment dwindled down, and was finally disbanded. But the material, to a great extent was left. Moreover,

not only was the population vastly increased, but a
peculiar element was introduced in the twenty thousand refugees, from the revolted colonies, who had
found an asylum in the Province. When, therefore, the
order from England arrived, Governor Wentworth
easily resuscitated the military body, and formed them
into a regiment, which was called " The Nova Scotia
Provincials." Owing to its geographical position, and
the capaciousness of its harbour, Halifax became as in
the time of the old French war, the great station for
the British Army and Navy. The town was thronged
with officers; the public service was in the ascendant.
Then, as now, young men were attracted by the profession of arms: Mr. Halliburton was one of them. He
closed Blackstone, and girded on a sword. This step
was in harmony with his character. Animated and
fond of society, the Army presented a more fascinating
field than the Barrister's office. Upon receiving his
commission, which bears date A.D. 1793, he assumed
his new duties with the same cheerfulness and vivacity
that had characterised him as a child.

When H. R. H. Prince Edward arrived at Halifax, in
the month of October, 1795, from the West Indian
Islands, where he had served as Major-General, under
Sir Charles Grey, in the reduction of Martinique and
Guadaloupe, Mr. Halliburton was one of the subalterns
of the "guard of honor" that received him at the "king's
wharf." Sir J. Wentworth was then Governor of Nova
Scotia, and continued to hold that high office during the
whole period of time that the Prince remained in
Halifax. As Mr. Halliburton afterward became very
intimately connected in his military capacity with the
Prince, it may not be inappropriate to recall the fact that

his Royal Highness was in command of the 7th Royal
Fusileers, and Commander of the Forces in the Province
of Nova Scotia at the time of his arrival. This rank
and office he enjoyed until the month of October, 1793,
when he returned to England, in consequence of a fall
from his horse in Hollis street, at the north-west corner
of the present " Province Building," as he was going
home from a garrison Field-day. For the benefit of sur-
gical advice he went to England. This, however,
was not his final departure. On the 17th of May of
the following year, 1799, he was appointed successor to
General Prescott, as Commander-in-Chief of the Forces
in British North America, and, returning in July, assumed his duties. He remained in Halifax until a severe
bilious attack, followed by alarming symptoms, rendered
it necessary that he should obtain immediate leave of
absence, and return forthwith to England, which he did
in July, 1800. During this period, Mr. Halliburton
was associated with the Prince, at first as a subaltern in
the before-mentioned regiment, but afterward more intimately as a Lieutenant, and then as Captain in his own
7th Fusileers. It was but a short time after his Royal
Highness' arrival that he especially noticed the young
officer whom he often met in the society of the day,
and offered him a commission in his own regiment.
Mr. Halliburton gladly accepted the exchange, which
was effected in 1795. The Nova Scotia Provincials
were of modern date and stationary; the 7th Fusileers
were of old standing and moved about the world; he,
therefore, preferred the latter. His new position
brought him into a closer contact with the Prince,
whose esteem and confidence he secured by his promp-

titude, resolution, and even course of conduct. Important duties were assigned him, which were so well and faithfully discharged that he soon became a busy and prominent man in the garrison.

On one occasion the officer in charge of the men at York Redoubt—a fort erected upon a promontory which forms one side of the mouth of Halifax harbour—was unable to maintain discipline. Inattention to duty, together with all its concomitants, had so increased, that it became necessary to adopt strong means for putting a stop to these irregularities;—a resolute will, and wisdom to guide that will, were required. Mr. Halliburton was selected for the purpose. The officer in charge was recalled, and he assumed the duty;—a change took place at once. He began with a firm hand: he issued his orders, and saw that they were promptly obeyed: he kept the men employed, and left them no opportunity to spend their time in gambling and drunkenness. Notwithstanding a great love of society, and the ample opportunity of gratifying it by the fact of so many friends and relatives living in the town, not more than two miles distant, he stedfastly resisted all temptation to leave his post. Such conduct was not lost upon the strict disciplinarian in command.

During his stay at the Fort, that sad catastrophe occurred—the wreck of the ship of war " La Tribune." As this story has been sometimes erroneously narrated, it may be well to state the circumstances which actually occurred, as often related by Mr. Halliburton, who was an eye witness of much that transpired, and himself shared in the attempt to rescue the noble vessel from her perilous position. An interesting account of the har-

rowing event was published in the Halifax Journal, a
few days afterward, which, together with some statements not heretofore made public, will place the matter
in its true light. Early in the morning of November
23rd, 1787, Mr. Halliburton was standing on the top
of the abrupt elevation upon which the fort is built,
looking out eastwardly toward the sea. It was a dark
autumnal day: the sky was covered with dull grey
clouds, the water was black, except where crested by
the foam of a broken wave; the rising wind blew
freshly from the E. S. E. Above and beneath were the
signs of a coming storm. Gazing upon this cheerless
scene there also stood a sergeant of the company, named
McCormack (who for many years afterward served the
Government as porter at the Engineer yard.) He
addressed Mr. Halliburton, as they were both noticing
a ship bearing down upon them : " If that ship does not
alter her course, sir, she will be ashore within a
quarter of an hour." His prediction was too truly
fulfilled ; within five minutes she was stranded upon
Thrum Cap Shoals. It is generally supposed that the
wind at this time was blowing violently, and that a
heavy sea was raging. This, however, was not the case.
Every thing portended a storm ; but it had not yet
arisen. There was the prospect of a gloomy evening,
and still more of a tempestuous night; but the gale was
in its infancy. It was the self-satisfied opinion of " the
master" that caused the stranding of the ship. As early
as eight o'clock she had made the harbor, and running
before a fair wind was rapidly nearing it. The
Captain, whose name was Barker, had suggested to the
sailing master the propriety of engaging a harbour Pilot

to conduct the vessel in; but that officer replied that there was no necessity, as he knew the harbor well, and having once taken in a forty-four gun ship against a head wind, he would have no difficulty with a fair one. This "a fortiori" argument prevailed, and the captain —fully confiding in the master's skill and knowledge— went below to arrange some papers which he wished, upon landing, to hand to Admiral Murray, who was then in naval command of the station. Now it so occurred that there was a negro on board, named John Casey, who had formerly belonged to Halifax: to this man the master looked for assistance in piloting the vessel safely to her anchorage; but he misplaced his trust. About nine o'clock the ship approached so near Thrum Cap Shoals, that the master himself became alarmed and sent for Mr. Galvin, a naval officer holding the rank of "master's mate," who was simply a passenger on board the Tribune. This gentleman, who knew the harbor well, had offered to pilot the ship, but his offer had been refused; and, not being well, he had retired to the cabin. On being suddenly summoned, however, he hastened to the deck; his opinion was asked, but before he could form it, the noble ship was stranded on the shoal. Capt. Barker rushed from below, and in his impetuosity asked Mr. Galvin how he could look on and see the master run the ship ashore. This charge was easily refuted.

Signals of distress were immediately made to the military posts and the ships in harbour. Mr Halliburton, whose station was the nearest, instantly manned his boat and proceeded to the scene of the disaster. He reached the ship, and stepping on board, ordered

his men to row a short distance off until he was ready
to return, when he would make a signal for them.
Presenting himself to the captain, he inquired what aid
he could render. The captain replied, " The only thing
you can do is to signal to the Dockyard for help." As
promptly as he went, so promptly he returned. Indeed,
so anxious was he to telegraph the news that he did not
remain on board more than five minutes. Calling to his
boat's crew to come alongside, he embarked and crossed
to the fort. The signal staff instantly repeated the facts
and the danger. The message was acknowledged, and
every thing apparently put in fair train for meeting the
emergency. Boats were manned both at the Dockyard
and the Engineer Yard, while others proceeded from
several of the military posts near at hand. Whilst
these were making their way to the shoal, the crew
of the Tribune threw overboard all the guns except
one which was retained for making signals of distress.
In the hurry and confusion which prevailed, they took
the easiest method of lightening the ship, and unhappily threw their cannons over to leeward. As the
wind grew stronger, and the tide arose, the ill-fated
vessel surged and beat upon these iron breakers for
many an hour.

    While she lay rocking to and fro, the large and heavy
boats sent from the Dockyard were making slow
progress against the storm. One of them reached her,
under the guidance of Mr. Rockmer, who was a boatswain at the Naval Yard. Several of those dispatched
from the Engineer Yard, having two miles less distance
to row, had accomplished their aim a little earlier.
Beside these, one or two, as already mentioned, had put

off from the military posts in sight of the disaster.* In
these were three officers, two of whom, Lieutenants
North and Campbell, belonged to the 7th Royal
Fusileers; one, Lt. James, belonged to the Royal Nova
Scotia Regiment. While these gentlemen were on
board it grew dark.

Capt. Barker, fretting under the probable disgrace
which awaited him for the stranding of his ship, grew
imperious and dogmatical. It appears that a short time
previous, a brother officer in command of a ship, had
been cashiered for abandoning her when in a similar peril,
though he saved the lives of his crew and passengers;
and this, it is supposed, influenced Captain Barker
to refuse permission to any one on board to leave the
Tribune. Whether he gave the tyrannical order that
none should disembark is now doubtful; but circumstances seem to bear out the tradition. He probably
feared that all might take alarm if any were allowed to
go; and that his ship and his prospects would alike be
ruined.

Between five and six o'clock P. M. the rudder was
unshipped and lost. At half-past eight, the tide had
so risen that the Tribune began to heave violently, and
in half an hour she was afloat. But no sooner was she
fairly free from the shoals than they discovered seven
feet of water in the hold. She had been beaten in and
shattered by her incessant rolling upon the guns which
had been so injudiciously thrown to the leeward side.

---

*An officer of the Army, who probably had come by one of these earliest
arrivals, advised Captain Barker to land his men and save their lives. But
he replied, "Ah! sir, I wish that your coat was blue instead of red," as had
that been the case it would have justified him at the time in taking the
advice; though had he done so, and the ship floated, the step would have
been fatal to him professionally.

Captain Barker who had been very indignant that no officer of higher naval rank had been sent to his assistance than the boatswain, now took his advice, and let go the best bow anchor. This failed, however, to bring up the drifting ship. Two sails were hoisted, by which they endeavoured to steer, and the cable was cut. But the ship was unmanageable, and she drifted to the western shore—a fearful coast of precipitous rock— against which the surf broke with terrific fury. As a last hope, they let go the small anchor in thirteen fathoms water. It held; and then the mizen was cut away. It was now 10 o'clock, and, at this juncture Lieutenants North and Campbell left the ship in their own boat, one of them having jumped out of the port hole into the water. But Lt. James unhappily could not be found at the moment. They had not gone half an hour when the ship gave a sudden roll, and, then righting again in the twinkling of an eye, sunk with her masts erect. " Then rose from sea to sky the wild farewell." Two hundred and forty men, women, and children floated for a few seconds on the boiling waves; some were dashed to pieces against the rocks : forty reached the two remaining masts that still stood some feet above the water, and clung with the energy of despair to the yards and ropes.

As the night advanced, the main top gave way, and all who were trusting to it were once more plunged into the sea. Dunlop, one of the survivors, described their cries and shrill shrieks as sounding fearfully through the moan of wind and waves. On the last topmast remained by morning light only eight of the large number who had clung to it. The cries of these were heard all through

the night by watchers on the shore ; but so fearful and
terrific had the storm become that they were either cowed
or paralysed, and made no effort to rescue the unhappy
people.

Nor was it until eleven o'clock of the following morning, that a noble deed was performed by a mere child,
which, had it been done in a country better known,
would have ranked him among heroes. This boy, who
had scarce attained his 14th year, boldly pushed out in
a little skiff, and braving the howl of winds, and surging
of the ocean, made an effort to save the survivors who
still clung to the mast. Bravely he buffeted the adverse
tempest, as his little boat rose to sight, and then sank .
from view. He reached the ship, backed in his boat,
took in the two most exhausted, landed them safely on
shore amid the cheers of his friends, and took them to
his father's house, where they were kindly cared for.
Returning once more he plunged with his frail barque
into the still boisterous sea ; but his exhausted strength
was unequal to the task, and after contending with the
raging elements for some time, he was obliged to give up
the contest, and seek safety for himself on shore. His
humanity, however, struck a chord in other hearts.
Strong men were ashamed any longer to stand and look
idly on ; they manned their larger boats and succeeded
in bringing to shore the remaining six. Thus ended the
question of life and death—of two hundred and forty-six,
eleven only lived to tell and retell the tale of this awful
catastrophe.*

---

*The courageous boy was brought up to town, and placed as a midshipman
on board the Flagship ; but he was so unhappy, and felt so out of his element that he could not bear the change, and voluntarily returned to his
former mode of life.

It is no wonder that this anecdote made a deep and permanent impression upon the minds of the community. It was calculated to excite sympathy and grief in a colony just springing into life, where the inhabitants were few, and each event was noted and discussed for a longer time, and with more earnestness, than when such scenes are more frequently witnessed, and a new disaster drives the preceding out. Hence the loss of the Frigate "LaTribune" has been a landmark in the history of Halifax, and is still referred to by the older inhabitants as a well known epoch. Such an interest did it awaken in the mind of the Duke of Kent, that he caused a tombstone to be erected in the church-yard of St. Paul's, with the following epitaph, which may yet be read by the curious : "This stone, sacred to the memory of Lieutenant B. James, of his Majesty's Royal Nova Scotia Regiment who lost his life in the attempt to render assistance to the 'La Tribune' Frigate, on the 22d of November, 1797, aged 29 years—is placed as a testimony of the high sense entertained of his spirited and humane exertions on that melancholy occasion, by Lieutenant-General H. R. H. Prince Edward, commanding the District."

The Duke of Kent highly appreciated the services of Mr. Halliburton, who was always prepared to receive, and able to execute his orders ; and when, at one time, he was promoted to a company in the 81st Regt. the Prince found means of retaining him in his own regiment. His Royal Highness gave him a letter to the Commander-in-Chief, requesting that he might be reappointed to the Fusileers. While in England, whither he went to join his new regiment, Captain Halliburton himself effected an exchange with a brother officer, and in three months he was on his way back to Nova Scotia, and took his place as a Captain in the 7th. Among other services which he performed, was that of establishing a system of telegraphic communication between the Provinces of Nova Scotia and New Brunswick. In effecting this, it became necessary to cross the Bay of Fundy, from the North shore to Cape Chignecto. The means of transit was a small flat-bottomed boat; certainly, a dangerous enterprize, as those will testify who have ever sailed upon these waters, or know the strength of the tide. From the entrance of the Bay to the strait formed by Partridge Island and Blomidon, the velocity of the current increases in proportion as it advances, while within it the tide rises higher than in any part of America. From Cape Sable, the flood passes through the Seal Islands and Bald Tuskets towards the Northwest at the rate of two or three knots; obstructed by these islands, its rate is increased to four or five, then taking the course of the shore, it flows past Cape St. Mary's, and then towards Brier Island. As the Bay becomes narrower, this vast body of water rushes forward with fearful rapidity, and fills the Basin of Minas and Chignecto Channel with tremendous impetuosity. In the latter place, it must attain the speed of seven miles per hour, and in the spring tides rises as high as seventy feet.* On these uncertain and treacherous waters he launched in a frail and easily overturned boat. He safely, however, reached the Cape on which a few Highlanders resided, though at some distance from the shore. As he did not find his party he proposed to return immediately by the same way as he came; and having been informed that the navigation was dangerous, he intended

---

* Haliburton's Hist. of Nova Scotia.

to give the Cape a wide berth; but as he was stepping into the boat, in the early dawn of a May morning, one of the settlers, and it is said, almost the only one who could speak English, came to the shore, and warned him that his safety lay in keeping as close to the shore as possible, or the skiff would be overwhelmed by the furious tide. This was the very opposite of his purpose, and thus, in all human probability he was saved from a premature death. While on this telegraphic service, he suggested to General Smith, at that time Quarter Master General in Nova Scotia, that system of telegraphing which was subsequently adopted and for a long time used, though whether entirely from his suggestion or not cannot be said. Amongst the families with whom he most intimately mingled was that of a loyalist, who, like his own father, had been obliged to seek refuge in this colony. This was the Rt. Rev. Charles Inglis, already mentioned, who for many years had been Rector of Trinity Church, New York, and who, during the Revolutionary Wars, had not only witnessed, but himself been a prominent actor in some strange scenes. During a time of great excitement in New York the churchwardens requested him to omit the prayers for the King and Royal Family; but he told them that if they thought the times too disturbed to open the church, they had the power to close it, but if the church was opened, and he performed the duty, he would do it according to the prescribed form. Public service was held at the appointed time, and a party of soldiers were sent to the church during the time of divine service, with fixed bayonets, to intimidate him. Although he saw them in the church, and knew their purpose, he read on as usual the collects for the King and the Royal Family. What the precise orders of this band of soldiers were, it is impossible now to tell. If they were told to prevent his uttering these petitions at all hazards, they failed in the discharge of their duty; for they permitted the courageous man to go on in the performance of what he believed a conscientious obligation. He was a subject of the king, and for the king he prayed.

The families had much in common—similar sentiments, similar circumstances, and similar social training. It was not strange that with this family Capt. Halliburton should form a matrimonial alliance. In 1799 he married Margaret, the Bishop's eldest daughter. He went with his bride to live in Hollis street, and the following year his eldest daughter, now deceased, was born. After his marriage, he continued for various reasons but a short time in the Army. At the peace of Amiens he determined to resume his study of the Law, and resigned his commission; his " friend and patron," the Duke of Kent, had left Halifax on the 30th of July, 1800. Thus ends his military history. Nor did he in old age forget his early profession, nor the friends of his youth, as may be seen from the following lines taken from a poem written by him when fourscore years of age, and printed for circulation among his private friends :—

> " Daughter of Edward ! such the warm desire
> Of one who knew and loved thy Royal Sire !
> What though his martial discipline was stern,
> Himself submitted to each rule in turn.
> But, when from his stern duties he sought rest,
> No kinder heart e'er beat in human breast :
> No tale of woe was poured in Edward's ear,
> But ever found a ready listener there :
> Witness, when down his manly cheek the tear

Flowed freely, Thomas, on thy mournful bier ;
Witness, when that sad catalogue of grief,
Which overpowered thee, Goldsmith, sought relief—
How readily he did relief extend,
And to thy dying hour remain thy friend.
Long were the tale to tell of all the good,
Which from that royal hand so freely flowed.
Tho' fourscore years have cooled my youthful blood.
Thanks to the gracious Giver of all good,
I still, in age, His mercies can enjoy,—
Still in His service would my hours employ ;
With friends, and family, and with plenty blest,
And waiting calmly, till I sink to rest
In those kind arms, where sinners seek repose,
When all life's anxious cares in death shall close.
Oft on my early years does memory dwell,
Reminding me of one I loved so well:
Thy faults, thy virtues, rising to my mind,
Nor to the one, nor to the other, blind ;
I bring this tribute from the shrine of truth,
To thee, the friend and patron of my youth !"
　3

CHAPTER II.

HALIFAX has been in existence but little more than a hundred years. During that period of time it has undergone a great change; it has risen from a small and dependent settlement, to the size and rank of a city of no mean importance. It has developed from a rude village, defended by palisades and block-houses, into a well-planned town, adorned with many public and private structures of admirable design and excellent workmanship, and protected from assault by numerous towers and forts. It has expanded from the contracted encampment of a few thousand settlers, governed by laws imposed upon them from abroad, and sustained by provisions bestowed as a gratuity, into a city spreading over a wide area, containing a large and intelligent population, framing its own code of regulations; and many of its inhabitants possessing much wealth, and conducting commercial business with almost every part of the world. In some respects the progress has been slow and inconsiderable, in others, rapid and great. Compared with many cities in the Western States of America the capital of Nova Scotia may boast of its antiquity, but should be silent on the subject of its growth. Within the compass of ten or twenty years from the felling of the first tree on a chosen site, towns have sprung up in the forests of the corn-

growing country of the far west, and on the borders
of the great lakes, which have quickly rivalled and
then surpassed in extent, in magnificence, in riches, and
in traffic the old cities of the Union, and the leading
cities of the British North American Colonies.

Many circumstances have contributed to this magic
change. An enormous population, growing daily by
natural increase, and continually augmented by almost
ceaseless streams of immigration—flowing chiefly from
Ireland and Germany—have crowded the sea-ports,
towns and villages of the Eastern States, and constantly
pressed out the surplus from their confines. Those
who have thus been driven away from overthronged
places, being partly natives and partly immigrants,
have combined the necessary elements of knowledge of
the country, and a willingness to labor, and so have
soon formed homes in the wilderness. The soil has
speedily repaid them for their venture and their toil,
and by their skill and perseverance its riches have
transformed themselves into dwellings, warehouses, and
factories.

The rise and progress of the metropolis of the small
Province of Nova Scotia, has been as nothing compared
with these. It has possessed certain advantages which
ought to have resulted in a marked material progress.
It is situated most favourably for expansion; having an
extensive area for building, with miles of water lots for
wharves and docks, surrounding it; and thus is fitted for
the conduct of an unlimited business with the interior
of a mighty continent, a large portion of which belongs
to the same country as the Province itself, acknowledges
the same sovereign as its Head, the same common law as

its rule, and is identified with it in all its great
interests.   With a harbour sufficiently capacious for the
navies of the world, accessible at all seasons of the year,
and shut in from the storms that may rage in the
Atlantic by an island several miles in length, lying
across its mouth; nearer to the British isles than any
other possession of the crown in America, except Newfoundland; and connected with New Brunswick and
the Canadas by a broad isthmus for its highway, Halifax
enjoys some at least of those inherent advantages which
contribute towards the formation of large and influential
cities in a new country.   A result equal to these
advantages, however, has not been attained: it has
reached no such ambitious summit as to its extent or its
dignity.

The confusion which has existed in the minds of the
inhabitants of Great Britain and Ireland, in reference to
the Province of Nova Scotia, by their commingling it
with Canada; the general impression—early made and
difficult to efface—that the climate is severe, and the
soil sterile; the culpable neglect of those whose duty it
was to make efforts for creating a flow of immigration,
such as imparting information to those in the old
world, and providing for such instruction to intending
purchasers and settlers of land on the moment of their
arrival, as would make their design easy of accomplish-
ment; the too great want of self-dependence on the
part of Halifax from its very inception; its too constant
reliance upon the mother country for support of every
kind; the fact of its being looked upon by the world
simply as a garrison town, and a station for the West
Indian fleet: these causes, combined with the effect

produced by the presence and expenditure of a large
army and navy, who kept up a circulation of money
just sufficient to support a limited business, and unhappily just sufficient also to prevent a spirit of enterprise,
have no doubt exercised a great influence in retarding
the growth of the city.

Into a proof of these statements it is not my intention
to enter. But having freely admitted that in comparison
with some cities and in view of the advantageous position which Halifax geographically holds, it has not
advanced with equal pace, it will be my purpose, in this
chapter, to show that the town has made substantial
progress—perhaps slow, but certainly sure.

That I may show of what material the community
was formed, into which the subject of this memoir was
thrown, and what were the influences which moulded it,
I shall attempt to draw a picture of Halifax as it was
during the first fifty years of its existence,—that is, from
its settlement under the Honorable Edward Cornwallis.
A. D. 1749, until A. D. 1800. This period will comprise nearly half of its history, and enable the reader
who is familiar with the present aspect and affairs of the
city, to draw a contrast for himself between Halifax as
it then was and as it is to-day. So marked, indeed, is
the change wrought in the town, both material and
moral, in the size, in the public buildings, the private
dwellings, the ships, the warehouses, the streets, the
vehicles, the equipages, the furniture, the manners, the
customs, the dress, the conversation, the business, and
the laws, that if one of the old habitues of the town in
those early days could return, he would become bewil-

dered with the new state of society and the altered
scenes, and be scarce able to recognize the neighborhood
in which once he lived.   A knowledge of the real elements of daily life, the social customs, the domestic
habits, and the material stage on which different parts
in the drama were played, will give us a clearer insight
into the history of the past, than a bare acquaintance
with the dates of certain events, and the precise periods
of the occurrence of political changes.   While these
epochs form the basis of all history, and the results arising from them for good or evil to a community, constitute the true ground-work for philosophical enquiry,
argument, and conclusion, they do not afford the necessary matter for becoming accurately acquainted with the
real condition of society in its personal relations and in
the elements most influential in creating and moulding
thought and habits.   A man who would rightly estimate
the progress of Halifax should certainly be informed as
to its condition in all those particulars named above:
they are essential to his forming a correct judgment.

A walk through Granville street, Hollis street, Bar-
rington, Brunswick, or Water streets, as they now are,
would astonish a townsman of the times of Governors
Lawrence, Hopson, and Belcher.   He would look in
vain for the house in which the representative of royalty
held his mimic court, the old balconied market, in
which he was wont to spend his afternoon of a sunny day
in spring, or of a rainy day in summer, and those re-
nowned hotels, at which gathered the officers of the
army and navy, so many of them in those stirring times
on field and flood distinguished by their valor and by

their noble descent, where Loudon and Colville, where Amherst and Wolfe dined and supped. These have long since fallen to decay and been replaced by other and better buildings.

In those days of old, the limits of the town were narrow. At first, but not for long, the harbor on the east, Salter street on the south, Jacob street on the north, and the citadel on the west, were the original boundaries; the whole being enclosed with a strong palisade of pickets, with block houses, or forts, built of hewn logs, placed at intervals along the different lines.* When the Indians, against whose midnight attacks it was found necessary to erect these barricades, forbore, by means of treaties and diminishing numbers, to assault the town, these limits were not so strictly observed, and the palisades were allowed to fall gradually into decay or to be removed. They appear, however, to have been still standing in 1760, inasmuch as a record remains of the ceremonial of proclaiming King George III., in the month of December, which states that it was performed, among other places, at the north and south gates. All immediately outside of these limits was considered as forming the suburbs of the town. The Dockyard, which was first established in 1758, extended and improved in 1769, and its present wall built, as the inscription over the gate informs the passing public, in 1770, was then considered as an establishment quite unconnected with, and at some distance from, Halifax

---

* I may say, once for all, that I am indebted to a valuable and most interesting pamphlet, published by T. B. Akins, Esq., for a very great part of the information contained in this sketch, especially in reference to the streets and public buildings. Much of the other matter has been gained from various sources, such as papers, almanacks, and letters. But without the aid of the above-named pamphlet, the sketch could not have been drawn

proper. Certain sailors, for instance, who met with a
serious accident on board of one of his Majesty's ships,
are spoken of in the newspapers of the day as "being
brought up to the town from the Naval Yard."

The small German settlement, originally composed of
some fifteen families of Protestant Germans from the
Palatinate, who preferred remaining in Halifax to ac-
companying their fellow emigrants to Merliguesh Bay,
the present Lunenburg, had fixed their residence in the
north suburbs, which had been laid out by the Government Surveyor and Engineer. So completely detached
was this little settlement from the town, both by position
and nationality, that a place of worship was erected in
1761 for the use of the German families, and a town lot,
on which originally stood one of the block houses,
granted as the site for the parsonage of the German
pastor. Two or three years afterwards the inhabitants
applied to the Governor and Council to officially name
their town Gottingen; the request was acceeded to; but
though used for a few years as the designation of the
whole district, it eventually was confined to one of the
streets running through it; which, within the memory
of persons living but a few years ago, had only one
house on its long line. In true devotion to the memory
of fatherland, Brunswick was applied to another street,
which early became the main thoroughfare, and most
thickly built portion of this suburb, where some of the
old houses with single stories and roofs of double pitch,
still stand. The remaining street, beside that which ran
along the water's edge, seems to have been named in
honor of an early settler, whose death and burial, which
occurred in 1779, is mentioned as having taken place in

this separated district. " On Friday last, died L. Lock-
man, Esq., 73, and his remains are (sic) on Thursday
evening last interred in the German church at Gottingen,
near this town." There was a long space between this
German town and Halifax, and between the Dockyard
and Halifax, so that the act of passing from either one of
these to the town proper, was viewed as quite a matter
of business. The intermediate road lay between fields,
gardens, trees, and a few isolated houses, with their
gables towards the streets, if going from the town to
Gottingen ; or between these on the one side and the
water on the other, if going to the Naval Yard.

The streets of the town continued for a long time in a
very rough condition, and not unfrequently so filled with
stumps of trees and jutting rocks, as to render the passage of carts and carriages an intricate and dangerous
task. Though this was the case, there were indications
of progress connected with these highways, for as early
as 1768 to 1777 the Government went to the expense of
lighting the town by placing lamp-posts at all the principal corners. An irregular street ran along the water
side, following the windings of the shore ; on the upper
or town side were built shops and stores, while the
owners of the water-lots built wharves and slips. Here
was transacted the mercantile business ; the name, however, was not Water street, as now, but all the advertisements mentioned the various sales as taking place on
" the Beach." This road, as it may be termed, beginning at the Dockyard, ran in a southerly direction along
the water side, through the Royal Engineer Yard, until it
reached Point Pleasant, the site first chosen by Governor
Cornwallis on which to build the town, but abandoned

in consequence of the shoal water in its immediate front. Traces of this way are even yet discernible in spots a little to the north and south of Steele's Pond. It early became a favorite walk for ladies and gentlemen, who had leisure to spend the afternoon in seeking health or amusement, and was kept in such excellent condition that Governor Fanning found it not inconvenient to make his residence in a house just below the " Tower." Another road, leading to the northern suburbs, also became a fashionable resort. This was made under the auspices of the Governor, Sir Andrew Snape Hammond, and formed part of the highway to Windsor. The fact of his residing on the road, in a house erected on the western boundary of the Governor's Farm, (near the head of the present road leading from the Richmond Railway station,) tended greatly towards rendering it a favorite walk. Near his Excellency's dwelling stood another, which became famed for breakfasts and suppers during the summer season. Not only did gentlemen walk out in the afternoon and order an early dinner, but it was a common, and one of the most popular modes of spending a holiday, for ladies and gentlemen to form a party, and start early in the morning that they might breakfast, dine, and sup, at one or other of the " tea-houses," as they were called, which were kept in various parts of the peninsula.

For lack of other amusements, a very rational and useful one was early substituted : while it provided recreation, it was a practical and substantial benefit. Public gardens were established and largely patronized. Not far distant from the site of the present Horticultural Society's Garden, and hard by the Artillery Park, was one containing a pavilion, in which grew a great variety of fruit trees and shrubs. Another was situated near the old burial-ground of St. Paul's or the English churchyard, as it was sometimes termed; while a third was kept by a provincial gardener, to whom the House of Assembly voted a salary. If the romantic pictures drawn by De Mont and Poutrincourt of the fertility of the soil and genial nature of the climate—who wrote of grapes growing on the banks of rivers, and dining in the cornfields under the warm rays of the sun in the month of January—were found by the horticulturists to be fiction rather than fact, they, at least, contributed to the welfare of the community, and as they cultivated their gardens, also cultivated a taste for a useful occupation in a young settlement.

Within the town, the Parade was a great land-mark, and although no buildings were erected upon it, save the Artillery Barrack, the common phraseology of the day, when speaking of a shop or dwelling situated at either side of it, was that such were " on the Parade." The names of the various streets were seldom used for many years, and the habit of designating a place of business or a private residence by its proximity to well-known public places, almost entirely obtained.

Immediately around the town were numerous fields, gardens and swamps. On the southern side of Spring Garden Road, leading to the North-West Arm, were pasture lands and meadows, which in the spring formed good shooting ground, where many a plover and snipe were bagged; and in the autumn, filling by the rain, became a sheet of water, which, a little later, turned into skating ponds for the boys. The Common was likewise a

marshy place, to which birds and sportsmen betook
themselves in the season; and as here and there were
spots on which alder bushes and low shrubs grew, it
was not unusual for wood-cock to find a cover. The
Eastern Shore of the North-West Arm was owned by
a few individuals, who took but little interest in their
property, and deemed it an unprofitable speculation to
attempt converting the many acres of which for trifling
sums they became possessed, into farms. Towards the
mouth of these beautiful waters, and about midway between it and their head, were several residences, around
which the land was cultivated, but the remainder stood
for a long period of time as it stood when the first fleet
arrived in the bay.

On either side of many of the streets the trees had
been permitted to stand, or, if removed, others were
planted in their place. This was particularly the case
in the southern portion of the town, adding very much
to its appearance, when seen from the water, or looked
upon from the citadel, and affording comfort to the inhabitants, by sheltering them from the Sun in summer,
and breaking the force of the winds in autumn. Here I
cannot forbear quoting the impression made upon a re-
fugee from Kennebec, the Reverend Jacob Bailey, who
arrived in Halifax in the summer of 1779, and was
kindly taken care of by Dr. Breynton, the Rector of St.
Paul's. " The house," says Mr. Bailey in his journal,
"which the Doctor had procured, belonged to Mr.
Justice Wenman ,keeper of the Orphan house, and stood
on the east side of Pleasant street, which runs straight
from the Grand Parade, near the church, to the water,
and is almost a mile in length. This is the most ele-

gant street in the town, and is much frequented by
gentlemen and ladies for an evening walk in fine weather.
After tea we perceive one gay company after another,
in perpetual succession, dressed in their finest apparel,
which affords a fine and cheerful appearance. At the
gate we have an extensive prospect of the harbor and
the adjacent ocean, which is closed by the southern hori-
zon, and can discover every sail coming from the westward the moment it proceeds round Chebucto Head.
To the northward, the street extends, adorned with the
Grand Provo, Assembly House, Church, and private
buildings, to a vast distance, and is limited by a cross
street, three quarters of a mile from hence. To the
west arise beautiful ranges of green fields, interspersed
with several remarkable structures, as Fort Massey, the
Governor's Summer House, the Work House: and beyond them the Citadel Hill, with all its fortifications
and warlike apparatus, towers aloft in majestic grandeur,
and overlooks both the town and the adjacent country.
We enter through a spacious gate into a decent yard,
with an avenue to the house, bounded on each side by a
little grove of English hawthorns, in this season, in all
their blooming glory. The house consisted of a convenient kitchen, a tight cellar, a chamber, and an elegant
parlor, papered, and containing two closets. Before the
door was a little porch with a seat. From the two
eastern windows we had a most charming prospect of
Mr. Newman's garden, in which were planted such a
profusion of willows, hawthorns, and fruit trees of
various kinds, that they formed a perfect wilderness,
extremely pleasant to the sight and grateful to the smell.
And indeed, when we looked out of these windows, we

rather fancied ourselves in the midst of a wooded
country than in the midst of a populous town." Such
were the impressions made upon the mind of this loyalist, who had reached Halifax under the most adverse
circumstances, and though his idea of the vast extent of
the town, and the grandeur of the edifices, provokes a
smile, it conveys to us a picture of what he actually saw.

The public buildings were numerous, as might be
expected in a town commenced and chiefly sustained by
Government.   Amongst the first erected, besides those
alluded to, were the churches—St. Paul's, for the
United Church of England and Ireland ; St. Matthew's
for the Protestant Dissenting congregation.   The site
for St. Paul's was selected immediately after the arrival
of the first settlers, and as there was not a sufficient
number of skilled artisans among them to undertake so
large a work, orders were dispatched to Boston for the
frame and materials necessary to a building of the proposed size.   In the course of a short time these were
brought to Halifax, and the erection of St. Paul's proceeded forthwith.   On the 2d September, 1750, the
sacred structure was opened for public worship, and
though not completely finished, was viewed with great
admiration by the town.   The most flourishing accounts
as to its size, appearance, and substantial workmanship,
were sent to England by those most interested in it.
The population consisting for the most part of members
or adherents of the Church of England, there was no
jealousy excited when the House of Assembly, a few
years afterward, voted a sum of £1200 sterling towards
finishing the Parish church, and the Members joined in a
subscription towards a fund for the purchase of an organ ;

indeed it was the custom, during the greater part of the half-century, for the House of Assembly, in its official capacity, annually to attend divine service in St. Paul's, and hear a sermon from one of the clergy. The organ was not purchased at once, but while waiting for either an increase to the sum collected, or for some good opportunity to send to England for it, a Spanish ship, on her way to South America, was brought into harbor as a prize. On board, amongst many other valuable articles, was an organ, with a solid mahogany frame, of plain, but chaste design, on its way to a Roman Catholic chapel. The organ was sold, and the churchwardens of St. Paul's became its purchasers. The instrument was many years after replaced by another, but the case still stands un-changed.

Owing to many circumstances, but chiefly to the natural ascendancy of the Established Church, St. Paul's became and continued for fifty years to be the centre of much of the history of Halifax. Not only did the House of Assembly make it their yearly resort with much ceremonial, but all the magnates of the land, and those distinguished military and naval men, who so often were their guests, were wont to assemble within its walls on different state occasions. It was once the scene of a somewhat strange but important transaction between the native Indian tribe and the new possessors of the land. In a political point of view it was a matter of much moment, occurring at a time when the Micmacs were really formidable foes, difficult as it may be for us who are acquainted with their miserable remnant, to imagine them ever to have been such. They had resolved to be at peace with England, and in order to testify their

sincerity, they determined to invest their act of entering into treaty, with the sanctity of religion. For this
purpose they met in Halifax, and after due arrange-
ment, they marched up in a body to St. Paul's, in order
that they might publicly proclaim before God and man.
their firm resolve to live and die as British subjects.
The representative of the Sovereign was in his accustomed place, the commanding officers of the army and
fleet were present, the members of Government and the
principal gentlemen of the town surrounded them, and
the inhabitants, of all ranks and ages crowded the
church. At the hour appointed for divine service, the
Indians rose from their seats and sung an anthem in
their own wild and plaintive strains. When the low
wail of the chant had died away, an influential chief
stepped forward, and as the representative of that once
dreaded people, he knelt down, and in the Micmac
dialect, prayed for a blessing on his Majesty King
George III., and for prosperity to his Majesty's Province. This prayer concluded, he arose, and Rev. Mr.
Wood, who with praiseworthy zeal had mastered their
language, interpreted it to the Governor in the hearing
of all the congregation. The solemn contract thus made
in the house of God, was then officially acknowledged
by his Excellency turning and bowing to the whole tribe
of Indians. Divine service, in English, then commenced, and at its conclusion, the Indians closed the worship by again singing in their own language another
anthem.

Upon the death of any leading personage, whether
civil, military, or naval, St. Paul's became the scene on
which great interest was centred, for the funeral obse-

quies of such were conducted with great pomp and ceremonial. When that popular and respected man, Governor
Lawrence died, the whole town assembled to attend his
funeral, and witness the sepulture in the vault beneath
the church; and when, still later, one of his successors,
Governor Parr died, the church was once more thronged
to witness the burial of the chief personage in the town.
During those troublous times which elapsed between the
death of these men in high places, St. Paul's was frequently the centre of attraction for all the populace.
Many an able officer of the army and navy was brought
to Halifax to die of his wounds, or already killed, to be
interred with the burial-rites of the Church. Their
names and heroic deeds are graven with the sculptor's
chisel on their tomb-stones. Of several, the record of
their lives and actions may be read on the mural tablets
which adorn the walls of the sacred edifice; of others,
there remain memorials in the escutcheons which hang
upon the pilasters. One of these was placed in the gallery
as the temporary remembrancer of the Baron de Seiltz,
the last of his line, who, according to an ancient feudal
custom of Germany, when the honors and titles of a
house become extinct, was buried with all his parapher-
nalia, in full uniform, and with his weapons beside him.
Presiding over the parish and church for well nigh forty
years, was a man of ability, indomitable energy, and the
most kindly, generous heart. This was the venerable
Dr. Breynton, to whom Halifax was most deeply
indebted, not only for the anxious care with which he
attended to his charge in spiritual things, but for his
wisdom, prudence, and humanity during the trying
scenes incident upon the American Revolution, when the

4

town was taxed to its utmost power by the influx of the
poor and distressed who found refuge among its loyal
people.

In December of the year 1749, a lot was granted by
Governor Cornwallis for the site of a church to the
" Protestant Dissenting Congregation." The frame of
the building was probably imported from Boston for the
same reasons as that of St. Paul's. Like the latter, it
was soon erected, and when finished, was called " Mather church;" no doubt, in compliment to the distinguished divine, Cotton Mather; for a large proportion
of the congregation were originally composed of settlers
from New England. The name " Saint Matthew,"
appears to be a corruption of the word Mather, and to
have been insensibly introduced : the Scotch prefixing
the title Saint, according to the custom which has prevailed from time immemorial in the old country. The
name of the first minister was Aaron Cleaveland, as
appears from inscriptions in the books of the congrega-
tional library ; but the early church records were
destroyed by a fire, and the members of the church are
thus left without the information which now would be
full of interest.

In the middle of the square now occupied by the
Province Building, stood the first Government House,
which was put up immediately upon the town being laid
out. Like the churches, so the frame and materials of
this were brought from Boston; but the work of completing it was far sooner effected; for in the autumn the
Governor took up his residence in it, and on the 14th of
October he held a Council there. It is described " as a
low building of one story, surrounded by hogsheads of

gravel and sand, on which small pieces of ordnance were mounted for its defence." As the house was small and inconvenient, it was removed by Governor Lawrence eight years after, who replaced it by a more spacious and convenient residence ; and this continued to be the Government House until the administration of that able man, Sir George Prevost, who caused it to be taken away, and the present noble building erected in its stead, while at the same time he settled on a new site for Government House, and not long afterward that now in use was built.

The House of Assembly, first convened by Governor Lawrence, and its business commenced by an opening speech on the 2d October, 1758, held its sittings for some time in a house erected at a very early period, and now used and known as the "Halifax Grammar School." As public property, this was one of the best known houses in Halifax, for it did duty for various official bodies, being at one time used as a Court House, at another, as a Guard House. Its position becoming familiar to the inhabitants in consequence of the various uses to which it was put, it was one of the grand land-marks or sign-posts by which inquirers were directed in their search for shops or dwellings.

One of the most noted buildings was the old Market House, which occupied the site of the present Police Establishment. A piazza or balcony ran along its front, and here gentlemen of all professions and business, officials and strangers, loiterers and newsmongers, were accustomed to assemble, for an hour or two of the day, to promenade, to hear and tell the news, chiefly to talk over the last information received from England. The

old French war, the American Revolution, and the great
Revolution of '89, furnished topics of discussion always
new and always stirring, and as may be gathered alike
from papers, letters, and journals, these were the subjects which most occupied the thoughts and absorbed
the conversation of those who thought and talked on any
thing beyond their personal wants.

Next in importance came the famous hotels ; and first
in order ranked " The Great Pontac." This was a
large building of three stories in height, and in its zenith
kept by a noted host, whose name was Willis. A creek
ran up from the harbor close to the hotel, and as there
were neither houses nor stores on the lower side of the
irregular and rough street which skirted the beach, a fine
view of the harbor was seen from the windows. Here
were held, on a grand scale, the assemblies, balls, and all
species of public entertainment. At several different
periods of time, varying in length, the town was thronged with officers of the army and navy. The loyal
colonists treated them with great hospitality, and they,
in turn, marked their appreciation of the attention by
entertaining them again with the most sumptuous din-
ners and expensive suppers. Such were the frequency
and extent of these hospitalities, that the host of the
" Great Pontac" was glad to receive assistance in his
culinary department, from the cooks of the ships of war,
and in his waiting department, from the officers' servants. The smoking dishes were brought in boats,
rowed by strong crews, while other sailors, dressed in
white, stood ranged along the creek to receive the cooked
meats, and carry them with all speed to the great
dining room. All through the summer season of many

years there was no busier scene in Halifax than the neighborhood of this once famous hotel. The constant presence of a large number of the army and navy, created this gaiety: and no sooner had one body of troops, and one portion of the fleet, received and returned hospitalities, than others arrived, and the same series of expensive receptions and returns were passed through again.

Some eight years after the settlement was commenced, Lord Howe arrived at Halifax with a fleet and army, on their way to make an attack on Louisburg. While his fleet rode at anchor in the harbor, Lord Loudon joined him, having under his command six thousand Provincial soldiers from New York. The attempt proving unsuccessful, some of the ships of war and some of the transports returned to Halifax for winter quarters, while the others sailed for England. Scarcely had the town settled into repose, when, early in the following spring, General Amherst arrived, with not less than twelve thousand men, partly provincials, enlisted in the New England States, and partly regulars, and in a few days more, the signal was made for the fleet under Admiral Boscawen. The whole armament, consisting of one hundred and fifty-seven sail, and fourteen thousand men, did not leave Halifax until near the end of the month of May. Amongst those who had enjoyed the hospitable attentions of the town and sailed for the siege, was that illustrious man, General Wolfe. Of him and General Amherst, Lieutenant Green, who was present at the capture of Louisburg, and was afterward the first Sheriff of Halifax, was wont to relate the anecdote so creditable to the bravery of Wolfe, and yet more creditable to the

humanity of Amherst: "Give me fifteen hundred men,
General," said Wolfe, "and I will take the place in two
weeks, with the loss of not over three hundred."
"Thank you, sir," was the reply, "I will take it in six
weeks, without the loss of one."

Upon the termination of this spirited and successful
assault upon the stronghold of the French, the fleet and
army returned to Halifax, and remained for some time,
in order to refit. But great as the stir which was made
by this enormous inundation of strangers upon the town,
much as it was enriched by the rapidly obtained and as
rapidly spent spoils taken from the captured city, and
gay as it was rendered by the triumphant victors, this
was but one of many such stirring epochs through which
Halifax was destined to pass, nor always for its good,
either in a social or business aspect. In the very next
year, General Wolfe arrived with another powerful fleet
and army. This time he was on his way to the siege of .
Quebec. Though he returned not, having fallen in the
hour of victory on the plains of Abraham, the ships and
troops returned to their rendezvous, and from this date
the harbor was constantly visited, for four years, by the
squadrons commanded by Lord Colville and by cruisers,
coming into port for orders and supplies. A lull, both
in the business and gaieties of the town, now set in,
which continued almost unbroken, until the breaking
out of that spirit which resulted in the American Revo-
tion. Then once more the old and familiar customs
revived, consequent upon the return of a large military
and naval force. The presence of so many men, a large
number of whom were possessed of ample means, and
freely spent them, together with the frequent distribution

of prize-money, paid in specie, by the Halifax department of the Commissariat, tended greatly towards the
promotion of that lavish expenditure and those frequent
entertainments which were less conducive to the permanent well-being of the town, than to the transient pleasure of its inhabitants. But all this supported the
" Great Pontac," and rendered it so noted an hotel.
Such, indeed, was its fame, that no doubt, in order to
draw custom, the conductor of a new and rival establishment copied the charmed name, yet presuming not to
put it on a par, he called it the " Little Pontac." Beside these were two others, both situated between the
Dockyard and the town; the one was the " Crown
Coffee House," in those days frequented chiefly by
country people; the other, the " Jerusalem Coffee
House," known even in modern times, but at first a sort
of halfway-house, between the Dockyard and Market,
whereat wearied gentlemen were supposed to refresh
themselves on the long walk between these two points.
In the middle of the enclosure now occupied by Government House, with its adjacent grounds, there stood a
wooden building which was used as a residence for the
Field Officers, and occasionally devoted to other military
purposes; while a little further north, on the site of the
" Freemason's Hall," was another ordinary wooden
structure, occupied at first by French prisoners brought
from Annapolis, and afterward by the Main Guard,
during the period of the Revolutionary war. These,
and the buildings erected at the expense of Government
at the Royal Engineer Yard, the Ordnance Yard, and
the King's Wharf, and the Jail House, were the most
noted for public purposes.

The private dwellings were usually small, covering a very limited area, and seldom more than one story in height, finished above with an attic. Although the town was laid out in squares, each containing sixteen lots, of forty feet in width and sixty feet in depth, each individual obtained, if he could, except in the central part, more lots than one. Thus the residences of many were quite detached, and ample scope afforded for gardens, which were assiduously cultivated by the proprietors. Great value was set upon these pieces of ground, for necessity laid it upon each one to be his own market gardener, notwithstanding the existence of the public gardens ; and being deprived of many other luxuries which could be obtained in older countries, the inhabitants diligently cultivated vegetables and fruit-trees, in order that they might have some variety on their tables. Not a few planted trees before their doors, under the shade of which the dairy cow loved to ruminate during the hot days of summer, and to lie down at night, to the inconvenience and danger of the pedestrian.

The furniture in the dwellings of those who possessed means, was of a far more substantial character than that now used by persons of the same class, and was considerably more expensive. The householder, however, was content with a far less quantity than is deemed necessary at the present day. It was usually made of a mahogany wood, of a rich, dark color ; the dining-room table was plain, but massive, supported by heavy legs, often ornamented at the feet with the carved resemblance of a lion's claw ; the side-board was high, rather narrow and inelegant ; the secretary, or covered writing desk, was bound with numberless brass plates at the

edges, corners, and sides; the cellaret, standing in the
corner, which held the wines and liquors brought up
from the cellar for the day's consumption, was also
bound elaborately with plates of burnished brass; the
chairs cumbrous, straight-backed, with their cushions
covered with black horse-hair cloth, were as uncomfort-
able as they were heavy; the sofa, though not common,
was unadorned but roomy; the great arm-chair deserved
its title, for it was wide enough and deep enough to
contain not only the master of the household, but, if he
pleased, several of his children beside. These for the
most part comprised the furniture of the dining-rooms
of the upper classes. That contained in the bed-room
was built of the same wood, and of a corresponding
style. The bedsteads were those still known as four-
posted, invariably curtained, and with a canopy over-
head, not only shutting out air, but involving serious
expense and labour to the matron, as at the approach of
winter and summer the curtains were always changed.
The chests of drawers and the ladies' wardrobes were
covered with the ubiquitous brazen plates, and being
kept bright, gave the room an air of comfort and clean-
liness. In almost every hall stood a clock, encased by
a frame of great size; a custom introduced by the Germans, from whose native land they seem to have been
imported in great numbers. The mistress of such an
establishment had no sinecure, in keeping such furniture
in order; and it was not an unfounded complaint which
they preferred, that the time of one servant was wholly
engrossed with the daily routine of burnishing the metal
on the furniture and doors, and polishing the wood.
For common use, rough tables were made by the me-

chanics of the town; and chairs, with rush-bottomed
seats, were manufactured in an old establishment in Hollis street, conducted by one of the early settlers. It was
necessary, however, to speak some months before the
chairs were actually needed; and if the good man happened to be out of rushes, the intending purchaser was
obliged to wait until the rushes grew, were cut down,
and dried.

The kitchen department, in those early times, was of
the greatest importance. The day's labor began at early
morning with the often unsuccessful attempt to produce
fire from flint and steel; baking and brewing, as well as
ordinary cooking, were, for the most part, attended to at
home, and all was done, for many years, at the open
hearth, on which hard wood was burned as fuel. For
twenty years the purchase of wood took place without
any special measurement; but as it then began to grow
more scarce, cord-wood surveyors were appointed by
Government, to protect alike the buyer and seller. The
coal brought to market from the Sydney Mines, after
this period, brought the same price as now before the
end of the century, being advertised for thirty shillings
per chaldron. Those who did not wish to consume fuel
in baking, or were not skilful in the art, bought their
bread at the bake-houses kept in Grafton and Pleasant
streets.

It was the habit to dine at an early hour, and take
supper between eight and nine o'clock. The fashionable
dinner hour was three o'clock, and on some state occasions it was made as late as four. As a consequence of
this custom, business ceased to be transacted, at least by
the public offices, soon after mid-day. It was too late

to return, when the somewhat lengthened meal was over. In the ordinary course, a custom prevailed of walking on a fine day, after dinner, sometimes towards the Point, sometimes to the North, and, in less favorable weather, to the Market, for a promenade beneath the balcony. On returning home, those whose resources in themselves were small, usually played cards until supper was laid : while among the more intellectual it was the admirable custom that the gentlemen should read aloud while the ladies worked at embroidery. The standard English authors were their text-books on these occasions ; they had but few, but these were the works of the ablest historians and the most distinguished poets. Few are aware how well-informed, in spite of many disadvantages, were the upper classes of society in those early times. There was much to hinder and very little to promote education ; the habits and occupations tended to withdraw the mind from the duty and pleasure of self-culture, and the opportunities of instruction were few and far between ; yet no mean amount of information was stored up by those whose libraries indeed were small, but contained the productions of the masters in literature. It is true that much noxious sentiment on religious subjects was introduced, subsequent to the French Revolution, and as a consequence, sacred matters were freely and flippantly discussed in the colonies as well as in the British isles. But even then, there were families in which divine truth was received with deepest reverence, and, as topic for unholy handling, was not allowed. The full and accurate acquaintance of many ladies with History, ancient and modern, with Milton and Shakspeare, with Pope and Dryden, and with others

of equal fame, may yet be traced through a few of their
daughters, who still survive—themselves old ladies now
—to adorn their native land.   The fact was, that they
had few books, but these they read diligently and mastered thoroughly.   Many of them learned the French
language, and both wrote and spoke it fluently and well.
So necessary a part of the good education of a young
lady was it considered, that the friends of one, not finding a good teacher in Halifax, sent her to Lunenburg for
the special purpose of being instructed by Rev. Jean
Baptiste Moreau, who resided there.

For the public and private entertainments so often
alluded to, there was no great variety of food.   The
market was supplied in a very different degree from
that which is enjoyed at present.   When the troops and
fleet, on some of the occasions mentioned, invaded the
town by thousands, their consumption almost created a
famine in the land ; on one occasion beef rose to two
shillings and sixpence per pound, and butter to five.
Except in these extreme cases, the absolute necessaries of
life were abundant.   Corned beef, pork, and salted
codfish, far more frequently formed the dishes of all
classes than fresh meat.   For delicacies and variety
anxious housekeepers were driven to ingenious devices
in cooking.   The same species of meat was dressed in
many ways ; and preserved fruits took a high rank at
the table, especially during the winter season.   Poultry
early came into fashion ; and for game a porcupine was
considered as the right thing.   For vegetables each man
was either dependent upon the produce of his own garden, or if he should live in the middle of the town,
where gardens could not be, he might purchase from the

public gardener, if he had any disposable produce.
When, after a few years, these public gardens were
abandoned, the want of vegetables was very seriously
felt, and it was then viewed not only as an enterprise on
the part of the proprietor, but as highly conducive to
the public welfare, when on Saturdays he sent one
wheelbarrow filled with " greens" and vegetables from
a well-kept garden near Fresh-Water-Bridge. All the
ungardened gentlemen kept watch for the passage of this
valuably laden train, and followed it down to the
market, that they might get their share. The butchers'
meat was carried round to the customer in the ordinary
tray by boys, or on small carts drawn by dogs : as was
also the bread baked at the two chief bakeries.

Thus were the original settlers supplied with food.
Unfortunately for themselves there was no lack of that
which they might drink. Pure water, indeed, was
abundant, and pumps were placed at the most convenient spots, at which the public could fill their pails
when they pleased. This was a sad annoyance to the
immediate neighborhood, for there was no cessation of
the noise of the pump-handle, and to an almost incessant wrangling between the lads and half-grown girls
who were sent for the morning and evening supply.
But the appetite of Halifax was not satisfied by such
simple liquid. It was too easily obtained to be held of
much value, and a craving for stimulants early became
the crying evil of the town. Wines and strong liquors
were brought in great abundance to the market, and
found a ready sale. It was an unhappy circumstance,
and exercised its baneful influence, to a very large
extent, upon men of all ages and ranks. On this it is

alike needless and useless now to descant. The bare fact is enough.

Carriages were owned by but a few of the inhabitants, even till towards the close of the century. There were some of different forms and styles introduced at a very early stage of the history, indeed quite enough, within eighteen or twenty years, to constitute a source of revenue to the Government, since at the end of that time all persons " having wheel carriages were called to pay tax at the excise office in Halifax." It seems, however, that amongst those who were strictly civilians, only one was the envied owner of a covered carriage, and, perhaps, this was owing to the fact of his having twice administered the Government as senior Councillor, when he may have thought it necessary to his dignity and position sometimes to drive instead of walk. On all grand occasions he was expected to send his equipage to the whole round of ladies who might be invited to an entertainment. If the ladies gained comfort in one way, they lost it in another. True they all drove, but the first on the list was obliged to be in readiness an hour before, certainly as awkward for her host as tiresome for herself. It was even worse with the gentlemen, as to the tax upon their patience. The fashion of the times was to wear the hair powdered, with a cue. This was a long and tedious process. As the hair dressers were few, they were compelled, in order to get through their task, previous to the hour appointed for a festivity, to begin it early in the morning. He was an unfortunate man whose turn came first, for he was obliged to sit the whole day in idleness, or move with slow and measured step, lest he should disarrange the handiwork; sleep he dare not, for one unlucky nod would spoil it all, and so he was forced patiently to wait until the time came, and then with cautious, wary step, proceed slowly to his host's. On such occasions the full dress consisted of knee-breeches, silk stockings, shoes and silver buckles, white neckerchief, of amazing thickness, straight collared coats ornamented with large buttons, a colored waistcoat, and hanging at the side, a sword or rapier; this last addition to the costume, which was more like a long dagger than a sword, as may be seen by those which are still preserved in a number of houses in Halifax, was looked upon as the distinguishing badge of one who was entitled to be considered as an esquire or gentleman. And this species of court dress was frequently called into use. The custom of constantly calling together the leading men, for consultation on topics of importance to the colony, resolved itself, as time passed, into the holding of levees. In the course of some years these official gatherings were held no less than nine times, and on all these occasions the streets leading to Government House were filled with the gentlemen of the powdered hair, the silk stockings, and the silver-hilted sword.

It is quite indicative of the general ease, and lack of urgent business in the community, that even as late as 1796, when Mr. Bulkely was still Secretary of the Province, as he had been for many years, that there were no less than twenty-four holidays, during which the public offices were closed.

Although not very common, it was sometimes the case that the gentry were served by slaves. That they were owned and dealt with as goods and chattels by the townspeople, is sufficiently clear, but there does not seem much proof that they were generally employed as domestic servants.   As early as 1769, an advertisement appears in the newspaper, which states that " on Saturday next, at 12 o'clock, will be sold, on the Beach, 2 hogsheads of rum, 3 of sugar, and two well-grown negro girls, aged 14 and 12, to the highest bidder."   Again, as late as August 17, 1790, another advertisement appears, which, in some respects, reminds one of modern days, in other lands.   The subscriber offers forty shillings reward for the capture of a negro boy slave, named Dick, whom he describes as to size, gait, and clothing, and winds up with saying, " Whoever will secure the negro slave in any of his Majesty's gaols, and give immediate notice thereof, shall receive the above reward, and if delivered to his master, shall be allowed all reasonable expenses."   There are not wanting the record of curious bestowals, by will, of slave property, but the information is sufficient, without adding any of these. It should be added, not merely as a set-off to this custom in a British colony, at so late a date, but as putting the matter in its true light, that so soon as the matter was seriously brought up, it was settled in a court of law that slavery could not obtain, and so was no longer tolerated.

In all matters relating to the government of the town, the machinery was far from complicated.   Certain taxes and fines imposed by the magistrates in session, went towards the few public works that were deemed necessary,—the constructing of drains, repairing of streets, making of gutters, and such other positively needful acts.   But the general business of keeping the citizens in order, was the duty imposed upon a very small force. Two or three constables, under the direction of a Chief Magistrate, constituted the staff which was to keep in awe the turbulent, and bring offenders to punishment. Yet they were not often too feeble for the duties assigned them, for the military and naval power took ward and watch over their own transgressors, and thus lightened materially the task of the civil officers. When, however, any special excitement arose, or danger threatened from housebreakers and thieves, the townsmen turned out and patrolled the streets for a few nights, until the cloud passed away. The punishments resorted to, for minor offences, were similar to those in use in older countries : the stocks for drunkenness, and whipping at the public post for theft. We find it noticed that two " were lately tried, convicted, and sentenced to receive twenty-five lashes at the public post for theft, for stealing sundry articles, * * * * and on Saturday last they received their punishment accordingly."

At a very early period a newspaper was published. It was in the month of January, 1769, that the first number of the first paper, called " The Nova Scotia Chronicle and Weekly Gazette," was printed and published by Anthony Henry, and edited by Capt. Bulkley, Secretary of the Province. In later years, and before the close of the century, others were published, by different proprietors and editors. They were modelled very much after the same pattern, the peculiar feature being that of a very full selection from the English and American newspapers From the advertisements, which generally occupied either a quarter or two-fifths of the whole, it is possible to glean with tolerable accuracy the

5

state of business, the situation of the chief houses, and
the names of the prominent and most enterprising men,
beside many other matters of interest as affecting the
condition or the progress of the town. The shops, as
we now term them, were rather receptacles for all manner of saleable articles. Each man, no doubt, had his
speciality, but he rarely, if ever, confined himself to this,
generally adding some stock of a wholly different genus,
the sale of which more properly belonged to his neigh-
bor. During the half-century the subdivision of labor
was little recognized as a principle, nor was it needful ;
the town was probably far better served by the general
importation of goods to each one's place of business.
Men in trade sent to England for any and every thing
which they thought it likely their customers would buy,
without regard to the fact that they were nominally
hardware, dry-goods merchants, or grocers. Hence the
ordinary shops bore a strong resemblance to those very
useful and lucrative places of business, in our country
towns and villages, known under the very appropriate
title of " stores."

Editorials were few and brief. Often the papers came
out without any observations from their conductors.
There was no attempt to influence or to reflect public
opinion, except on rare occasions. The space devoted to
local news, even including the shipping lists, and notices
of deaths and marriages, seldom exceeded half a column.
Reports of the debates in the House of Assembly were
very meagre, and in comparison with the portion of the
page occupied by the grand questions discussed in the
British Parliament, they held no place. If the press
met the wants of the public mind, it is clear that the in-

tellectual appetite desired " Old country" information
in preference to " New." When a " leader" did appear,
within the first thirty years, it was not always couched
in the language " best understood of the people." It may
not be amiss to quote from one of them, perhaps the most
remarkable, the aim of which is sufficiently intelligible,
though the terms in which it is expressed are rather
high sounding. The writer, no doubt, meant to say,
that much damage was done in the harbor, the mouth
of which opens toward the south-east, in consequence of
a storm from that point of the compass taking place at a
time of spring-tide; but the wording is at least curious
in a paper not specially devoted to science: " The vast
damage done to the wharves during this storm must be
attributed to the extraordinary height of the tide and
force of the winds, acting in conjunction with one
another; for it must be observed that neither wind nor
tide of itself could have occasioned such damage to the
wharves. Therefore, if we allow the tide to be either
primary or secondary, in the cause, we had little less to
expect, when we found to what degree the wind arose;
for the moon being full and near her perigeum, the
earth far advanced in its perihelion, and the wind at
S. E., it would be absurd to suppose the contrary of an
extraordinary tide, while every influence thereon conspired to increase it." The selections from the English
newspapers were made with admirable judgment, and
afforded a most comprehensive history of passing events.
Although they improved in many respects, such as appearance, type, execution, and wider range in selection,
they continued in a remarkable degree to be counter-

parts of the first in the matter published and in its management.

The communication with England was uncertain, and at some periods, infrequent. There was either a constant succession of arrivals and departures, or an almost total absence of them. At those seasons when war, or the anticipation of war, brought His Majesty's ships to Halifax, there was no lack of mails, either coming or going, and those gentlemen who were anxious to cross the Atlantic, often found a passage on board. When they were not fortunate enough to do this, their accommodation was not of the best kind; a schooner was most frequently the style of vessel in which they were compelled to sail, and oftentimes the passage in one of these pent-up craft was painfully tedious; and even when the Falmouth line of packets was established, the transit, though more agreeable in its mode, was not more rapid. The number of ships entering and clearing, bears a really marvellous contrast with the present list. It was often the case, except in the great national excitements already spoken of, that not more than two vessels arrived or sailed during a week. This, indeed, never occurred during the spring and autumn, for at these periods the importations insured a steady flow, for several weeks, of craft of various size; but then followed a period of stagnation in the harbor and around the wharves.

To pass on to the number of the population and give anything like an accurate statement of it, during this era, would be almost impossible. It fluctuated in a most extraordinary manner, varying from four thousand to twenty thousand; now rapidly increasing from immi-

gration and the settling of some of the officers and men
of both army and navy, then as quickly diminishing.
At one time, owing to the great influx of military and
naval forces, the town would suddenly rise to momentary energy, and manifest enterprize and prosperity ; in
a little while the fervor would pass away, and it would
appear to be following in the wake of some of the old
colonial settlements, and destined to fall into ruin and
decay like its short-lived rival, Shelburne, on the western shore. The letters written to England often allude
to the changing numbers, and ascribe the decrease, not
infrequently, to the fact of some going into the country,
and others to the coves where fishing-stations had been
formed. Many, no doubt, were disappointed, and
either returned home, or found their way to the New
England States, and thence scattered to others of the old
colonies ; while on two different occasions the tide
turned, and brought to these shores a vast number of
people from the continent : the first, upon the proclamation of Governor Lawrence, subsequent to the expul-
sion of the Acadians, the second upon the outbreak and
conclusion of the American Revolution. On the former
occasion, only an indirect influence was exerted upon
Halifax, for those responding to the appeal, were for the
most part farmers, who went to the different counties in
which the unfortunate Acadians had resided, and entering into other men's labors, took possession of houses
which they built not, and wells digged which they digged not, vineyards and trees which they planted not.
But their arrival in the Province exercised a beneficial
influence on its capital, creating business, and so affording employment of different kinds for a greater number

of persons within it. The latter emigration was more
direct in its bearing upon the population of the town.
Hundreds came to Halifax, who knowing nothing of
agriculture, were glad to find employment as labourers,
servants, mechanics, clerks, and book-keepers, while
others set up various kinds of business, or opened, on
their account, shops in which to conduct their own
trades. There is nothing more remarkable in the history of Halifax, during the first half-century of its existence, than the fluctuation of the population; it far more
resembled the tide than the stream; in place of a steady
flow increasing gradually in volume, and emptying itself
into the reservoir, it now rushed like the tide at full
moon, until it reached its highes tmark, and then re-
ceded with an ebb as rapid, leaving only the original
number, as the main water is left in the channel of an
estuary. And thus at the close of the century there
was but a very slight difference in Halifax, as regards
its population, from the beginning of it.

To one other feature of the town it is necessary to
advert, vastly more important in its nature than any of
those already described, and yet such as must be more
briefly discussed: it is that of its religious condition.
Our proximity to those days is too close to admit of a
searching scrutiny into the moral phase of the community, or to delineate it with the same minuteness of detail
as its material state. But it would be unjust to pass
over in silence a subject of so much moment, and to
withhold a portion of the truth most necessary for
drawing a contrast between past and present. Unhappily, those days were eminently irreligious days. The
laxity of sentiment, and the disregard to the doctrine

and precepts of the Gospel were painfully manifest.
Noble exceptions there were—bright spots amid the
murky clouds—refreshing oases in the desert. But the
testimony left on record of those whose opinion is worthy of trust, is unanimous, that religion was treated with
indifference by the many, with scorn by some, and with
reverence by but few. To cite none others, the first
Bishop of the Diocese was so impressed with the fearful
condition of the community, the general tone of society,
and the debasing tendency of the opinions prevailing,
that he wrote a letter to some in high places, which is
still extant, bewailing in no measured terms the terrible
degeneracy of the days, and urging that some steps
should be taken to erect barriers against the impetuous
torrent which threatened to overwhelm religion and
morality. The lament was the same from such men as
the pioneers of the Scottish Church and the Wesleyan
denomination, in whose biographical memoirs these
views are to be found. And from a letter of the late
Chief Justice, we gather like sentiments on the subject.
There were zealous clergymen, but their efforts were
productive of comparatively little good in the town itself.
Some heard and took heed : but the majority turned a
deaf ear to their warnings and counsel. Many, under
the cloak of their not being members of the Church of
England, kept themselves aloof from its sanctuary and
its clergy, and not being provided with ministers and
teachers of the denomination in which they were profes-
sedly brought up, were left to their own devices. For
some time there were but few places of worship beside
those of the Establishment ; but towards the end of the
century others arose : the Wesleyans, the Roman

Catholics, the Baptists, as well as the Churches of
Scotland and England, had their churches and their
ministers ; but the labors of each and all combined produced but little apparent benefit. It would be alike
painful and unprofitable to enter into this subject ; and
as no good could arise from a record of the facts which
would prove the strong statements made, it is better to
leave them, in order that they may sink into oblivion.
The knowledge of the fact is enough—the particulars
are unnecessary. While on the one hand it would be
a culpable omission to pass over in silence the general
truth, on the other it would only pander to a morbid
taste, to recall the errors and vices of the age. Happily,
that period of indifference and carelessness has long
since passed away, and, we may trust, never to be repro-
duced.

Such was the condition of Halifax, material and
moral, during the first half century of its history.
Although the changes which took place have not been
strictly traced in their chronological order, it will not be
difficult for any one to distinguish between those
circumstances, habits and customs which belong to an
earlier or a later period. With the exception of that
which is expressly mentioned as belonging to the very
infancy of the town—such as its limits and defences—
the details belong almost as much to the middle and
close of the fifty years, as to the commencement. The
inattention to the order of time is designed, in reality
there was but little permanent change between, 1750
and 1800, either in the material condition of the town,
in the number of its inhabitants, in the nature and
extent of business which they transacted, or in their

manners, habits and customs. The fluctuations have
been fully noticed, and the tendency of these transient
gleams of prosperity not darkly hinted at. But whatever changes took place, there was a singular uniform-
ity preserved in all that constituted Halifax proper. It
always returned if not altogether, at least, nearly, to its
own level.

Into this place with its customs, habits, manners, and
amid society framed and moulded by the events and
circumstances described, the subject of this memoir was
thrown at an early age. The influences under which
his boyhood and early life passed may be clearly seen :
and as they were not calculated to expand the mind or
cherish the moral qualities, it elevates and ennobles his
character, that amid so much to depress and so little to
enlarge the mental powers, he acquired so much knowledge and trained his intellect with so much discipline,
and that amid so much to blunt the moral senses, he
preserved his integrity, his reverence for God, and his
firm resolve to act his part in the great drama of life
upon the principles and motives inspired by Christianity.

CHAPTER III.

CAPTAIN HALLIBURTON having resumed his study of
the Law, with Mr. Stewart, Solicitor-General, was, in a
short time, admitted to the Bar. He signed the Roll
on 12th July, 1803, as Attorney, and on the same day
was admitted as a Barrister. Seated on the Bench of
Nova Scotia at this time, were Chief Justice Blowers,
and assistant Judges Monk and Brenton. He could
have but little supposed at the time of his admission
and of commencing the practice of his profession, that he
himself so soon should occupy a seat upon the Bench.
The practice at the Courts was lucrative and important,
consisting chiefly of causes arising out of the shipping
interest. The general war, in which all the European
powers were more or less involved, had the effect of
making the mercantile marine of the United States of
America the carriers of a great part of the commerce of
the world, and particularly of that connected with the
American continent. Hence arose constant difficulties,
seizure of vessels, charges of illicit traffic, and a host of
similar troubles, prolific of litigation. Mr. Halliburton
was engaged in some of these cases, and proved himself a
successful practitioner. Nothing remarkable, however,
appears to have transpired during the short period of
time that he practised at the Bar. There can be little
doubt that he occupied himself diligently in the dis-

charge of his duties, and in accumulating information on all subjects of general interest, as well as of a local nature. In addition to his legal studies and business, we find him, during the time that he was practising at the Bar, acting as Secretary to the Board of Governors of King's College, Windsor. He then became interested in that young institution, nor did his interest in it ever flag. Down to the day of his death he continued to be one of its ablest supporters. For half a century and more he was so identified with it, that a long succession of students associated the name of Judge Halliburton with College and their College days.

The change from military life to the confinement of an office, affected a constitution not then very strong, and though his professional prospects were so good, he felt that his health would be seriously injured by their pursuit, and was somewhat doubtful as to the propriety of pursuing them. At this juncture a vacancy occurred on the Bench, by the death of Mr. Justice James Brenton, and to this responsible post he was elevated at the early age of thirty-three, on the 10th of January, 1807. On the 13th of the month he received from Mr. Gautier, the Clerk of the Council, his Commission as Assistant-Judge of the Supreme Court, went to the Council Chamber, and there took the oaths of office. Shortly after his appointment he removed from the town to Sherwood, on the Bedford Basin, where he resided for several years. His mind was very solemnly impressed with the nature and responsibility of the arduous duties which this high preferment imposed upon him; and highly gratified as he was at the promotion, he did not permit himself to be carried away by his new honors,

but seemed more conscious of his own need of wisdom
and grace. To men of the present day who are acquainted with the opinions which prevail now among all
classes, and which have prevailed during the last thirty
or forty years, it will not seem at all remarkable that he
should have had a profound reverence for revealed religion in early life. His character was so moulded, and
his conduct so guided of late years, by the doctrines
and precepts of the Word of God, and society in general—however there may be many and sad exceptions,
outwardly at least acknowledging a belief in religion
and a respect for its consistent exponents—that we are
not surprised at finding true religious feeling animating Judge Halliburton. He was just the high-minded
and amiable man, who would appear likely to adopt
religion; in his position it would seem incongruous not
to have manifested at least an external reverence for
God, and an outward respect for His will. But the
views entertained on religion were far different in the
outset of his career; society was in general but little
leavened by it, and vastly influenced by scepticism and
infidelity. A looseness of conduct, and an open indifference to moral as well as religious law, prevailed to a
fearful extent. The French Revolution, at the close of
the last century, had been productive of evil in a vast
variety of ways. In social life the greatest laxity of
conduct had sprung up,—sacred ties were broken without remorse,—self-gratification was the ruling principle,
—and men learned to smile at and applaud the most
unhallowed scenes of dissipation. In the political world
the most unprincipled demagogues ruled and advocated
the overthrow of all ancient laws; and while they kin-

dled the hopes, fired the blood, of those who had nothing
to lose and every thing to gain.   The religious community was held up to scorn by the Encyclopedists, whose
unquestioned learning in literature, art, and science,
rendered them formidable foes.   Not only the Continent
of Europe and Great Britain and Ireland were flooded by
men who openly avowed themselves unbelievers in Christianity, but the United States and British North America
were equally invaded by them, either in person or in their
writings.   The Colonies were especially innoculated
with their baneful notions.   Volney, Tom Paine, and
Voltaire, Hume, and Gibbon, were favorite authors in
England.   As the chief, and nearly all the offices of
Government were filled up by the Crown, (and sometimes perhaps more for the purpose of finding a living
for some needy relative of a minister, or an impatient
hanger-on, than out of regard to his fitness,) there was
a constant renewal of this element of scepticism introduced.   It was thought not only manly but fashionable
to deny the truth of Christianity.   Questions of doctrine
were freely discussed, in order to show how inharmo-
nious they were with the attributes of God,—infidel
authors were the grammar and text-book.   Their axioms
and opinions were quoted glibly at the dinner-table and
at those evening feasts which were the custom of the
times.   The great topic was not in the back-ground, but
brought to the fore, only, however, as an object of assault.

Those were irreligious days, and as might be proved,
pre-eminently so in Halifax.   Witness the following

letter, from the late Chief Justice himself to the author of the life of the Duke of Kent :—

" At the time of his arrival, the habits of the garrison were *very dissipated*. The dissipation, indeed, was not confined to the military ; the civil society partook of it largely. It was no unusual thing to see gentlemen join a company of ladies in a state of intoxication, which would now be deemed very disgraceful, but which was then merely laughed at by the ladies themselves. His Royal Highness at once discountenanced such conduct. Among the military he soon put an end to it by parading the troops every morning at five o'clock ; and as he always attended himself no officer could of course feel it a hardship to do so. The improvement which thus took place among the military gradually extended to their civil acquaintances, and his Royal Highness thus became instrumental in improving both.

" Gambling also prevailed to a great extent : but his Royal Highness never touched a card ; and as the early parades compelled its former military votaries to retire early to bed, gambling, as well as drinking, fell into disuse.

" I must mention a circumstance which occurred about this period, which interested many at the time. A very kind-hearted captain of the regiment had been sent to Newfoundland to recruit. He was not well calculated for that service, and in the hands of an artful sergeant had returned much in arrears to the paymaster. He was an amiable but easy-going man, and a few days after his return, he dined at a party where cards were introduced in the evening. He had never been in the habit of playing, but was easily prevailed upon to join the party ; and by one of those runs of good luck by which the tempter frequently seduces novices, bore off all the money of the evening. It was a sum quite sufficient to relieve him from his difficulties.

His great luck was the engrossing subject of conversation throughout the following day. 'But of course,' said
the losers, 'Macdonald will give us a chance of winning
our money back again, when we meet at Esten's, on the
next Thursday evening.'

"Every body knew that Mr. Macdonald would be
easily persuaded to do so, and his friends feared that he
might become a confirmed gambler. His Royal Highness heard of it; sent for him; and after conversing
with him, very seriously and kindly said, 'Mr. Macdonald, you have never been in the habit of playing,—
these gentlemen requested you to play, and if, by com-
plying with their request, you have won their money, it
is much better that they should bear the loss, than that
you, from a false notion of honour, should run the risk
of acquiring a bad habit. I request that you will give
me a positive pledge, on honour, that you will not again
play at games of chance.' Macdonald did so. *The
Prince made it public.* Of course, after that, no gentleman could solicit Macdonald to play; and as he was not
inclined himself to do so, he escaped the snare in
which, had it not been for his Royal Highness's friendly
interference, his good luck might ultimately have en-
tangled him. Poor, kind-hearted Macdonald! he fell a
victim to the climate in the West Indies not long afterwards.

" His Royal Highness's discipline was strict, almost
to severity. I am sure he acted upon principle; but I
think he was somewhat mistaken in supposing such un-
deviating exactitude essential to good order. Off the
parade, he was the affable prince and accomplished gentleman. At his table every one felt at ease; but while
it was evidently his object to make them so, his dignified manner precluded the possibility of any liberty
being taken by the most forward.

" I cannot close without mentioning *his benevolence to
the distressed.* A tale of woe always interested him

deeply, and nothing but gross misconduct could ever induce him to abandon any whom he had *once been induced to befriend.* I have much pleasure in giving these recollections of his Royal Highness, under whom I served for several years, and from whom I received very great kindness.

" I return Mr. Neale's letter herewith, and have the honour to remain,

" Your Excellency's obedient servant,

" BRENTON HALLIBURTON.

" His Excellency Lieut. Gen.
Sir John Harvey, K. C. B., &c., &c., &c."

It was in the midst of society like this that Sir Brenton Halliburton embraced and held fast to religious principle. No doubt there were honourable exceptions to the class alluded to, but they were few. Yet Sir Brenton was emphatically a religious man, not indeed as he was in later life, but having much light in the midst of great darkness. His views of this all-important subject were clear and strong. That he was a man of private prayer, amid all this worse than coldness, is amply proved by his own journal of those days. And it is really marvellous that such a man should have existed at all. He who speaks in private letters, which he never supposed would come to light, of the state of his feelings and heart in this way, must have had a high sense of the value of the Gospel :

" I do not remember any time when I have joined in public prayer with more continued attention. Mr. —— officiated. He was inaccurate in several instances, and gave notice that the Sacrament of the Lord's Supper would be administered on Christmas day, without *reading the exhortation.* This was particularly exceptionable. Clergymen should never give the congrega-

tion the idea that any part of the service is useless, or
merely formal, and that *they* can substantially and *more
briefly* answer the purposes intended to be effected *by it.*
Neither the head nor the heart of a man who thinks so,
can be quite right. It is true it may be done without
the intention of *doing* ill ; but thoughtlessness in such
characters and in *such cases*, is a sad excuse. He gave
us a very good sermon. If I was inclined to criticise it,
I would say he went rather too diffusedly into the general character of Christianity, without sufficiently enfor-
cing its peculiar duties ; in the language of my *former*
profession it would be called a *parade sermon*, prepared
and reserved for great occasions. Perhaps it may be
very fair for a clergyman, preaching in a parish where
he is a stranger to the congregation *at large;* but a
Parish Priest should confine himself in a single sermon
to the enforcement of particular duties ; let him recom-
mend sobriety at one time, honesty at another, chastity
at another : they will each provide him an ample subject for one discourse. But when I say he should thus
bend all his force to the illustration of *any* particular
duty, I mean that he should enforce faith in Jesus
Christ (on which all depend) at all times.

"Rose, and endeavoured to impress my mind with
the feelings this day ought to excite,—this day which
we commemorate as the anniversary of the birth of our
blessed Lord—of the advent of Him who forms the sole
connexion between heaven and earth,—who redeemed us
from the bondage of sin and misery, to which we were
everlastingly doomed by the decrees of justice,—who
paid the price of His precious blood for the purchase of
our freedom, and atoned for our sins by his sufferings,
—by whose wonderful love mercy was extended to depraved. sunken, and sinful creatures, without wounding
the immaculate character of justice in the *moral* world.
I trust the mercy of God, through our Lord Jesus
Christ, will enable me to feel the value of this stupen-
dous exertion of goodness. May I never cease most

6

humbly and ardently to implore Him to do so. ....
visited me before church, and introduced the subject
which occupied my mind yesterday, (the seat on the
Bench). I did not wish to divert my mind from a more
important subject, and told him I would not engage to
do anything about it to-day. We had a numerous congregation, and I think the worst sermon I ever heard
.... deliver,—inconclusive in its arguments, (if it
contained any,) and very ill-adapted to the day. The
communicants were numerous. I partook of this Holy
Sacrament with more satisfaction than usual, and humbly trust my gracious Creator, Redeemer, and Sanctifier
will extend to me the graces He has promised to all that
seek Him there."

Nor can a more touching scene be painted than his
course on that day on which he was promoted to the
Bench, January 12, 1807 :—

"This day I rose between eight and nine o'clock,
breakfasted alone, and afterward went in search of Mr.
Gautier, the Clerk of the Council, to obtain my Commission as Assistant Judge of the Supreme Court, to
which office I had been appointed by His Excellency
the Lieut. Governor, on the 10th inst.; procured it from
him at the Secretary's Office; went to the Council Chamber, and there took the oaths of office before the Chief
Justice; returned home and prostrated myself before
the Almighty to thank him for this instance of goodness
to me, and to beseech Him to enable me to do those
things which are pleasing in His sight, and act with
diligence, integrity, uprightness, fidelity, and independence; and that in the discharge of my public duty I
might fear Him and Him alone. May He grant these
my petitions for the sake of my blessed Saviour."

For the next day we find the following entry :—

"Rose, and offered up my prayers, and again peti-
tioned for grace to enable me to perform the duties of
my office."

His attendance upon public worship was regular, and when in the House of God, his journal shows him to have been most attentive and devout.

Judge Halliburton had not been seated long on the Bench when fresh troubles arose between England and the United States. The pacific relations between these countries were violently disturbed by the discovery of several English deserters on board the American frigate "Chesapeake," from which they were taken by his Majesty's ship "Leopard."

As a consequence of this collision, a very hostile feeling arose, and unhappily was fostered by too many restless spirits, so that war was confidently anticipated as an inevitable result. Exports of provisions from Nova Scotia were prohibited; and the American Congress, in retaliation for the commercial restrictions of Great Britain, imposed an embargo on all American vessels, and commanded all British ships to quit their ports. Into all the questions arising from this trouble, whether directly or indirectly, Judge Halliburton entered with great zeal. He thought, he talked, he wrote upon the topic. The ability which he displayed was equal to the interest which he felt. Whether he viewed the subject as one grand whole, or analyzed its separate parts, he proved himself capable of mastering it. He grasped the great question at issue, with all its accumulated complications, and he severally weighed the minute details with accurate justness. Although much occupied with his professional duties, he took the liveliest interest in everything connected with the welfare of the Colonies. It was for this reason especially that he turned his attention so much to the dispute between Great Britain

and the. United States.   The consequences to the Canadas, New Brunswick, and Nova Scotia were, in his estimation, of the highest importance.   Hence he spared no
pains nor opportunities to place' them in a right light
before the British Government.

Judge Halliburton did not confine himself to the cir-
cumference which the colony formed ; while he ever
had it uppermost in his mind, he took a wider range,—
looked at events abroad,—entered deeply into all the
great questions of the passing day : and this gave his
mind an expansive cast.   But those affairs occupied him
most which had a bearing upon the colonies.   It was
by them that all his abilities and all his sympathies
were evoked.   The impressment of sailors by British
vessels out of American,—the commercial relations between Great Britain and the United States,—the state
and condition of trade between the Colonies and the
Republic,—the true relative position between England
and the Provinces,—and the manner in which the mo-
ther-country should treat the colonists ; these, and all
such matters as these, were constantly engaging his
mind.

In 1810 he wrote a very long and able letter, ani-
madverting upon the conduct of the American Government, in so abruptly breaking off negociations with the
British Commissioners.   It would be, at this date,
uninteresting to the general reader to quote portions of
this closely-reasoned document, although to those who
take an interest in American history, and especially the
conduct of the American towards the British Government, it would be by no means devoid of instruction.
All through the period of misunderstanding and disa-

greement, bad temper, and wilful perversion of facts, Judge Halliburton watched the course of events until they reached the crisis in 1812. War was formally declared, and the arrival of his Majesty's ship "Belvidera" at Halifax, announcing that she had been chased and fired into by an American squadron, proved the necessity of meeting the declaration with vigor. Measures were immediately adopted to meet the case. A press-warrant was granted to the Admiral on the station, the Militia were called out and armed, letters of marque were issued, and privateers fitted out against the Americans. So much was Judge Halliburton's mind occupied with all that was now transpiring, and the causes which led to this unhappy state of things, that early in the following year he published a series of letters upon the subject over the signature of "Anglo-American." These letters are valuable, and especially worthy of being again brought to light at the present juncture in America. Indeed, it is no less to preserve, as far as possible, some of the best productions of his mind than to delineate impartially his character, that this memoir is written. For this reason the following letters are introduced :—

[For the RECORDER.]

MR. HOLLAND,—

Sir,—As a constant reader of your paper, I request that you will accept of my thanks for the publication of the eloquent and interesting speech of Lord Liverpool, in support of his Royal Highness the Prince Regent's message to Parliament, recommending a grant of money, to relieve those patriotic Russians, who have made such important sacrifices for the benefit of their Country and the World. I trust, sir, that it has arrested the attention of all your readers; and that the passage, in which his Lordship so feelingly describes and deplores the miseries to which a people are exposed, who inhabit a country that becomes the theatre of war, has excited mingled feelings of detestation against the unprovoked author of such calamities, and of admiration of those, who have so heroically endured them.   Such feelings, sir, will naturally arise in every generous bosom : but unless we have some personal interest in the events which excite them, their duration will be momentary.

The whole civilized world, it is true, is concerned, and deeply concerned, in the recent transactions in the North of Europe, but the inhabitants of these Colonies have a peculiar interest in dwelling upon them with attention.

During a warfare of twenty years, in which our parent state has not only maintained her own independence, but has interposed a barrier to an ambition that would know no bounds, we, sir, have dwelt in peace ; and while pursuing our usual avocations could scarcely realize to ourselves that so great a portion of the human race was enduring the miseries, which were inflicted upon it by that ruthless Tyrant, who has long ruled a nation that, under every form of Government, has been the disturber of Europe.

But, the rulers of a neighbouring country have thought proper to light the flame of discord on this side of the Atlantic ; and, as even successful war may have its attendant miseries, I would wish my fellow-subjects here, to dwell upon those feelings of indignation, which the description of the calamities of the Russians could not fail to excite against the author of them, and then direct them against those men, who have done their utmost to introduce similar horrors among us.   That the war, which the American government has declared against Great Britain, is wicked, wanton, and unjust, must be evident to all who have paid attention to the transactions between the two Countries: but as the majority of your readers may not have had leisure to mark them as they passed, and general assertions are not calculated to produce conviction, I shall endeavour to supply satisfactory testimony in support of this position. The Americans will not, I trust, object to my proof, when I resort to their own official documents to obtain it.

Among the numerous pretexts for the commencement of hostilities, which disgraced the pages of Mr. Madison's message to Congress of the 1st of June last, the orders in council were prominent and pre-eminent; and it is highly probable that, without the aid of the feelings that had been excited against this retaliatory measure, a majority of the Congress could not have been obtained in support of the darling object of the American administration. When they laid so much stress upon this grievance, they were not aware that sound policy would be obliged to yield to popular clamour, and that a combination of interested and factious men had driven the British Cabinet to abandon the Orders in Council, at the very moment when America had declared war on account of them. So firmly had they taken their stand upon this ground, and so completely had the attention of the British Government been drawn to this subject by the American Ministers, that it was considered in England as the *cause* of the war. It was confidently expected there, that, as the *cause* was removed, the *effect* would cease; and in that expectation the British Admiral on this station was directed to devote to negotiation that time which would perhaps have been better employed in vigorous hostility.

But whatever may have been the honest construction which British candor gave to American declarations, the conduct of the American Government has proved that they had very different views. The revocation of the Orders in Council certainly took them by surprise, and well indeed, sir, it might. The foundation of the war

was gone, but the superstructure, which the Legislature
alone could erect, remained, and American ingenuity
was at no loss to devise a support for it.   They have
chosen one which, they are well aware, cannot slip from
beneath the fabric they are so anxious to maintain.
The war now rests upon a stable foundation.   It rests
upon a right which no British minister will, I trust,
have the boldness or the treachery to abandon : " The
right to employ our own subjects in our own defence."
By referring to the Report of the Committee on Foreign
Relations, made to the House of Representatives at
Washington on the 30th of January last, you will perceive that the American Government are now determined to persist in the war until Great Britain relin-
quishes the exercise of the right of impressment on
board of American vessels.   This report, which occupies
three columns of a paper, is one labored tissue of false-
hood and sophistry.   But I shall not at present impose
upon myself the task of exposing all its misstatements,
but confine my attention to what may be truly termed
the burden of the song.

The report, in order to impose upon the understand-
ings and inflame the passions of the American people,
dwells, with wonderful pathos upon the evils that attend
the impressment of American citizens into the British
Service, and states in so many words, that " *the impressment of American Seamen being deservedly considered a
principal cause of the war, the war ought to be prosecuted
until that cause was removed.*"   But, that Great Britain may
fully understand how long the war is to be continued,
and by what sacrifice peace must be purchased, the
report subsequently states : " *With the British claim to
impress British Seamen the United States have no right to
interfere, provided it be exercised in British Vessels, or in
any other than those of the United States.*"

Inhabitants of Nova Scotia ! listen to these declarations, and learn from them the determination of the
American Government to inflict upon you the cala-

mities of war, until Great Britain shall be so far lost to every sense of honour and of interest, as to direct those gallant officers, whose achievements occupy the brightest page in our history, to forego the right of reclaiming British seamen, deserters perhaps from their own ships, from American vessels;— until the Commanders of our ships of war shall be told by their own Government: If when the carnage of battle, or the ravages of disease, have thinned your crews, you should meet an American vessel, whose decks are crowded with British seamen, you must not presume to claim from them the performance of that duty which they owe their Country! True it is, that by the immemorial customs of the civilized world, by the laws established among nations, and by the feelings implanted by the God of Nature, every man is bound to protect and defend the country which gave him birth. But the President of the United States of America wills it otherwise; the American Congress hath spoken, and the laws of nations and of nature must be silent!

Every man, sir, must feel the insolence and arrogance of this demand. I must acknowledge that it has excited no small degree of indignation in my breast. But I shall endeavour to dismiss those sensations, and in my next letter, calmly, and I trust impartially, examine the justice of the American claim.

An Anglo-American.

In the two letters which followed in order he enters into the *justice* of those claims, and with great logical acumen proves the propositions which he lays down: and though they would afford to the reader an excellent specimen of his reasoning powers, their introduction would make this brief memoir too voluminous. The selection without them is ample, and except for their bearing upon great questions now thrust upon the

notice of England and British North American colonists, might be thought by some, more than ample.
The close of his fourth letter is written with so much
nerve and vigour, that it is worthy of being read:—

"Great Britain, I trust, will not be the first of the
European Powers to abandon a principle so essential to
the preservation of social order. She will not be the
first to consign to the grave that virtue which the poet
has delighted to celebrate, and the orator to inspire;
which the historian has labored to perpetuate and the
moralist to instil; the *amor patriæ,* which is the parent
of those honorable sentiments that stimulate the wise,
the worthy, and the brave to conquer every selfish feeling, and to devote their talents, their integrity, and their
valor to the service of their country. No, sir, let
America, who is yet unknown to fame, let the progeny
of that motley mixture which she has deemed it wise to
introduce into her bosom, be the authors of this code of
selfishness and depravity; let them lay the corner-stone
of the tomb of disinterested virtue and of genuine patriotism; let it remain for them to obliterate those early
impressions which endear to us even inanimate objects,
those pleasing recollections of our infant years, those
ardent friendships for the companions of our boyish
days, that generous interest in the partners of our youthful joys, and that delightful association of personal and
local attachment which have hitherto bound mankind to
the land of their nativity; let it remain for them to
banish all these ennobling feelings from the human
bosom; to listen solely to the selfish suggestions of interest, and carry themselves to market, to sell their allegiance to whatever Government will promise them the
most advantageous bargain. Yes, sir, let Mr. Madison
and his associates, if such means of acquiring celebrity
are most congenial to their feelings, transmit their names
to posterity as the incendiaries of the temple of patrio-

tism. But let Englishmen, and let us who participate with Englishmen in their inestimable privileges, ever fondly cherish those sentiments of enthusiastic attachment to the land of our forefathers, which have animated our long list of patriots and of heroes from our Alfred to our Nelson. Let these pretenders to philanthropy and philosophy instil into that part of the rising generation which may come within their baneful influence those principles of frigid indifference and gloomy scepticism, which will leave mankind without a home here or a hope hereafter; but let us firmly adhere to those sound doctrines which have stood the test of experience; let us instruct our children early to know and deeply to revere the sacred volume, which will present to them the most animating prospects of future felicity, which, while it tells them that they are not vagabonds upon the earth, will teach them to exclaim, when the fond recollection of the land of their nativity rises in their minds: 'If I forget thee, O Jerusalem, may my right hand forget her cunning; if I do not remember thee, may my tongue cleave to the roof of my mouth.'

"May such, sir, be the sentiments of every
                    " ANGLO-AMERICAN."

[For the RECORDER.]

Sir,—Having closed my examination of the justice of that complaint against Great Britain, which the American administration now assign as the chief cause for the continuance of the war; and having endeavoured to place in its proper light, their insolent and unprincipled claim for the restitution of native British subjects as American citizens, I shall now attempt to prove, that these are the mere *pretexts* for hostilities; that they were not actuated by the motives, which they avow; and that the real causes, which have induced them to assume the awful responsibility of arming their fellow-creatures against each other, are of a very different nature.

This undertaking, I admit, is in many respects dis-
similar from that in 'which I have hitherto been engaged.   Whether a professed motive justifies the conduct
which has been adopted in consequence of it, is a question which every man who is capable of comprehending
the subject, and who is made acquainted with its attendant circumstances, may decide upon the common principles of justice.   But when we attempt to dive into the
recesses of the heart, and pronounce an opinion not
upon the actions but upon the motives of men, we require not only correct sentiments of justice, but a knowledge of the human character, to guide us in forming a
decision.   This, however, is not one of those cases
which require an uncommon depth of penetration, or
quickness of apprehension, to assist us in its investiga-
tion.   Notwithstanding the infinite variety of characters
which human nature presents to our observation, there
are certain fixed principles of action which are common
to all, and by which mankind in general are actuated,
while they retain their reason ; and when men assign
motives for their conduct which are manifestly insufficient to account for, or are directly inconsistent with it,
we do not hesitate to pronounce that they have not
revealed the truth.

If we view the situation of the United States of
America, and consider the different habits and interests
of the separate governments which form that confederation, the conduct of those who represent them in the
American Congress, and to whose care their interests
are confided, we must be convinced that the motives
assigned by that portion of the Union which constituted
the majority, for plunging the country into war, are
manifestly insufficient to account for their conduct, and
quite inconsistent with their situations as the representatives of those States which are not injured by the evil
of which they complain.   It is notorious that the States
who are concerned in navigation, and whose citizens
must of course be almost the only sufferers by the prac-

tice of impressment, are unanimous in their opposition
to this war. No person, I think, who is in the least
acquainted with the situation of America, can entertain
a doubt of this fact. When the question of war was
carried in Congress, its main supporters were the representatives from the States not engaged in navigation,
and its opponents were those whose constituents derived their chief support from it.

It is true that some of the members from Massachusetts and New York, two of the most wealthy and
populous of the commercial States, voted for the war ;
but it must be recollected that those members were
elected before it was known that such a question would
be proposed for their decision, and the general sentiments of their constituents have since been strongly
expressed upon this subject by the unanimity which
prevaled among their electors for the Presidential chair.
The author of this war was unanimously rejected by
New York and Massachusetts, as well as by all the
other commercial States of the Union, and he owes the
continuance of his authority to those who are as little
affected by the injury for which they have sought such
awful redress, as they will be by the misery and ruin
which this disastrous remedy will bring upon those
whose interests they profess to defend. It is in vain
that the commercial States exclaim ' *Non tali auxilio,
nec defensoribus istis.*' Their Southern confederates have
substantial reasons for pressing them to the earth by the
weight of their protection. It is in vain that they ex-
postulate with the representatives of those portions of
the Union who do not own a single seaman, upon the
inconsistency of their stepping forward as the cham-
pions of the rights of the ocean! It is in vain that they
conjure them to leave the care of their own interests to
themselves ; that they assure them that the means by
which they would secure a few of their seamen from
impressment, will condemn the whole of them to impri-
sonment ; that the measures which they have adopted to

vindicate the rights of commerce, will consign commerce itself to destruction : regardless of arguments, which they cannot answer, and deaf to entreaties to which they were predetermined not to listen, the guardians of American seamen and of American commerce have resolved to expose all the former to captivity, to preserve a few of them from temporary restraint, and to annihilate the latter, to secure it from a partial restriction.

That these men, sir, have reasons for their conduct I do not pretend to deny; but that they are not the reasons, which they have assigned, must be evident, I think to every man of common understanding. Should we not be surprised, if the Tin-miners in Cornwall should rise in rebellion to redress a grievance, which only affected the Coal-miners in Newcastle; or if the men, who hew Timber at Pictou, were up in arms to avenge an injury sustained by those who quarry Plaster of Paris at Windsor ; while neither of the parties immediately interested thought the injury of sufficient consequence to excite a tumult. No man of common sense would be so credulous as to believe that these rioters had assigned the real motives for their turbulence ; and the case of America is still stronger than that which I have put, for the commercial States not only do not consider this grievance as a sufficient cause for war, but they earnestly deprecate having recourse to that measure ; they implore their Southern masters not to extinguish a partial conflagration from which they do not apprehend any serious consequences by a general deluge, which will overwhelm them with ruin. But their petitions are unheard; they are not permitted to have a voice in the consideration of evils which are exclusively their own ; and they must degradingly submit to a remedy, which is indeed in a tenfold degree worse than the disease.

What the real motives of the prescribers are, I shall attempt to develope in my next letter ; and, if I am

right in my conjectures respecting them, the inhabitants
of these colonies are deeply interested in dwelling upon
them with serious reflection.

AN ANGLO-AMERICAN.

<hr>

[For the RECORDER.]

Sir,—I think it must be evident to every man of
plain sense that the representatives from the southern
states of America, who in conjunction with the cabinet
at Washington now rule over the Union, could not
have been induced to involve themselves in war, for
the mere purpose of avenging the wrongs of their
northern brethren, when the injured parties did not
seek their assistance; nor for the still less colourable
pretext of vindicating the cause of those British subjects
who have been naturalized in America. The spirit of
chivalry, when it existed in full force, seldom influenced the conduct of governments; and we shall
require very strong testimony to induce us to believe
that it now actuates the minds of the American administration, and their adherents in Congress, who are
neither so disinterested as to expose themselves to evils
for the benefit of their political opponents; nor, low as
our opinion of their talents may be, so foolish as to
suppose that they could protect Commerce by a
measure, which, it is evident to men of the meanest
capacities, can only tend to its destruction. As we
cannot therefore believe their own account of their
motives, we must endeavor to discover the causes of this
unnatural war, as it is termed, by an examination of the
circumstances and situations of the men who have declared it, and of the country which they govern. And,
however bold the assertion may appear, I cannot refrain
from pronouncing, that this war, which is termed *unnatural*, has grown very *naturally* out of the situation of
the United States of America, and might have been ex-

pected by every intelligent man who had attended to
the affairs of that country ; who had watched its general progress, the distinct and clashing interests of the
northern and southern portions of the Union, and the
growth and comparative strength of the political parties
in that country.

The majority of the writers in America who are opposed to the Government, attribute this war to French
influence, to the subserviency of their own Cabinet, to
the views of the Tyrant of Europe, and assert that America has declared war against Great Britain in obedience
to the dictates of that usurper. That the " hand of Na-
poleon," to use the phrase of one of their own orators,
" is in this thing," I do not entertain the smallest doubt.
But the question then presents itself, how came it there ?
And why is American blood and American treasure to
be lavished in support of his views ? It is more difficult
to suppose that the rulers of America have entered into
this war *solely* in compliance with the orders of Bona-
parte, than that they declared it for the motives which
they themselves assign. As my wish is to take an impartial and a liberal view of this subject, I will not con-
descend to consider the baser motives of bribery and
corruption, which have been urged, without any proof,
against the leading men in America, until such charges
are substantiated. An unprejudiced mind will never
admit them for a moment. If they have had any foundation in fact, their opponents would delight to detail
and triumph in exposing them ; and while they rest upon assertion only, we must attribute them to political
animosity.

It is to the distinct and clashing interests of the Northern and Southern States of America that we are to
look for the real and original causes of this war. But
although we are to consider these as the *primary* sources,
I certainly admit that there are *secondary* causes, and
among these, French influence is predominant.

Nothing could be more natural than that confedera-

tion, which was formed by the thirteen colonies of Great
Britain after their separation from the parent state.
They had almost every motive, which can influence the
minds of men to induce them to unite with each other.
Born the subjects of one general government they had
long considered themselves as fellow-countrymen. Engaged in one common cause, they had persevered together in an arduous struggle against a powerful nation,
until success had crowned their efforts. Looking to one
individual as a leader, who had guided them to independence, they could not but desire to form a government under his auspices, by which those sanguinary
contests might be prevented, that have generally prevailed among small independent states. Thus influenced both by their reason and feelings, they formed
that confederation which we have long known as the
United States of America. But, although this step was
recommended by the wisest men among them, and was
certainly the most prudent plan which they could adopt,
it could neither remove nor remedy all the evils to
which they were exposed in their new situation. It
prevented those scenes of bloodshed, which the history
of their parent state exhibited to them during the period
of the Heptarchy, and which, without such a Union,
would have been repeated among them, until the most
powerful government had gained the dominion over the
others. But it could not prevent that desire of sovereignty, which ever exerts itself in those who embark
in political life. It restrained the passions of the men,
who, actuated by the thirst of power, would have delu-
ged the fields of America with blood; but it could not
preserve that political independence and entire quality
among the separate states, which it was designed to establish and perpetuate. Their jarring interests had
until this period been adjusted by the disinterested decision of the mother country. They were now to be settled by interested delegates from the respective states
of the Union; and influence and intrigue would not fail

7

to exert themselves in that field, from which actual war
had been prudently banished, and they might prove
equally efficacious in the acquisition of political ascendancy. If the situation of the Union had produced a
variety of conflicting interests and opposing parties,
these under the guidance of able and upright men,
might have been managed in such a manner as to con-
duce to the general interest of the whole; or at least
might have been so balanced as to make the general
good preponderate upon all important occasions; and
had several parties existed, none of which decidedly
overpowered the others, men of talent and integrity
would have stood a fair chance of holding the reins of
government.   But when once the separate interests of
the country had divided it into two great parties, the
leaders of each must consent to be led; and when their
own opinions did not concur with those of their political
associates, they must either have abandoned their posts,
or have acted in subserviency to their views.   Such is
the situation of the United States of America.   The
Congress is not divided into a number of parties contending for the various interests of the respective states,
which its members represent; but as the interests of the
southern and inland states are identified from natural
causes, and are distinct from those of the northern and
eastern portions of the Union, which last are also held
together by the same firm and common bond, so it
necessarily follows, that the Congress is divided into
two parties, and that the struggle for ascendancy, which,
if they have entered into the confederation, would have
been decided in the field, is now contested between the
northern and southern states within the walls of Congress. I am aware that men, who do not consider
questions of this nature upon general principles, but confine their observations to particular facts, will enquire
how it happens then, that many of the members from
the northern states have coalesced with those from the
south, and uniformly acted with them prior to the de-

claration of war. But the answer to this question is very obvious. In the first place, the interests of the southern party led them to favour the views of France, the enemy of Great Britain. To France many of the northern representatives were attached by the recollection of the services she had rendered to them during their revolutionary war; and the political animosity, which had subsisted in the minds of others against Great Britain, was too keen to allow them to listen even to the suggestions of interest. It is no answer to my arguments to observe, that they did not universally overcome the influence of prejudice and of prepossession. It is sufficient for my position to establish, that the *majority* of the commercial states, in defiance of that spirit of hostility against Great Britain which the war had excited, felt that it was their interest to preserve a good understanding with her; and that the *majority* of the southern states did not feel any such interest, but were disposed to favour the views of France, not from any positive benefits which they promised themselves from a connection with that country, but because, in their contest for superiority in their own, it was their interest to depress their political opponents, whose enterprising spirit, if it received no check, would acquire a degree of weight and influence, which might perhaps counterbalance the numerical advantages of their more indolent rivals. I cannot suppose it will be disputed that the interests of the northern and southern inhabitants of America are not the same. The former are a hardy, active, enterprising people, whose country is not rich in native productions, and who can only rise to wealth and power by industry and commerce. The latter, though they may be as intelligent, are by no means as active as their neighbors. Nor is it necessary for them to be so, as they possess a country which yields them abundantly all the necessaries of life, and whose surplus produce will always bring purchasers to their shores. The inhabitants of the northern states have hitherto been their carriers, but it is of greater consequence to the southern party, who have obtained the reins of government, to prevent an increase of wealth and power, and its attendant influence, in the hands of their rivals, than to preserve the convenience which the navigation of the northern states has hitherto afforded to them.

Since the recognition of the independence of America by Great Britain, four individuals have successively filled the Presidential Chair. Washington was called to it by the general voice of the country. But, even during that early period, the northern and southern inhabitants of America began to entertain different ideas of their respective interests; ideas which naturally arose from the difference of their respective situations, and which they must therefore ever entertain. Massachusetts produced his successor in office. But, although that powerful state was the originator of that resistance to the mother country, which success has deprived of its harsher name, and America should therefore have considered her as the parent of the revolution, yet the southern states reluctantly submitted to the sway of Adams. A regular systematic opposition was perfected during his administration, and, at its expiration the reins of government were placed in the hands of a Virginian, about twelve years ago, and have never since been resumed by the northern portion of the Union; nor, while the people of the south persist in their present measures, can those of the north ever acquire sufficient power and influence to regain them.

I consider the question then, sir, in this point of view. If the confederation had never been formed, it is probable that those different portions of it would, long before this time, have contended for the dominion over each other at the point of the sword. As they are already united under one general government the political contest for superiority, though carried on without bloodshed, is quite as serious and as interesting to those who are engaged in it, as if their forces were encamped against each other, in the open field. Each party will look abroad with as much earnestness for support, and will avail itself of the passing scenes in other countries, either to advance its own interests, or to depress those of its opponent, and nothing could have a greater tendency to depress the Northern and Eastern States than a war with the greatest maritime power in the world. This, sir, I consider as the sole *primary* cause of the war in which we are now involved, though there are secondary causes, to which I shall turn the attention of your readers in my next letter.

I cannot, however, close this, without observing that I by no means assert or think, that every individual member of Congress who voted for the war, was induced to give his vote by these considerations. Various are the motives which lead different men to the same determination; intrigue and influence, prejudice and partiality, friendship and hatred, interest and passion, may separately act upon the members of a popular Assembly, and induce them to concur in one design. But I am firmly of opinion, that that disposition to remain at peace with Great Britain, which prevails among the majority of the commercial states, and that subserviency to the views of France, which is so evident both among the leading men, and in the great bulk of the inhabitants to the southward originates in the distinct interests of each, and in the political rivalship which subsists between them; which, after a long train of hostile conduct against Great Britain on the part of that faction which has possessed itself of the government, has finally terminated in open war. The only difference between the two parties is, that the previous prejudices and animosities of the northern people were in opposition to their interest; and therefore we do not find such decided unanimity among them, as we meet with to the southward, where their prejudices and prepossessions unite with their political views.   I am, sir, &c.,

AN ANGLO-AMERICAN.

[For the RECORDER.]

Sir,—In my last letter I stated that that Confederation, which was designed to establish and preserve the
independence and equality of the separate States of
America, was not calculated to effect that purpose ; that
it only caused those who were desirous of obtaining
superiority to adopt different means of accomplishing
their object, and to carry on their plans of conquest in
the Congress instead of arming the Northern and Southern hosts against each other ; and I consider the war with
Great Britain into which the Southern people have
plunged the whole country, as a very natural consequence of the measures which they had adopted to establish their ascendancy over the Northern portion of
the Union ; that it is in reality a war of the Southern
and Inland against the Northern and Eastern States of
America, and that the Executive Government and the
majority of Congress intended the Act, which declared
it, as an authority to the British cruisers to seize the
property and to destroy the power of their political
rivals.

I am quite aware that many persons will consider
these as very extravagant positions, and though they
may not be disposed to think very favourably of Mr.
Madison and his confederates, they will not believe
them so depraved as to act with such determined
hostility against their fellow-citizens ; but it must be
remembered that the fellow-citizenship of an inhabitant
of Boston and of Baltimore is not a very strong tie,
and the maxim " *nemo repente fuit turpissimus,*" is as
applicable to the progress in political as in any other
species of depravity. Men who have been long eagerly
bent upon one object, whose principles have become
habituated to bend to their passions, and whose percep-
tions of right and wrong have consequently lost their
original acuteness, will adopt measures with indifference
which, at one period, they would have shuddered even

to contemplate. I have no doubt that Mr. Madison when he first became jealous of that commerce which was elevating the Northern States, could not have believed that he ever would have resorted to so violent a measure to effect its destruction. But when his enmity and that of his associates had once been *exerted* against the commercial part of the country, each year would silently increase it, and every succeeding measure which they directed against it, would probably prove stronger than its predecessor. Many of the inhabitants of the commercial states are convinced that the war has originated in the causes which I have assigned, and inveigh with much bitterness against those anti-commercial prejudices which actuate their rulers. But we, sir, though deeply interested in the subject, may discuss it with less partiality than either of the political parties in America; and if the discussion should convince us that the antipathy which the men of influence in the Southern States entertained for Commerce, does not originate in mere prejudice, but in a well grounded apprehension that the wealth and consequent influence which it would introduce into the commercial districts, would eventually insure to them the superiority in the Union, we must necessarily conclude that those who are now possessed of power will persist in the measures by which alone they can preserve their ascendancy; and consequently if they should succeed in their attempts upon these colonies, *they would have the same motives to oppress us,* which now induce them to devote the property of their commercial fellow-citizens to destruction, and their persons to captivity.

In the consideration of this subject it is necessary for us to bear in mind the distinguishing characteristics of the northern and southern inhabitants of the United States of America; both are sagacious and acute, but the former are active and enterprising, the latter indolent and luxurious. Notwithstanding the fertility of their country, the love of ease and pleasure has always rendered the natives of the southern states more dependent upon those with whom they were accustomed to traffic, than those of the north whose country afforded them less to give in return for what they received. For a long time prior and indeed subsequent to the Revolution in America, the inhabitants of Virginia, of the Carolinas, and other southern states, were so deeply indebted to the British merchants that it might be said that the agriculture of those countries was carried on with British capital.

But when America began to reap the advantages, which she derived from the confusion introduced into Europe by the French Revolution, when the ships of France and Holland were seen no more on the ocean, and those of America were substituted for them, the consequent influx of wealth, though generally felt throughout America, was peculiarly beneficial to the inhabitants of the Northern States, who owned by far the greater part of the vessels so profitably employed, and whose activity and energy was unremittingly exerted to increase the number of their shipping. From the mere carriers of the productions of the Southern States, an increase of capital very soon enabled many of them to become the purchasers of it, and they then not only derived the benefit of the freight, but the profits upon the sale of the cargo when carried to its ultimate market; their capital likewise enabled them to purchase such articles as were calculated for the consumption of the Southern States, and by supplying them with these they secured a profit upon the return cargo also. The same indolent and luxurious habits which had plunged them into debt to the British merchants, still prevailed among the southern inhabitants of America, and they would very soon have become generally indebted to their more active fellow-citizens. It is true that there were many merchants of opulence, enterprise, and activity in the commercial towns to the southward, but these would soon have borne no proportion to the num-

ber of those from the north who were engaged in trade
in the manner that I have described, as the shipping
generally and the American seamen exclusively belonged
to the northern states.

These circumstances early excited much alarm and
jealousy on the part of the leading men to the southward, and although they did not think that the commerce in which the country was engaged was directly
injurious to them, but on the contrary was beneficial, as
they participated in the wealth which it introduced,
foresaw it would produce a serious effect upon their
relative situation with their northern confederates ; as it
would not only give them a much greater comparative
accession of wealth, but would occasion a direct state of
dependence upon them in a numerous body of the
southern planters and traders.

While the inhabitants of the Southern States were
indebted to England or to any other foreign country,
although such a state was not desirable, the disadvantages attending it were by no means so great to the men
of influence there, as they would have become if they
had fallen into debt to those who lived under the same
elective government with themselves. Foreigners would
not have the same inducements to exert that influence
in their elections, which a creditor ever has with his
debtor ; indeed, if they interfered at all they would
probably be disposed to forward the views of those who
were indebted to them ; but if this influence should be
transferred from those who had no immediate interest in
the event of their elections, to their political rivals, it
was highly probable that they would exert it most
actively and successfully. It was obvious, therefore, to
men of reflection that commerce not only increased the
wealth of the northern states in a greater degree than
those of the south, but that it had also a direct tendency
to render the latter dependent upon the former.

Some of your readers may not immediately compre-
hend the political consequences which would have

ensued, if the southern states should have become
generally indebted to the commercial states; and others
may be at a loss to imagine how it could happen that a
fertile country possessing many articles of export should
become indebted to the consumers of many of those
articles who had no native productions to give them in
return.   But I would turn the attention of this class of
your readers to a very common case in our own
Province.   We frequently see in the different townships of this young and flourishing colony, and particularly in the new settlements, the sons of some of our
farmers commence, what is termed a *country trader ;* the
father is probably no richer than his neighbors, and the
trader therefore commences without a capital, and relies
solely for success upon his own activity and prudence ;
if he bears a fair character, he very easily procures a
small supply of goods from a merchant in town : these
he retails to his neighbors and receives their produce in
payment, which he brings to market, and with the
proceeds of it pays for his first supply of goods, and
obtains another.   In this manner he continues to
traffic for some time, and if he has only a tolerable
share of prudence and judgment he will not fail to
amass a fair portion of wealth.   If the inhabitants of
the townships are extravagant, and indulge themselves
in articles of luxury or dress beyond their means, which
has been the case in some of the settlements, they
become generally indebted to the trader, who is then
the first man in the township; and need I ask the
inhabitants of this country if they have not often
witnessed the effects of the influence which a man thus
situated, exerts at an election.   Now the same causes
will generally speaking produce the same effects upon
the great scale as upon the small, and the case I have
mentioned illustrates the relative situation of the northern and southern States.   The southern states yield the
articles with which America is to pay for those foreign
productions which she consumes ; so in the case I have

mentioned, the extravagant farmers produce the articles with which the merchant in town is to be paid for his merchandise which they consume. But when the trader steps in as a middle man between the farmer and the merchant, although he has no capital and produces nothing himself, yet by deriving a profit both upon his sale of country produce in town, and upon the articles which he carries into the country, he creates a capital by his industry, and renders his extravagant customers dependent upon him. So the inhabitants of the commercial states, by purchasing the productions of the south from their extravagant owners, and deriving a profit upon the sale of them in Europe, and returning to the southern ports with wine and other articles of luxury of European growth, which suit the taste and habits of the natives of the southern states, create a source of wealth by their superior industry and economy, which it is probable would eventually introduce a state of dependence on the part of those they supplied, similar to that experienced by the extravagant farmer on the country trader.

The Northern States of America though deficient in native productions, would have become to the Southern States, what Holland was to those nations on the continent of Europe who were but little engaged in navigation and commerce; and it is notorious that the Dutch merchants, although they had no native articles to export, were among the richest in Europe. Nor was there any reasonable prospect of preventing the northern states from deriving this advantage but by the destruction of that commerce which threatened to bestow it upon them. The original causes were beyond the control of those men whose political consequence was thus brought into jeopardy. They originated in those distinguishing characteristics of indolence and extravagance, of activity and enterprise, which climate had introduced and habit had confirmed. It is true, if we consider the United States of America as one nation sl.

was materially benefited by commerce, in the southern
as well as the northern portion of the Union, and had
she been under a monarchial government, or indeed
under any government where the care of the general
interest was the actuating principle, it would have been
carefully cherished. But as it would certainly have
diminished the political importance of the great land-
holders and planters to the southward, they early determined upon its destruction.

We, sir, have indulged ourselves for years in laughing at what we termed the Chinese schemes, the philosophical reveries, and the Utopian dreams of Mr. Jefferson and his political associates; but although they
have sacrificed the good of their country to their own
ambitious views, yet I confess it appears evident to me
that they could not have devised better means to secure
that personal superiority and political power which
they are so anxious to retain, than those to which they
have had recourse. If commerce had flourished as it
would have done, if it had not been assailed by embar-
goes, non-importation acts and those other measures
with which the American government pretended to
defend, but really meant to destroy it, it is highly probable that the mere agents of the northern merchants·
would soon have acquired a greater degree of influence
in many of the southern States than the greatest landholder and planter. This influence would of course
have been exerted in favour of those candidates for the
Presidential Chair and for seats in Congress, who were
supported by the northern states, and the dictatorial
voice of Virginia would have been heard no more.

It is then to preserve the power of the landholder to
the southward by the destruction of American commerce
and navigation, that war has been declared against Great
Britain. To commerce itself they are not inimical; and if
Sweden, Denmark, or any other European nation should
be permitted to withdraw from the great contest in
which the world is now involved, and to maintain the

character and privileges of a neutral, there are no ports on the borders of the ocean to which they will be more welcome than those in the Southern States of America. If we do not blockade them strictly, they would then not only accomplish the object of destroying the wealth and power of the Northern States, but they would accomplish it without a sacrifice of their own trade; they would much rather encourage the navigation of Sweden or of any other European power than that of Massachusetts Bay, as their own commerce may be carried on quite as conveniently in neutral vessels as in those of their political rivals, who would thus be deprived of the means of acquiring that aggrandizement so much dreaded by the present rules of America.

We have heard much, sir, lately, of an embassy from the United States to Russia, to seek her mediation between Great Britain and America. If this mission has any object beyond that of cajoling the American people, it is probably designed to impress upon the mind of the Emperor the necessity and convenience of allowing one among the northern nations of Europe to remain neutral; if this point was once carried, it would release the southern people from most of the evils of the war (except at such times as they should be blockaded) while the navigating states must inevitably sink beneath its pressure.

The impositions which have been practised upon John Bull have frequently exposed him to ridicule; but if the good folks in America can really be persuaded that their government have undertaken this war in defence of their commerce, when every school boy sees that it must inevitably lead to its destruction, or that they are sincere in seeking the good offices of Russia to induce Great Britain to grant them that peace, which I blush to acknowledge, she has been soliciting from the Court of Washington; honest John must then cede the palm of credulity to his American offspring; but as the wresting of this trophy from his brow is not one of their

most undutiful acts it will excite more surprise than
anger ; let the act, however, be their own, for I trust
the deception is too gross to impose upon a single

ANGLO-AMERICAN.

It is needless to remark how half a century ago,
Judge Halliburton foresaw and prognosticated the hostility of North and South towards each other. True,
the proximate cause of the present difficulty is not
specially pointed out, as the spark for kindling that
flame which now burns with such fury throughout the
late Union. But the ultimate issue arising from all
causes was distinctly perceived by him and foretold.
But the documents may speak for themselves ; they, at
least, prove the interest which he felt in the colony,
and the ability with which he could wield his pen in
furtherance of any great cause.

Upon Mr. Madison's message he wrote and published
some severe strictures, particularly examining it from a
legal stand point of view. These letters, and those of
the "Anglo-American" were, without doubt, written
for more eyes and heads than those in Nova Scotia.
Sir John Sherbrooke at the time was Lieutenant-Gover-
nor of the Province ; and there can be little question,
but that through him the views of one close at hand,
and familiar with the whole business from beginning to
end, were read and studied with deep attention, at home.

Two more papers of this class were written by Judge
Halliburton some ten or twelve years later ; one of
them was published, the other was not. They were
both written during the administration of the Government by Sir James Kempt. The one consisted of cer-

tain observations upon the Governor's instructions delivered to Sir James during his term of office, and contains sentiments on free trade so enlarged and liberal as to be worthy of a later age. The other is a pamphlet seen by very few of those now living, originally printed at Halifax in the year 1825, and afterwards printed in London in 1831. The value of these colonies to England in her position as mistress of the seas, is set forth with arguments so sound and language so powerful, that it may not be amiss in the present day to call attention to the unalterable facts. The extracts immediately following are from observations on the Governor's instructions :

"It does not occur to me that any alterations are required in the remaining sections, and I would venture to suggest a hope that no very material alteration will be made in the *General Instructions*.

"The instructions which have been given to Governors with their Commissions on the first formation of a Colonial Government have been generally considered to be the basis of the Colonial constitution, and the Colonists have thought that as far as they conveyed to, or recognized rights in his Majesty's subjects, within the Colony, they could neither be altered nor rescinded, so far indeed as they were restrictive, it has never been questioned that the restriction (if it depended solely upon the instruction) might be lessened or removed.

"This idea has been carried so far that some have supposed that a Colonial Constitution, derived from his Majesty's instructions rests upon a more secure foundation than one created by Act of Parliament, upon the ground that the Parliament has the *power* to repeal any law which they have previously enacted, but that his Majesty cannot recall any rights which he has *granted* to his subjects; and the advocates for this opinion de-

clare that if the Parliament were to repeal the Quebec
Bill without making any provision for the Government
of Canada, that the power of governing that country
would revert as a matter of course to its old channel,
and the people would lose their right of being represented; but they assert that the inhabitants of Nova
Scotia would not lose their right of representation by
the revocation of the Governor's instruction to call
assemblies of the freeholders.

"Without discussing the soundness of this opinion I
would merely suggest to your Excellency the impolicy
of making any important alterations in the General Instructions. The mischievous might represent the measure as a remodelling of the Colonial constitutions.

"But this argument does not apply to the instructions
relative to trade; these are generally speaking restrictive upon the Colonies, and a relaxation of them is most
ardently desired. My situation and pursuits in life have
not afforded to me the opportunity of acquiring sufficient knowledge upon this subject, to give to your
Excellency any opinion upon these instructions in detail; but no one who takes any interest in the welfare
of the country can reside long in the Colonies without
making general observations upon this important subject; and the first consideration which presents itself is
the effect which the erection of an independent government on this side of the Atlantic must ultimately produce in the mind of the colonist in his view of the
relations between the colony and the mother country.

"While the whole of America was subject to one or
other of the European powers, the system of confining
the trade of the colony to the mother country, extended
all over the western continent, and while every inhabitant of America was subject to it, no invidious compa-
risons presented themselves to excite discontent.

"But when a merchant, residing in Quebec or in
Halifax, is now called by the course of his business to
visit New York or Boston, and sees the wealth which

the inhabitants of those cities have derived from unrestricted trade with all the world, it is natural for him to desire a participation in that advantage, and although he may be warmly attached to the British constitution, he is insensibly led to condemn the restrictions which debar him from it.

"It may, however, be said with justice, that an interested individual is not the proper person to judge of interests, so various and so complicated as those which are involved in the system of commercial restrictions, which the European Powers have hitherto imposed upon their Colonies. But it is the duty of the statesman to consider the effect of every material change in the situation of public affairs and of public feeling; and to decide whether a system, which may have been wise and useful at one time, may not under other circumstances become impolitic and mischievous.

"I am aware that some are of the opinion that the period of separation between a Parent State and its Colonies, must inevitably arrive, and that no system of policy can avert this event, when the colonies have attained sufficient wealth and strength to assert their independence; and politicians have existed, so narrow-minded as to suppose it expedient to cramp their exertions, and stint their growth, in order to preserve them in a state of dependence.

"Whatever opinion may be entertained by his Majesty's Ministers, upon the first point, we have no reason to suppose that any one of them is actuated by the narrow-minded principle to which I have last alluded. I am persuaded that they take a lively interest in the affairs of the Empire at large, and that they would gladly adopt any measures to advance the growth of the colonies, which did not interfere with the general interests of the country.

"It can scarcely be supposed that any person in his Majesty's confidence, can think the separation of the colonies from the mother country a desirable event; if

8

there be, I address no arguments to them. But to those who think it inevitable, I would suggest that the present colonies in North America are differently situated from those formerly possessed by Great Britain, which now compose the United States. When disputes arose between them and the parent state, the popular leaders were animated by the prospect of erecting the country into an independent nation; but no reasonable man in these colonies can ever entertain any such view. We can never become sufficiently strong to stand alone, and must, therefore, either continue our connexion with Great Britain, or form one with America. In considering the *probabilities* upon this subject, I would introduce no high-flown sentiments of loyalty on one side, or of liberty on the other; but adopting the lower, though sounder principles, that the colonies, like the rest of mankind, will be ultimately guided by their interests, I think it may be made to appear probable at least, that interest would induce them to desire a continuance of their connection with Great Britain, if a liberal system of policy should be adopted towards them.

"In the first place, it is certainly true that no citizen in the United States of America has his personal liberty more firmly secured to him, than his Majesty's subjects have in this Province.

"*Secondly*, it is equally true, that whatever property we acquire is guarded as sacredly by the laws which prevail in the colonies, as it is by those which exist in the United States.

"Upon these important points, therefore, we have no reason to desire a change. It must, however, be admitted that the facility of acquiring property is greater in the United States than in these colonies; and that a wider field is opened there for commercial enterprise. Should this continue to be the case, it cannot be doubted that the interest of the colonists will lead them ultimately to prefer a connexion with a country which will permit them to participate in those benefits, rather than to continue subject to one which withholds from them such privileges.

"It is for his Majesty's ministers to decide, whether it would not be wise to prevent this desire, by *gradually* removing the cause of it. I say gradually, because too sudden a relaxation of those restrictions, would certainly injure that class of his Majesty's subjects at home, who have hitherto engrossed the colonial trade, and might prove injurious to the colonies themselves, by exciting a wild spirit of speculation in branches of commerce, with which they are as yet unacquainted.

"It is for them to consider whether it would not be proper now to view the colonies in a different light. They have hitherto been viewed as a *property*, by which the sources of the wealth and commerce of the parent state might be increased; not as an extension of territory, by which the physical force of the empire may be augmented. So far, indeed, from adding to its strength, they have generally presented vulnerable points to an enemy, and have required a considerable portion of the British forces to be employed in their defence. But the time will soon arrive when they must either add to the strength of Great Britain, or of America. In the event of a war between those two countries, it is evident that, if the feelings of the colonists were not favorable to Great Britain, it would be difficult to retain them; and few persons will be so romantic as to suppose those feelings would be in favour of Great Britain, if interest leant the other way.

"It will be easy to prove that the addition of these northern colonies to the United States, would not be a desirable event to Great Britain. It would increase in a very great degree the naval strength of America, by giving to them many commodious harbours, and a hardy race of seamen which our fisheries must produce; it would add to the wealth and consequently to the national resources of that country, by the possession of

those fisheries, and the mineral productions in which
these provinces abound. •

"The retention of these provinces would not merely
prevent America from enjoying these advantages; but
if the affections of the people are also retained it would
be an important weight thrown into the opposite scale.
The population of the colonies, it is true, neither does
nor will enable them to cope single handed with
America; but it must be remembered that the United
States of America are not composed of a people well
adapted for recruiting armies, to carry on conquests.
The inhabitants of that country are a formidable enemy
to invade; but they are, generally speaking, too comfortable in their own homes to engage in distant expe-
ditions; and their Government could seldom raise a
disposable force, which the colonies, if hearty in their
opposition, could not with a little assistance from the
mother country, successfully resist.

"The question which his Majesty's ministers, therefore, have now under consideration, relating to the
colonies, is not merely commercial, but involves important political considerations. Should they be induced,
after mature deliberation, to decide that it would be
sounder policy to act upon the principle of relaxation,
rather than upon that of restriction, and determine to
pursue a course which would ultimately give to the
colonies a much greater freedom of trade, it may be
doubted whether that event would prove injurious to
the commerce of Great Britain. The wealth which a
free trade has enabled the inhabitants of the United
States to acquire, has made them better customers to
Great Britain, than they could have been, had they
continued cramped by restrictions; and should the
liberality and indulgence of the mother country even
produce the effects of making the colonies in a series of
years, *virtually* independent, their *nominal* connexion, if
it should be nothing more, would prevent their falling
into the hands of America. The pride which they now

feel, in considering themselves as forming a part of one of the greatest empires in the world, would in all probability still continue. If the *power* of the mother country over the colonies should not be as great, after they had attained to a state of maturity, as it was in their infancy, her *influence* would still be felt; as those angry feelings which successful rebellion excited in the revolted colonies, would never be called into existence among a people who must attribute their prosperity to the fostering hand of an indulgent parent."

Each reader can make his own observations on the tone and judgment manifested in this document. It surely proves that he was not pent up by contracted notions, or the mere servant at will of Governments and Governors. He had an opinion of his own, and he exercised it. Though all may not agree with the conclusion at which he arrives, it is evident that he carefully weighed in the scale any matters brought beneath his notice, and endeavoured to ascertain just what they came to in the balance. His mind was more enlarged and his sentiments more generous than men of his day are usually accredited with.

In the year 1816, Judge Halliburton was appointed to a seat in the Council, then consisting of twelve members, and discharging the combined executive and legislative duties. The names of those with whom he was thus associated, were as follows :—

Hon. S. S. Blowers, *Prest.*
Rt. Rev. Robert Stanser,
  Bishop of Nova Scotia.
Michael Wallace.
Charles Hill.
Richard John Uniacke.
Charles Morris.

James Stewart.
Thomas N. Jeffery.
John Black.
Brenton Halliburton.
Philip Wodehouse.
Rupert D. George, *Sec'y.*

His value as a working man was soon felt, and he was rarely absent from his post. Scarcely a measure of importance came up, that he was not chosen as one of those most competent to take it in hand. In looking over the minutes of Council, we cannot help noticing the frequent recurrence of his name. In the years 1817, 1818, and 1819, he was very busy with all those questions of local interest which came before the Council; and when, a year or two later, the province took a fresh start, he specially interested himself in all that pertained to its true interests. Like the law lords in the British House of Peers, he watched and moulded all questions with a legal eye and hand. In all matters relating to education he took the deepest interest. He was a warm advocate for granting provincial aid to the Pictou Academy, and for many years strenuously supported its claims. Nor did he cease to uphold its cause until the injudicious character of the resolutions passed by its trustees, compelled him most reluctantly to withhold from it his further advocacy: for he was no blind adherent to party, but gave reasons for his course,—reasons always clearly expressed with orderly connexion and simplicity of language. Nor was it in the Council only that he was busily engaged. In everything which concerned the welfare of the province he came forward prominently to lend his aid. When the mercantile community were anxious to improve their position as a body, and to possess at once a recognized status amongst the merchants of British North America, and a bond of union and mutual intercourse, Judge Halliburton was to be found in their midst, helping them with information, and furthering their cause. At the public meetings his speeches were among the most lengthened and able. When social matters attracted the attention of the community, he was at his post, ready to work, as he was willing to advise. Of the Poor Man's Friend Society—an institution which circumstances seemed loudly to call for—the Judge was an active member. At the public meetings for the furtherance of its objects, his voice was seldom unheard. Unhappily this last public movement seems to have been early blasted by the introduction of politics. The newspapers were filled with correspondence, breathing strongly of bitter feeling and insinuating unworthy motives. The society soon broke up, and its name was soon forgotten. Thus busily employed with public affairs, and the special duties of his office, his time was diligently and usefully spent in the province. Nor does he seem to have sought any respite from labours which were at once toilsome and responsible, until the year 1821, from which date until the year of his elevation to the Chief Justiceship, will comprise the period of time contained in the following chapter.

CHAPTER IV.

On the 23d June, 1821, Judge Halliburton made one of a party who embarked with Admiral Griffith on board H. M. S. " Newcastle," on a voyage to Quebec. Of this pleasant trip to Canada he kept a journal, the brief notes of which testify to his powers of observation, the vivacity of his disposition, and his love for nature. The voyage was made without any special incident but one, which he describes with a good deal of interest as bearing witness to the order and discipline maintained in the British Navy. The ship was beating through the narrow Strait of Canseau, and in tacking touched the shore near Ship Harbour, and the quiet and prompt manner in which everything was done struck him so much that he made the following note of it :

" Nothing could have been more interesting than this scene. Instead of the hurry and bustle which might naturally have been expected to accompany the exertions to get the ship off, they were made with so much quietness and regularity that a person seated in the cabin would not have known that anything unusual had happened ; everything was done with the utmost promptitude : but the officers issued their orders without the appearance of haste, and the crew received them in silence and obeyed them with alacrity."

As the ship sailed up the St. Lawrence, the weather

was gloomy, and the passengers saw but little of the scenery. On the third day, however, after entering the mouth of the river, the fog cleared away, and Judge Halliburton enjoyed the scene unfolded to him very much. "July 3d, 1821. Until this morning the weather had been wet and hazy from the day of our entrance into the St. Lawrence, and consequently we could discover but little of the banks of that majestic river; the occasional glimpses, however, which we gained through the fog inspired us with an idea of the grandeur of the scenery. But on this morning the sun rose in all his majesty, the atmosphere was clear and cool, the wind fair, and everything conspired to heighten the natural beauties of the country. Confined as I had been for years to the tame scenery of Nova Scotia, I was not merely surprised, I was astonished on opening the view of Quebec, which presented itself to us. About half-past 8, the wind baffled us a little off Point Levi, which afforded to us the opportunity of seeing the prospect from different points. The bold grandeur of Cape Diamond excited my admiration much more than the Falls of Montmorenci, which (although a beautiful feature in the scene,) I must acknowledge fell short of my expectations. Cape Diamond has the advantage of contrast in the soft view which Point Levi presents on the opposite banks, and its rude and abrupt height is augmented to the eye by the buildings which cluster at its base. We landed with the Admiral at 11 A. M., and viewed the town, which by no means fulfils the expectations which its appearance from the water excites. We ascended the heights of Cape Diamond. The approach to its precipitous bank towards the river made me so dizzy that

I was glad to turn my eyes in the opposite direction, and the eye cannot turn any way from the magnificent eminence without meeting much to gratify it. The country on the banks of the Charles, which runs into the St. Lawrence below Quebec, is delightful, and the distant mountains make a very fine termination to the scene."

After a short visit at Quebec, the party proceeded to Montreal, and in their walk through the city, Judge Halliburton made some observations on the buildings, which it will be as well to transcribe: " The town is very superior to Quebec. The generality of the private houses are substantial and apparently comfortable, and many of them indicate that the owners are or should be wealthy. I afterwards learned that these buildings had enriched the town, but impoverished the builders. The public buildings are very good, and appear quite consistent with the present state of the country. They have not fallen into our error in Nova Scotia of building for posterity. There is a lofty monument erected near them to the memory of Nelson, which speaks more for the inhabitants of Montreal than it does for the taste or skill of the artist employed to erect it. The representation of some of his naval victories is displayed on the faces of the pedestal. If they are at all correct, the fire from Nelson's ships must have indeed been terrific, for the very smoke appears as if it would sink whatever vessel it fell upon. I wish the hero had been enveloped in such a cloud on the memorable 19th of October; a musket-ball never could have penetrated it."

The Earl and Countess of Dalhousie who had left Quebec some time previously, for the purpose of

making an excursion through the United States, were
now at Kingston, having accomplished their purpose,
and been highly gratified therewith. It had been
arranged that the Admiral's party should meet them in
Canada, and together proceed to visit the Falls of
Niagara.

A letter from a friend to Judge Halliburton, announced that the Earl and his friends were at
Kingston, anxiously awaiting the arrival of himself and
the Admiral, that they might start immediately for their
destination. Of the journey between Montreal and
Kingston, Judge Halliburton gives the following account: "We thus accomplished our journey from
Montreal to Kingston, in three days, and were only
thirty-seven hours and three quarters actually in the
carriage. The road as far as Prescott is very good;
from that to Kingston, it is extremely bad. There is
not, however, a bad hill in the whole extent; the
country is uniformly level and very fertile. Throughout Lower Canada it is almost studded with churches,
whose glittering spires (for all are covered with tin)
enliven the scene very much. The system of Agriculture, however, is most wretched; and the land which
appears originally to have been of an excellent quality,
is quite exhausted. The crops were thin and miserable; the farmers' houses, small, but well calculated
to resist the cold. In Upper Canada, the appearance
is directly the reverse of all this. You travel for miles
without meeting with a place of worship; but the
private houses are very superior to any thing in the
country parts of Nova Scotia, and I might say (with
few exceptions) to those in the towns also. Their

farms are apparently well cultivated, and the crops in general look extremely well. As to the characters or manners of the people of either Province, it would be presumptuous to speak, as we merely passed through the high road. The soil in Upper Canada, on the banks of St. Lawrence, is of a very superior quality, The road passes through a great extent of intervale. occasionally through a sandy loam, and sometimes, though rarely, through a loamy sand. One of the drivers, (a very decent man) assured me that they frequently took a crop of potatoes, or Indian corn, and two crops of wheat off the burnt land, before they laid it down, and this, of course, without manuring."

As soon as arrangements were made, the whole party started for the Falls. If it were proper to quote from the Judge's " journal," the entire description of the journey and the actual visit to this wonder of the world, the whole would be read with interest. The account, however, is so interspersed with remarks and anecdotes of a private nature, and only meant for the perusal of his own friends, that it would be a breach of confidence to transcribe them. But there is a simplicity and vivacity in the running comment that lends a charm to the diary, and makes one desire to travel over the same ground.

A few extracts, necessarily shorn of much of their value by their severance from the context, are introduced, in order to show the pleasure which the scene afforded him :

" After breakfast we proceeded to the Falls, but as the Admiral's party had not experienced the pleasure of travelling in canoes, his lordship proposed that we should accompany the ladies, who preferred that mode of travelling. The two canoes which had brought the Earl's party from Lower Canada, and were to convey his lordship to Drummond's Island, on Lake Huron, were accordingly launched. They were thirty-three feet in length, five and a half in breadth, and about three feet in depth, and manned with eight Canadian voyageurs, besides a steersman aft and another forward. Mr. Shaw, a gentleman of N. W. Company, who was with us, assured me that these canoes would carry four and a half tons of merchandize, besides provisions for their crews, for sixty days. The canoemen commenced singing and paddling almost at the same time. The day was fine,—the water smooth,—the surrounding scenery beautiful,—the party pleasant; in short the *toute en-semble* was delightful. The two canoes kept within a few feet of each other. One of the canoemen led the song, and the crews of both joined in the chorus. The singing was in a very different style from our batteau-men on the lake, and although we could not get at the sense, we were highly delighted with the sound of the songs. In this manner we proceeded to Queenstown, about seven miles above Fort George. Here the rapids commenced, and we quitted our canoes very reluctantly to proceed by land. After viewing the spot where the gallant Brock fell, we repaired to the carriages which had been prepared for us.

" We were now within ten miles of the Falls, and anticipated the pleasure of witnessing this great wonder of nature in less than two hours. Her ladyship, how-ever, proposed that we should quit the road and drive to the whirlpool, as we might not have leisure to stop there on our return. She proposed this without inti-mating that it was an object deserving of much atten-tion, and we proceeded towards it, without having our expectations highly raised. You may judge, therefore, of our surprise when we found ourselves, after a short walk through the woods, on the edge of a precipice,

which appeared to be two hundred feet high. The
opposite bank corresponded in height; and the whole
waters of the St. Lawrence were rushing between in a
narrow channel to a point where a sudden turn in the
river produced an ever-boiling whirlpool. You cannot
understand the effect by mere description.

"We remained admiring the whirlpool about a quarter of an hour, and then resumed our course towards
the Falls, which we reached about two o'clock; and
here the pen should drop, for bold would he be who
would attempt to describe them, or even to communicate
an idea of his own feelings, when they first burst upon
the view, as it respects the Falls of Niagara. Therefore I
have only to say, that to know, you must see them.

"The Horse Shoe Fall on the English side, which is
infinitely grander, burst upon us, and we were really
lost in admiration and astonishment. I do not remember to have experienced similar feelings. I could
neither speak nor be silent, but left the whole party behind and hurried towards the Horse Shoe with an inex-
pressible mixture of wonder, of delight, and of awe. I
never longed so much at once to dive, to swim, to soar,
to glide, as at this moment, and wished that I were sufficiently etherial to float in safety upon the waters which
rolled so majestically over the precipice, near to which
I stood. The rest of the party soon joined me, and we
remained nearly two hours at the Table Rock."

After mentioning a number of separate visits paid
during two or three days to the Falls, and viewing them
from various stand-points,—sometimes by the light of
the early sun,—sometimes by that of the moon, far on in
the hours of the night,—we have a description of the visit
now so ordinarily paid to the Falls. Here are his
notes. Those who have lately done the same, may
institute a comparison between the present and forty
years ago :

" 16th. I rose early this morning, having engaged to accompany his lordship and Col. Beresford under the Falls. We left our clothes in the shed which covers the staircase, and proceeded along the bottom of the bank about half a mile *sans chemise* in a nankeen jacket and pantaloons only. The morning was very favorable to our enterprise, and we advanced many yards (I should think thirty,) under the tremendous torrent without any difficulty. His lordship led the way, and seated himself near to a slanting rock, which impeded our progress farther. We could scarcely hear each other's voices. There was at times a momentary difficulty of breathing from the rush of the waters inwards, but the adventure is not attended with any risk. The situation produces a mixed sensation of awe and admiration. One would not go to the Falls without paying a visit to the cavern, which does not appear designed for human entrance ; but when the visit is once paid there remains no wish to repeat it. On my return home it appeared to me that the following lines might be conceived, though they could not easily be penned there :—

" Here, seated mid the rush of mighty waters,
    We look aloft to that stupendous height
    From whence the roaring cataract descends,
    And tremble, lest the torrent in its fury
    Should dash this massy rock into the flood.
    But 'tis not fear, when such a scene as this
    With awful grandeur overpowers the soul,
    When mixt emotions thrill through every vein,
    Astonished man seems raised above himself,
    Nor knows if pain or pleasure 'tis he feels."

" The countess and the ladies were to return under our escort to Montreal. Soon after breakfast we paid a farewell visit to the Falls, where, as I was lying upon my breast looking over the precipice at the Table Rock, I heard Lord Dalhousie utter an exclamation which at first alarmed me, but I was soon relieved by his calling out, " The hat, the hat." I looked up and beheld my poor broad-brimmed hat (upon the acquisition of which Judge Stewart congratulated me so warmly) gracefully floating upon the air between the Table Rock and the abyss below. Notwithstanding the half-formed wish which I entertained on my first visit to the Falls—that I could take a similar flight—I was well pleased my head was not in it. I had taken it off, before I laid down, and placed it upon the rock. to avoid the very evil which occurred, but a sudden breeze bore it away in despite of my precaution. His lordship immediately took Lady Dalhousie's arm, who was upon her hands and knees looking over the precipice beside me; and reminding her ladyship that as she was not very weighty the wind might seize her drapery and bear her off also. It was supposed that my poor beaver was irretrievably lost, but I dispatched a man after it, with the promise of half a dollar if he would look for it, to be augmented to a dollar in case he found it; and I very soon regained the felt, and felt what I regained. Of course its value is very much augmented, as I imagine very few hats have floated down the Falls of Niagara and returned to their own *blocks* again."

The Judge soon returned home, and was once more engaged in his duties at the Council board, and on the Bench. It has been already mentioned that he wrote and published, in the year 1825, some "Observations on the importance of the North American Colonies to Great Britain," which were republished in London in 1831. At a time like the present, when the question of throwing these colonies upon their own resources for defence, has been seriously brought forward in the British Parliament, and advocated by some of the ablest writers of the British press, it will not be inappropriate to reprint the pamphlet entire. Indeed the reproduction of this treatise will give a value to this memoir which it would not otherwise possess, inasmuch as it not only shows the compass of his mind, but may also be of service at that juncture of affairs towards which we are fast hastening.

OBSERVATIONS ON THE IMPORTANCE OF THE NORTH AMERICAN COLONIES TO GREAT BRITAIN : *By an Old Inhabitant of British America.*

CHAPTER I.

IT should afford great satisfaction to the inhabitants of British America to observe, that the attention of our statesmen is every day called, more and more towards the colonies of this continent, not only by those who have an opportunity of expressing their opinions in parliament, but by numerous writers in the public prints and periodical publications of the day.

The minds of his Majesty's Ministers have been so much occupied, by the important events which have occurred in Europe during the last five-and-thirty years, that they have been unable to allow themselves time to inquire into the real value of these colonies; and we should therefore rejoice, if this subject is brought to their consideration even by those who deny our importance.

It is contended, by some writers of the present day, that the North American Colonies are not worth the expense which it will cost the mother country to maintain and defend them. These writers do not say that the colonies are positively mischievous, or that Great Britain would sustain any injury from retaining them if they cost her nothing; but they lay down this position —'that no colony is worth retaining, unless the mother country derives a *revenue* equal to her expenditure upon it.' But may we not ask the advocates of this opinion, whether pounds, shillings, and pence should alone

9

engross a statesman's mind ; and if the adjustment of an account of profit and loss is the whole duty of a politician ?

It behoves those who would wish to form a correct opinion of the propriety of retaining or discarding these colonies, to consider well the present situation of the United States of America. During the long contest which so recently distracted Europe, the feelings of a large portion of the population of that country were decidedly hostile to us ; and their government chose to declare war upon us at a time when the freedom not only of Great Britain, but of the whole world, might be said to have depended upon the event of the invasion of Russia by Buonaparte.

Circumstances may again occur, to excite a similar disposition, and it may be roused into action at a period still more inconvenient than that which has just been alluded to. Should not our statesmen, then, reflect upon the means by which this hostile disposition may be best averted ; and how it may be rendered least formidable should it unfortunately be excited ?

When we look to the United States of America, we see a people of British descent ; who speak our language, adopt our laws, and who inherit our love of freedom and our spirit of enterprise. We see this energetic people rapidly spreading themselves over an immense continent, containing every variety of climate, and capable of yielding the richest productions of the earth. We can set no bounds to the population which such a country may in future maintain ; and we cannot refrain from asking ourselves if they are not destined to become formidable rivals to the nations in Europe ; and whether it does not behove the statesmen of that portion of the world to keep a watchful eye upon their growing power ?

Now it may be safely asserted, that no circumstance would have so great a tendency to increase that power, as the surrender of these colonies to the United States ;

nay, we may go further, and declare that it is almost the *only* measure that can render these states formidable enemies of Great Britain.

Separated from Europe by the Atlantic Ocean, they can only become formidable to nations of that continent as a maritime power. This truth is so obvious, that it cannot have escaped those who direct the affairs of the present mistress of the sea : but it ought not to be taken for granted (as it unfortunately is by many) that America *must inevitably* become a great maritime power : many predict that she will be so, because she possesses a great extent of coast, has the means of supporting an immense population, and abounds in rich productions, with which she can carry on an extensive foreign trade.

It must be admitted, that a country so situated may become very powerful upon the ocean : and it is highly probable that the navy of the United States will very soon be a valuable addition to the fleets of any of the European powers in future wars. But let it be recollected, that France and Spain possess all the advantages which have been enumerated, and yet their united naval force has ever been unequal to overpower that of Great Britain. And to what is it owing, that thirty millions of Frenchmen, aided by ten millions of Spaniards, are unable to equip and man fleets sufficiently powerful to destroy the navy of an Island which does not possess half that population? Principally to this, that the inhabitants of the inland parts of France and Spain, which form so large a portion of their population, reside in a country which affords them the means of subsistence, without obliging them to seek it abroad, and they are therefore indisposed to encounter the hardships of a seaman's life. Whereas Great Britain is everywhere surrounded by the ocean; the most inland parts of the island are not very distant from the sea; and as the productions of the soil would not support a very numerous population, a large proportion of its people are compelled to seek their subsistence by

engaging in the fisheries, or in the coasting and
foreign trade.   And it is from this hardy and enterprising portion of her subjects, that Great Britain derives
the means of establishing and maintaining her superiority upon the ocean.

Now it is evident, that the United States of America,
even now, resemble the countries of France and Spain,
in this particular, more than Great Britain ; and as
their people recede from the ocean, and plant themselves in the valleys beyond the Alleghany mountains,
the resemblance will be still greater.   By far the greater
part of the inhabitants of those distant regions will live
and die without ever having placed their feet upon the
deck of a ship, and will consequently add nothing to the
maritime population of the country ; the rich productions of their fertile valleys will find their way to New
Orleans,* and there provide abundant means of carrying
on foreign trade ; but the carriers of these productions
to the foreign market will either be foreigners, or
natives of the Atlantic States.

It is to these States, then, that America must look to
provide the seamen who are to man her navy, and
among these New York and New England will stand
pre-eminent.   The southern states of Virginia, the
Carolinas and Georgia, it is true, carry on an extensive
foreign trade ; but, independent of their being destitute
of any very commodious harbours for ships of war of
the larger classes, their climate, and the nature of their
population, equally unfit them to produce hardy and
enterprising mariners.   They have few, if any, vessels
engaged in the fisheries, and are therefore destitute of
that first great nursery for seamen.   The mercantile
sea-ports to the southward of the Delaware would,
doubtless, produce a very respectable number of sailors

---

* It may be observed here, that the exclusive use of steamboats
upon the Mississippi will even lessen the number of *fresh-water*
sailors which must otherwise have been employed on that immense
river.

at the commencement of a war; but as it is notorious that merchants usually navigate their vessels with the smallest possible number of hands, the employment of these men in the navy, in a country where the labouring classes cannot provide substitutes for them, will not only be productive of great inconvenience to the mercantile interest, but will render it difficult, if not impracticable, for the American Navy to procure further recruits from the southern states after it made its first sweep from the ships of the merchants; for surely those who are destined to wrest the sovereignty of the sea from Great Britain will not be selected from the indolent slaves of the southern planter.

I submit it, then, to the consideration of those who will reflect seriously upon this subject, whether the maritime population of the United States of America must not be principally derived from New York and New England. I do not deny that seamen will frequently be met with from other portions of the Union, but I mean to contend that these are the only states in that Union, who possess a population which, by their habits and pursuits, are calculated to raise America as a naval power. Let us, then, view their present situation, and consider whether there is much probability of their increasing the means they now possess of adding to the naval strength of their country.

The states of New York and New England are now old, settled countries : the population of the former may become more numerous in the back parts of the country, but an increase in that quarter will add but little to her maritime strength. But New England, and the south-eastern parts of New York, are already so fully peopled, that frequent emigrations take place from them to the inland States. Massachusetts does not, and we believe we may say cannot, raise within herself bread to support her present population, and therefore can never expect to increase her numbers very rapidly; while the western territory offers to her youth the tempting prospect of obtaining a livelihood in that rich country upon easier terms than they can procure it within her limits.

Let it not, then, be deemed chimerical to say, that America has no immediate prospects of becoming a great naval power.

If the confederation of these states continues, they will no doubt become rich and powerful to a degree that may defy all aggression; but it does not follow, that they will acquire a naval force that will prove formidable to the powers of Europe. Germany has been among the most powerful nations of Europe, and Austria and Hungary now produce valuable articles of export; but these countries, from their geographical situations, cannot produce a maritime population: other nations have, therefore, become the carriers of their productions, and they have never possessed any power upon the ocean. The inland states of America are precisely in the same situation; and I close these observations by repeating, first, that the sources of the naval power of America must be principally derived from the states of New York and New England; and, secondly, that there will be no great increase of the maritime population of those states until the western territory is fully peopled. When these fertile valleys are all occupied, and no longer hold out a temptation to the youth of the Atlantic States to remove thither, then they must follow the example of their ancestors in Great Britain; and if the soil of their country will not yield them a subsistence, they must seek it from the sea which washes its shores. But that day, I think it will admitted by all, is far distant: ages must elapse before that vast country, through which the Ohio, the Missouri and the Mississippi roll, will afford no further room for the enterprising emigrant.

CHAPTER II.

IF there is any truth in the preceding observations, that the United States of America can only become formidable to the nations of Europe as a maritime power— that their maritime strength must spring from the maritime states, and can only increase with the increase of the maritime population of these states—it follows inevitably that the addition of other maritime states to that confederation must increase their maritime resources, and accelerate the period when they will become formidable upon the ocean.

I have before ventured to assert that no circumstance would have so great a tendency to increase that power as the surrender of these colonies to the United States ; and I shall now endeavour to prove this assertion.

America would thereby gain an immense addition to her sea coast, and of a description, too, very superior to the greater part of that which she now possesses, for the formation of a maritime population.

This coast may be divided into three portions.   The first, commencing at the Bay of Passamaquoddy, where the American line now terminates, along the shores of New Brunswick and Nova Scotia, to Cape St. Mary's. The second, running from Cape St. Mary's along the Atlantic coast of Nova Scotia and Cape Breton, to Cape North.   The third, running from Cape North, along the western side of Cape Breton, to the Gut of Canso— thence along the northern shores of Nova Scotia, to the Bay of Verte, and from thence along the coast to that part of New Brunswick and Canada which lies upon the Gulf St. Lawrence, to the mouth of the noble river from which that Gulf takes its name.

Each of these three divisions contains an extent of coast equal to that which runs from New York to the Bay of Passamaquoddy ; which may certainly be deemed the most formidable part of that now possessed by America, for naval purposes.

In the first section, we commence with the fine Bay of Passamaquoddy, containing several islands, whose inhabitants, from their situation, will always be seafaring persons; the town of St. Andrew, in this bay, is already rising into mercantile importance, and is resorted to by numbers of European fishing and coasting vessels. At no great distance from St. Andrew's is the town of St. John, situated at the mouth of the fine river of the same name, which supplies it, and will for years continue to supply it, with immense quantities of timber: many hundred vessels are engaged in carrying this timber to Great Britain, and bringing out the supplies of British goods which the wants of a rapidly increasing population annually demand: ship-building is carried on to a great extent up the river, as well as in many other situations farther up the bay, on the New Brunswick and Nova Scotia shores; and, as the capital of the country increases, more attention is paid to the construction of them, and they will very soon bear a high character. As we proceed round the Bay of Fundy to the counties of Westmoreland, in New Brunswick; Cumberland, Colchester, Hants, King's County, and Annapolis, in Nova Scotia, we meet with a country, the greater part of which can scarcely be exceeded in point of fertility. The upland is of an excellent quality, and thousands of acres of most valuable marsh have already been reclaimed from the sea, and are capable of maintaining ten times the number of people which now inhabit these districts.

This section of the coast has no good harbours, but it has numerous rivers, inlets, and creeks, into which the rapid tides* of the Bay of Fundy enable vessels of large size to enter; and when those tides recede, the soft

---

* These tides rise in some parts of the bay, 30, in others 40 or 50, and in some from 60 to 70 feet.

muddy bottoms of these inlets and creeks render it perfectly safe even for heavy-loaded vessels to rest upon them.

Great numbers of small craft, owned and navigated by the inhabitants of the country, are now met with on this bay, carrying from the places I have mentioned, gypsum and lumber (in which the country abounds) and agricultural produce, to the ports of St. John and St. Andrew; and if these colonies were possessed by the United States, it would be filled with vessels of a larger description, conveying, not only such articles in much greater quantities, but coals also (which are found in abundance at the head of the bay) to the populous towns of Boston, New York, Philadelphia, &c., where their cargoes would meet with a ready sale. The navigation of the Bay of Fundy is at all times difficult, and in particular seasons of the year it is dangerous; but the people who reside upon its shores are a hardy, enterprising race; and you can scarcely enter the house of a farmer in that part of the country, in which you will not find some member of the family quite capable of taking charge of one of these small vessels, and conducting her in safety up or down the bay. The difficulty and the danger, therefore, will only tend to make more expert seamen of those who undertake to convey the productions of that country to market.

At Cape St. Mary's, the fishing-coast, as it may be termed, commences, and runs without interruption along the whole southern and eastern shores of Nova Scotia and Cape Breton, to Cape North. This line of coast is peculiarly adapted to produce hardy and enterprising seamen. With the exception of the small county of Lunenburg, which lies about forty miles to the westward of Halifax, no part of this coast can support an agricultural population. The land upon these shores is, generally speaking, rocky and barren, containing many spots capable of affording the fisherman potatoes to eat with his fish; but few which can

repay the man who devotes his labour exclusively to
the cultivation of the soil. But perhaps no part of the
world is more favourably situated for carrying on
extensive fisheries; it abounds with numerous and
commodious harbours, accessible at all seasons of the
year,* and capable of affording shelter to the largest
vessels. The shores swarm with fish, and, notwithstanding the injurious effects of the restrictions upon
our commerce, which the liberal policy of the mother
country is now about to remove, the natural advantages
of this part of Nova Scotia have induced many enterprising merchants in the settlements along the coast,
not only to carry on the shore fishery to a great extent,
but to employ vessels in the Labrador and Bank fishery
also. Now that these restrictions are removed, and the
commerce of the world is laid open to us, there cannot
be a doubt that our population upon this coast will
most rapidly increase; the numbers of the fishermen will
very soon be more than doubled; and the supplies which
these fisheries will require will increase the coasting trade
in the same ratio that the fisheries themselves increase:
thus producing, in a vigorous and healthy climate, a
most extensive nursery for hardy seamen.

At Cape North we commence the third section; and
although it is true that the navigation of this part of
the British possessions in America is closed during four,
or, in unfavourable seasons, during five months of the
year, yet during the other seven or eight months, the
whole gulf may be said to be whitened with the canvas
of vessels engaged in the timber trade, in the Labrador
and coasting fisheries, and in carrying supplies of
European and West India produce, not only for the
consumption of the inhabitants of this coast, but of the
rapidly increasing population of Upper and Lower

---

* As I wish not to mislead any one who may favour these observations with a perusal, I must except the harbours of Cape Breton,
lying between Scatari and Cape North.

Canada. Seven hundred sail of vessels annually proceed up the river St. Lawrence; upwards of three hundred go to Miramichi; and as many more may be divided among the ports of Merrigomish, Pictou, Tatamagouche, Ramsheg, Richibucto, and other harbours, between the Gut of Canso and Miramichi.

It may be said, that by far the greater part of these vessels are owned in Great Britain, and that if these colonies were ceded to America, their inhabitants would still wish to dispose of their timber, and would continue to require the same supplies which they now receive from the mother country, and would, therefore, afford the same employment to British shipping.

We will admit that this *might* be the case during a state of peace; I say, *might* be, because it is certainly more probable that American vessels would be substituted for British, to carry what would then be the productions of an American country to market, and also to bring back the supplies which that part of the country would require. But, in a state of war, all communication would cease; and, in the event of a mischievous alliance between America and the northern powers of Europe, where, we may ask, would Great Britain obtain those supplies of timber and other articles which these colonies are capable of producing, and which she may command as long as she retains them in her own possession?

The supply of timber is almost inexhaustible in the immense forests of this part of British America, and, as the forests are cleared, the land, particularly along the western side of Cape Breton, the whole of Prince Edward Island, the Gulf Coast of Nova Scotia, and the greater part of that of New Brunswick, is well calculated for cultivation, and is capable of maintaining an immense population. Numerous settlers are already established upon the shores, some of whom devote themselves to agriculture, others to the Gulf and Labrador fisheries, and some engage in the coal trade and in foreign commerce. When this part of the country is more fully peopled, the inter-communication of the numerous ports and harbours in the Gulf must create an extensive coasting trade, which will be carried on exclusively by the vessels of the power that owns the surrounding country.

I do not proceed to describe the coast northward, from the river St. Lawrence to the Straits of Bellisle, and from thence along the western side of Newfoundland to the entrance of the Gulf, because, although the first part of that coast is British, yet it affords *no home* for fishermen, and, as visitors, during the fishing season, it is open to American vessels as well as to our own, and the remainder belongs exclusively to the French.

Under existing circumstances, therefore, the coast of Labrador may afford equal facilities for forming seamen, both to Great Britain and America; but if the whole of the British possessions in North America should be surrendered to the United States, it may be doubted whether they would then be equally complaisant to us. It is not improbable that they would soon deem both the French and ourselves to be intruders on any part of the coast of North America. The President of the United States stated to Congress, upon a late occasion, that he had availed himself of the opportunity to which he then alluded, to intimate to the powers of Europe, that the continent of North America was no longer subject to colonization from that side of the water; and if Great Britain were once expelled from it, the slight hold which France has would soon be loosened.

Let us here pause and behold this young gigantic republic in possession of this vast addition to her sea-coast, a great part of which would deny to the people who inhabited it a subsistence from the soil, but would afford to them not merely a subsistence, but the means of acquiring wealth from the sea; and the remainder capable not only of supporting a numerous population, but abounding in minerals of various descriptions, in inexhaustible forests of timber, and other means of supporting an immense foreign and coasting trade.

Let us contemplate the numerous inhabitants of this extensive coast, who, from their pursuits, their habits, their laws, their language, their religion, and their feelings, bear a greater resemblance to the inhabitants of Great Britain than any other portion of the known world, and who are now well disposed to continue her subjects. Let us, I say, view these persons ranged upon the side of her enemies; let us see them manning the fleets of hostile America, and engaged in endeavouring to subvert that power which they are now desirous to support; let us see the treasures of Great Britain lavished to carry on a maritime war with America, into which, but for this accession of strength, the latter would not, perhaps, have engaged; and then let us ask ourselves if it would be wise in those who can retain them as subjects of Great Britain, to relinquish them to America, merely because they do not *directly* pay into her treasury a revenue equal to the expense of their establishments.

Are all the wholesome principles which formerly regulated the conduct of British statesmen to be forgotten? When France endeavoured to establish a nursery for seamen on this side of the Atlantic, Great Britain viewed her proceedings with the most jealous eye; and the city of London was illuminated for three successive nights, when the news of the capture of Louisburg was announced. Was it the acquisition of this small town, which is now reduced to ruins, that occasioned this burst of joy? Nay, were the rejoicings which took place on the reduction of Canada itself, owing to any positive advantages the nation expected to derive from this addition of territory? No, it was the blow which these events gave to our natural enemy; it was the diminution of her means to do us further harm, in our future contests with her, that excited our exultation;—

and it was then thought that the money which the reduction of these places, as well as that which the retention of them would require, would be well expended in
wresting and preserving them from the hands of France.
And shall we now, for the sake of saving a few
pounds, abandon a much more important country to a
nation who, when she once obtains possession of the
coast which I have described, will become more formidable upon the ocean than France has ever been?

That nation has already evinced a disposition to rank
herself among the enemies of Great Britain; and the
events of the last short war had a strong tendency to
increase the national vanity of the Americans, and to
induce them to believe, that they alone are capable of
coping with Englishmen upon the seas. Nor let us con-
ceal from ourselves that there is some foundation for
this idea; they are descended from Britons; they have
the spirit and the energy of freemen; the climate of the
northern portion of their country is calculated to make
them hardy; and it must not be supposed that they are
even now contemptible foes.

It remains for Great Britain to decide whether the
maritime population of the country which I have described shall add to her own strength, or that of this
growing rival.

The inhabitants of British America have no desire to
change their national character, and will feel disposed
to cling to the mother country as long as she fosters
and protects them. Does not sound policy, then, require that she should do so? Should a country which
will be capable of adding so much to her own maritime
strength, and the loss of which would add so much to
that of another, and a rival nation, be voluntarily abandoned by Great Britain?

CHAPTER III.

It may be said, by those who are unfriendly to the retention of these North American Colonies, that the very arguments which I have adduced to prove how much they would add to the naval resources of the United States show their value to that country ; that the retention of them, therefore, must lead to contests with the Americans, and that if they were once surrendered to them, all subjects of dispute between Great Britain and America would be removed.

These two positions, that the retention of these colonies must lead to contests between Great Britain and America,—and that the cession of them to the latter would remove all causes of future difference,—appear to be very plausible. But let us inquire if they are sound.

I admit, that if America were governed by a monarch, or even if that country consisted of one vast republic, that the acquisition of these colonies would be so great an addition to their maritime strength, that those who administered their affairs would never rest until they had achieved a conquest which, under either of those forms of government, sound policy would urge them to make. But, instead of being one entire republic, they consist of a confederation of republics, and the Congress is composed of persons who receive a delegated power from various states, that are not only destitute of common interest upon many essential points, but whose interests frequently clash with each other.

The southern states on the Atlantic have no desire to increase the political influence of New York or New England. The Virginians, who take the lead among the former, look with great jealousy upon Massachusetts, which state has twice wrested the presidency from their hands ; and the inhabitants of the western territory begin to look upon both as usurpers of that power and influence in the general government, which their growing importance teaches them to believe should belong to them.

Under these circumstances, neither the representatives from the western territory, nor those from the southern states, would be very desirous to engage in a war which would interrupt the safe transmission of their valuable productions to market, merely to acquire a country which would add so much to the political weight and influence of New England.

If the coast, which I have described, were added to the American possessions, its interests and those of New England would be precisely the same, and the *citizens* of Nova Scotia and New Brunswick would certainly enlist under the banner of Massachusetts in all political contests, either in congress, or for the presidential chair.

Mr. Jefferson, the former leader of the politicians of Virginia, was so well aware of the influence which foreign commerce was calculated to give to the states concerned in navigation, that he invariably endeavoured to instil into the minds of the inhabitants of the southern and inland states, that they had no interest in encouraging the American carrying trade; that it only tended to embroil them with foreign nations; and that it was their best policy to remain at home, and sell their native productions to the foreigners who came to their own shores in search of them. This policy was indignantly resisted by the New England States, who saw that it must prove ruinous to them; but it had numerous advocates to the southward, and in the states beyond the Alleghany, until the French influence, which prevailed in the American cabinet, involved that country in a war with Great Britain.

The unexpected brilliancy which attended some of the American achievements at sea, during that war, enlisted the national pride on the side of the seamen, and we have recently heard but little of this doctrine of Mr. Jefferson; but the principles upon which it was founded still subsist in, and are perhaps inseparable from, the

American confederation. We cannot therefore, expect to see the same earnest desire to make this conquest, on the part of the American Congress (with whom the power of declaring war is solely vested,) that we should witness in a government, where these conflicting interests did not exist.

It is, therefore, very probable, if Great Britain manifests a resolute determination to retain her possessions in North America, that the representatives of the southern and inland states, who form a vast majority over those of New England, will not subject their property to spoliation, by engaging in a contest with the mistress of the sea, for the purpose of adding to the power and influence of a portion of the Union which both consider as a rival.

But, secondly, will it follow that if these colonies were ceded to America, all causes of difference would be removed between the two countries? It will be admitted that this measure must increase the power of America; and in politics it is too often deemed that *power is right*—for those who have power to assert a claim which it is their interest to make, generally conclude that they have the right also so to do ; and, therefore, in all the differences which may hereafter arise between the conflicting interests of two commercial nations, America, when her power is thus increased, will assume a higher tone, and feel more disposed to support her claims by arms, than she will do if she should not acquire this accession of maritime strength. It may be also observed, that while the inhabitants of these colonies remain subjects of Great Britain, it is their interest that she should retain her possessions in the West Indies, on account of the advantage which their character as British subjects gives to them over the Americans in those islands.

But as soon as they became American citizens their interests would be directly the reverse, and they would join with all the Atlantic states in America, in urging.

10

the American Government to seize the first opportunity
of possessing itself of those islands. What the result
would be I do not attempt to predict, but I think it
will not be denied that the augmentation to her naval
force, which the possession of these colonies would give
to America, and her vicinity to the scene of contest,
would enable her to become a much more formidable
enemy to Great Britain in that quarter than France or
Spain have ever proved; and the natives of the British
West India Isles (who have frequently manifested a
sufficient portion of republican spirit) would feel much
less repugnance in yielding to the dominion of America,
than they would to that of any of the foreign governments of Europe.

They would recollect that a large proportion of the
rulers of that country are themselves interested in
guarding the *rights* (as they consider them) of the proprietors of slaves, and might, perhaps, think that their
interests as slaveholders would be taken better care of by
the American Congress than by the British Parliament,
with whose recent proceedings upon that subject the
West India planters are very generally dissatisfied.

These things should certainly be maturely considered
before it is decided that the North American Colonies
are of little or no importance to the mother country.

CHAPTER IV.

THE preceding observations have been directed
against those writers who have assumed, as a general
position, ' that no colony is worth retaining unless the
mother country derives from it a revenue equal to her
expenditure upon it ;' and an humble attempt has been
made to induce his Majesty's Ministers to think that the
North American Colonies are valuable appendages to
the British crown, independently of all considerations of
pecuniary profit and loss.

The writer of these pages does not boast of that intimate knowledge of the principles of political economy which would enable him to unravel all the intricacies of that perplexing science, and to prove to demonstration that, although these colonies do not directly pay into the treasury of Great Britain a sum equal to that which is annually issued from it for their support and defence, they do indirectly increase the commerce and manufactures of the mother country in a degree that renders her no loser by them upon the whole; yet he thinks, that might well admit of proof from the pens of those who have devoted themselves to the consideration of such subjects.

Indeed, the Edinburgh Reviewers, who are strong advocates for ridding Great Britain of the incumbrance of her Colonies, do not deny that she derives advantages from her commerce with them, in common, however, with that which she carries on with the rest of the world; but they are of opinion that she would derive the same advantages from them which she now does, if they were independent of all connexion with her.

They contend that as long as the manufactures of Great Britain are superior to, and cheaper than those of other nations, she will ever experience the same demand for them that she now does; but they gravely tell us that it will be of little importance whether these manufactures are carried to market, or the returns from them are brought to Great Britain in foreign or in British ships: that it is erroneous to suppose, 'that an extensive *mercantile* is necessary to the possessions of a great warlike navy;' 'that all that is required for the attainment of naval power is the command of convenient harbours, and of wealth sufficient to build and man ships;' and 'that, however paradoxical it may at first sight appear, it is nevertheless unquestionably true, that *the navy of Great Britain might be as formidable as it now is, or, if that was desirable, infinitely more so, though we had not a single merchant ship.'*

These sage reviewers proceed to tell us very gravely that the merchant service is a very *' round about method of breeding sailors'* for the navy, and that it would be a much better plan to *' breed up sailors directly in men-of-war :'* to effect which, these advocates for discarding the colonies, *on account of the expense of maintaining them,* propose that Great Britain should always keep afloat a sufficient number of men-of-war, manned wholly *during peace* with able-bodied seamen, to enable her, on the breaking out of war, with the addition of the proportion of landsmen and boys allowed by the admiralty, to equip a fleet worthy of the mistress of the sea ?

Had the wise gentlemen who conduct this review had the conduct of the affairs of the nation during the last ten years, those rows of floating castles which have so long been lying in idleness at Portsmouth, Plymouth, and Chatham, would not have excited the anxiety which John Bull so lately felt lest his bulwarks were mouldering with the dry rot; they would have been ploughing their own element, contending with, and, of course, sometimes suffering from, its fury; filled with the choicest seamen, who would have been withdrawn from the servile task of adding to the nation's wealth in the employment of humble individuals, and would have been nobly occupied in consuming the revenues of the country, and cruizing in quest of a non-existing foe. For I take it for granted, as these sailors are to be *trained up* in men-of-war, that the fleets in which they are *to be trained* are not to lie like guard-ships, at their moorings. No, these costly nurseries, with their full complement of able-bodied seamen, whose services will only be obtained by paying to them the highest rate of wages, must proceed to sea, and there encounter the dangers of the ocean, and such of them as escape from it will return into port to refit, and give ample employment to a numerous host of carpenters, shipwrights,

ropemakers, blacksmiths, &c., &c., &c., who would all
be rescued from the degradation of looking up to private
persons for a subsistence, by procuring employment in
the shipyards of our merchants, and become respectable salaried servants of their king and country.

But this is really too serious a subject for badinage,
and at the same time it is difficult to bring one's self to
answer people seriously who hold the monstrous position
that a nation, whose greatness is founded upon her naval
power, should be indifferent to her mercantile marine;
who tell us that convenient harbours, and wealth sufficient to build and man ships, is all that is requisite for
the attainment of naval power.

Has not France, has not Spain, convenient harbours,
and have they not each had ample revenues in the days
of their prosperity, to build, and to pay for the manning of fleets; have they not also been animated with
the most earnest desire to crush the naval power of
Great Britain? and have they not been unable to do so,
because, although they had abundance of *men* to place
upon the decks of their ships, they were destitute of
seamen to manage them?

That great statesman, Mr. Burke, laid it down as an
axiom, that experience was our surest guide, either in
political or private life, and until these gentlemen can
point out to us an instance, in which a nation, possessing commodious harbours and abundant wealth, has
attained to permanent naval power without a respectable
maritime population, let us pursue the beaten track.*

Let us leave our merchants, who are engaged either
in foreign commerce, in the coasting trade, or in the
fisheries, to devise schemes for the cheapest and most
effectual mode of procuring those seamen in time of
peace, which their respective pursuits require, and we

* I hope the Edinburgh Reviewers will not refer us, in support of
their position, to the fleets of boats, of ancient days, with their three
banks of oars, armed prows, and legions of *soldiers* to fight them.

may depend upon it, that individual interest and sagacity will effect the object of creating and preserving a maritime population more effectually, and upon better terms, than the government can do.   Let us not, by the adoption of this scheme, withdraw from their service thousands of the best of seamen, to eat the bread of the nation either in idleness or in unproductive activity; and increase the expense of navigating our merchant ships, by raising wages in the degree that this demand, or rather this unnecessary employment of seamen, would inevitably occasion; and thus drive those whose interest it now is to give bread to British seamen, to carry on their business in the ships of foreigners.

Let us not too hastily adopt the opinion, that as long as British manufactures are better and cheaper than those of other nations, that we shall always enjoy the same share of commerce that we now do, and that it is unimportant whether this commerce is carried on in British or in foreign vessels.   While all things flow smoothly, the *individuals* of every country will naturally seek to supply their wants upon the best terms, and will therefore resort to that country which can supply them with the best and cheapest articles: but governments may take a different view of the subject, and control the wishes of their people in this respect.   Great Britain is equally hated and feared in Europe; and the governments of that continent would willingly see the sceptre of the ocean transferred to this side of the Atlantic. Distant America might not interpose that barrier, which the naval power of Great Britain has so often enabled her to do to European ambition; and if that power were once lost, where should we find a counterpoise for that of France, whose ambition has so frequently threatened the *liberties* of the continental nations, and the *destruction* of our own?

Let us remember the declaration of the greatest politician and warrior that France has possessed for ages: that all he required, to render that country

powerful upon the ocean, was *Ships, Colonies,* and
Commerce; and as the result of his observations upon
the wants of France is confirmed by experience of the
advantages which have resulted to Great Britain from
such possessions, let us support and cherish them with
the most anxious care.

Let speculative politicians amuse themselves with
their discussions upon minor subjects, but let them not
be encouraged to SPORT WITH OUR PALLADIUM.

Some few years after the publication of this pamphlet,
Judge Halliburton—deeply interested in the political
affairs of that great country to which he felt it a high
honour to belong—drew another sketch, but in a very
different style. It is a humorous account of the changes
wrought in the English constitution, under the influence
of Earl Grey and Lord John Russell, and is added here
as a specimen of that kind of writing in which he occasionally indulged his playful mind, and by means of
which he pointed a shaft with sharp satire, or turned
into ridicule a selfish or unsound measure. The leaders
and prominent parties of the day, the Duke of Wellington, Earl Grey, Lord John Russell, Lord Brougham,
Lord Althorpe, Birmingham, Sheffield, and Manchester,
will easily be recognized through their disguise :

CRITICAL STATE OF THE BULL FAMILY.

FEW folks have made more noise in the world than
the family of the Bulls. They were a roaring set of
blades, always up to their work, and equally prepared
for a frolic or a fight. There were two branches of the
family, the elder descended from old Mr. John Bull, a
sturdy farmer in the north, and the other descended

from Paddy Bull, the drover, who said he was a half
brother of John's, by a different father and mother.
Pat was a riotous, good humoured fellow, who cared
not much how the world went, provided he had plenty
of potatoes and whiskey.

The mode in which the Bulls managed their concerns
attracted great attention in the neighbourhood. In all
the other families in the parish, the head of the house
gave law to every individual in it, and no one dare
question the propriety of his measures; but among the
Bulls the old gentleman could do little more than propose plans for cultivating the farm; and Mrs. Bull, who
lived much among her children, generally talked the
matter over with them, and with the trustees of the
estate, before they were adopted, owing to which, all
hands generally went to work with hearty good will,
and if the seasons were tolerably fine, they could always
reckon upon a good crop. It must be acknowledged
that this had not always been the case. Old Mr. Bull,
in his younger days, was disposed to be as headstrong
as his neighbours; and his wife, for some time after her
marriage, was obliged to be mighty obsequious. It was
then, " As you please, my dear, I cannot pretend to set
up my judgment against yours; but, if I might venture
to suggest," and so on. In this way, by degrees she
wheedled herself into the old gentleman's confidence,
and exercised a good deal of influence in the management of the family. In looking a little more into the
matter, she satisfied herself that she had good right so
to do; she inspected the title deeds of the estate, and
found that the old gentleman held it in right of his wife,
and that it was entailed upon his descendants, male and
female. She therefore, felt great interest in preserving
it for her children; she would not allow the trustees to
interfere with the rents; but insisted that the marriage
articles gave her the right to do so, and that they were
only appointed to prevent these articles from being in-
fringed upon by either party. She thus got possession

of the strong box, and then the old gentleman had to make his bow to her, whenever he wanted either to frolic or to fight, for he could neither pay a tavern bill, nor buy a rapier unless she gave him the money. In fact, the gray mare had completely become the better horse; and if all families, in which the ladies bear sway, were as well managed, we should have little cause to complain of petticoat government. The whole parish admired her prudence, and many fruitless efforts were made by the neighbours to imitate her.

Among others, the Frog family, who had long been rivals of the Bulls, and generally opposed them at all parish meetings, were determined upon trying Mrs. Bull's system. But as soon as they met to adjust their plans, the greater part of them got drunk, and set fire to the house; not content with this, the drunken dogs knocked every man's brains out, who attempted to extinguish the flames: and actually caught Mr. Frog and his wife, as they were attempting to escape out of a window, and chopt both their heads off. The whole neighbourhood was struck with horror at such atrocity. But the ragamuffins did not stop here: they threatened to burn down every house in the parish, and actually sent a parcel of drunken rascals into the streets, with fire brands in their hands, to carry their threats into execution.

The Bulls were not people to submit quietly to such conduct. They turned out manfully to defend their property, and after a long struggle they brought the Frog family to their senses; but what with the payment of constables and firemen, the purchase of engines and water buckets, and the expense of maintaining watchmen to guard the Frogs, until they got sober, they expended a world of money, and found themselves encumbered with a heavy debt at the end of the contest. This obliged them to economize in the management of their affairs, and the younger branches of the family, who were compelled to work hard to get a living, and

contribute their share of the interest of the debt, began
to manifest a good deal of discontent. The farm, it is
true, continued to be very productive, but still the debt
bore hard upon them ; and forgetting that they had
incurred it, to prevent the Frogs from destroying the
whole estate, they complained loudly of their mother's
management, as if she had been the whole author of the
evil. The old gentleman and lady set their wits to
work to put matters to rights ; they employed their son,
Wellslay Bull, who had put an end to the fray with
the Frogs, by knocking down their great champion, Nap
Frog, with his own hands, to be their steward, and
directed him to work the farm at the least possible
expense.

Wellslay was a thorough man of business, went to
work at once to discharge all the able-bodied servants
and labourers, that could be dispensed with ; but,
like a true son of John Bull, he would not turn
those who had grown gray in the service of the family,
into the streets, nor take away the parish allowance
from their widows and orphans. He also thought it
right to keep a good number of constables in pay, to
watch master Frog's movements, as he knew that the
only way to keep him quiet was to show him that he
would get the worst of it, if he kicked up another
row ; he also thought it would be bad economy in the
end to discharge too many of the workmen, as the
harvest might be lost by such a measure. At the end
of the year, therefore, notwithstanding Wellslay's re-
trenchments, the necessary expenses of the farm, and
above all, the interest due upon the mortgage, pinched
the family sadly ; and the young folks, who of course
knew least about the business, grumbled loudly against
Wellslay's management.

These roaring blades held a meeting at the Split
Crown, kept by Batterdown Bull, the most drunken
dog of the whole family, where, after draining the
punch bowl to the bottom, they decided that all the

difficulties they laboured under were owing to their
mother's listening so much to old Sam, and his
brothers, who, they decided, had no longer any right
to interfere in the management of the farm.   Old
Sam and his brothers had once been thriving men,
but it must be confessed that they were not now so
well to do in the world as they had been.   The family
mansion had gone to decay, and some of them had
scarcely a shed left to protect them from the weather.
The young Bulls, therefore, said that it was a shame
for their mother to continue to advise with such a
set of paupers, when such thriving men as Brummage
Bull the Blacksmith, Shuffle Bull the Cutler, Manshuttle
Bull the Weaver, and many other rising members of the
family, were not permitted to have a word to say about
the management of the farm.

   The old lady seemed to think there was something
like reason in what the young rogues said, although she
did not like their rudeness; but placing much confidence in Wellslay's judgment, she asked him what he
thought of it. " Why," says Wellslay, in his plain
blunt manner, "My dear mother, good advice is good
advice, let it come from rich or poor.   Some folks, now-
a-days, seem to think that it is of more consequence
who is to give you advice than what advice they give,
but that's not my way of thinking.   Now you know
that though old Sam and his family have not as much
of the ready in their pockets as they once had, they are
shrewd, sensible folks, and have frequently given you
better advice than you could get elsewhere.   Our affairs
are now in a ticklish state, and that confounded mortgage hangs like a millstone about our necks.   But we
must not turn rogues and rob a church, or refuse to pay
our just debts, as I am afraid master Brummage and
Shuffle and their crew would willingly do, although the
fellows would never have been the men they are now,
if it had not been incurred.   Why should they complain
forsooth of your acting upon the advice of old Sam's

family, when they have prospered so well under it, and poor Sam has scarce a house over his head. Try no experiments, my good mother, in these ticklish times, but just manage matters as you have done, at all events till you can pay off, or reduce the confounded mort- gage." There was a terrible uproar at the Split Crown when they learnt that Wellslay had given this advice to the old woman : Batterdown, Brummage, Shuffle, and Manshuttle, roared like mad bulls, and in a short time made so many of the labourers drunk that Well-slay said he would manage the farm no longer, and left them to their own misdoings. In an evil hour John applied to the old Gray Bull to become steward. He was as stiff-necked and wrong-headed a bull as any that bore the name, but was supposed to have much influ-ence with Brummage, and that set, because he had for years said that every bull, let his skull be thick or thin, had an equal right to give his advice about the management of the farm, and that old madam was in justice bound to listen to it, and to follow it too, said he in a thundering voice, which always set the disorderly bulls outside roaring — " Grey forever," " Grey for-ever." When Mrs. Bull saw that this old codger had become steward, she began to think she should find it expedient to let Brummage and Shuffle, and a few other roaring bulls into the hall, where she usually consulted with her children, and consoled herself with recollecting that she should have many a steady and sturdy farmer to keep these upstarts in order, and above all, that old Sam's family would still be there, upon whose discretion she could always rely. The good lady therefore walked into the hall to meet her children, with tolerable composure, and had made up her mind to let those noisy fellows in, with as good a grace as she could. She knew that little Johnny Bull, of Bed-ford, was to make the proposal to her, and as he was a desperate proser, the old woman seated herself in her arm chair, expecting to enjoy a comfortable nap, while

he was drawling out the threadbare arguments, which
had been so often refuted in favour of their admission;
but judge of her astonishment when, instead of the old
story of Brummage's and Shuffle's rights, he began by
proposing to kick the whole of old Sam's family out of
the hall, and ended by declaring that it was necessary
for John to divorce his present wife, and get a new one.
The old lady at first burst out a-laughing in his face,
but she soon found it was no laughing matter, and that
the new set of clothes with which Grey had furnished
John, was actually intended for his wedding. She was
so staggered by this intelligence, that instead of boldly
telling little Johnny she would not listen to another
word upon the subject, she gave a sort of half promise
to take it into consideration. The truth was, the old
woman was not quite as good stuff as she once was.
She had seen so many strange things come to pass of
late, that she scarcely knew whether she was upon her
head or her heels. She remembered when master Nap
Frog wished to get rid of his rib, he made mighty short
work of it. He walked up to madame's room, made
her one of his best bows, pressed her hand to his heart,
gave her a tender embrace, heaved a deep sigh, kicked
her out of the window, with an earnest entreaty that
she would fall upon the softest stone in the pavement,
and then returned to the parlour, whistling " Ca ira,"
—recollecting this, she feared that Grey might try to
persuade Mr. Bull to play her some such scurvy trick,
and to gain a little time to recover herself, she stam-
mered out something about taking it into consideration.
Grey, however, saw how she was likely to consider it,
and that he had little chance of getting the old lady's
consent in her present humour; he therefore proposed
to John to send her down into the country, where the
young bulls were keeping it up; and he hoped, between
wheedling and bullying, to cajole the old woman into
giving her consent, as the thing could not be done without it. John was not very fond of these trips to the

country, they cost a plaguey sight of money, and it was
a long time before the family got to rights after one of
them.   He told Grey that Mrs. Bull had just returned
from the country, and he did not see much use in sending her there again so soon; but Grey reminded him
that Wellslay was steward when she paid her last visit,
and that things then went on in the old dull jog trot
way; "but since I have had the management of the
farm, Mr. Bull," said he, "the servants have learnt
that they are as good as their masters, and ten to one if
some of the chaps don't run some rig upon the old lady,
that may show her that there is as good men as you in
the world."   "Well, well," said Bull, in a surly tone,
"take your own way about it, but I expect no good
on't, remember that."   Away went the old lady, and a
pretty time she had of it: there were rare doings at the
Split Crown.   Batterdown filled the well with Hollands,
so that there was no getting a drop of pure water for
love nor money.   During the whole of her visit, Mrs.
Bull scarcely met with a sober man.   "Evil communi-
cations corrupt good manners," said the wise man of
old, and so, alas, did it prove with Mrs. Bull!   She returned to town, more than half drunk, took little Johnny
in her lap, hiccup'd that he was her darling boy, and
she could refuse him nothing; and Johnny, before the
old woman got sober, wheedled her into consenting to
let Grey have his will and cut her connexion with the
old man.   But there was still a stumbling block in the
way.   The divorce could not take place without the
consent of the trustees, and they vowed they would
listen to no such doings.   Grey rated and raved at them
at a great rate, and threatened to apply to Chancery to
appoint other trustees, who would do his bidding; but
they snapt their fingers in his face, and said they didn't
care that for his threats: as long as they were trustees
they would do their duty like honest men.   Sober folks,
therefore, began to hope, that notwithstanding these
drunken bouts, the divorce might yet be prevented, and

the family saved from disgrace and ruin; and so perhaps it might have been, for John had still a sneaking regard for the old lady, although he did not like to let it out before Grey, and he thought if he could get her to listen to Wellslay's advice again, she might soon be prevailed to give up the low set at the Split Crown, and conduct herself once more like a decent woman. He gave Wellslay a pretty broad hint of this; but Grey saw them exchanging mighty significant glances, and as he had opened a correspondence with Batterdown, and his ragamuffin set, he persuaded them to waylay John, as he was coming to town to consult with his old steward, and to threaten to knock his brains out, if he didn't break off with Wellslay altogether. These rascals kicked up such a riot that they frightened the trustees into fits, which were succeeded by a state of lethargy, in which they all laid for several days. Before they had recovered from their stupor, Grey read old Mrs. Bull's consent to the divorce over to them. Whether they really nodded assent, or whether it was a mere involuntary paralytic nod, which they could not control, has never yet been ascertained; but Grey immediately brought down old John to the hall, where the trustees were assembled, sent for the old woman, and *there* all these looking more dead than alive, ratified the divorce. That same evening, old Sam and the whole of his family were found dead in a dismal hole, called skull-dell A. Some of their friends told Grey they thought that they were entitled to christian burial, but he swore it would cost too much money, and the beggars might rot where they were. Grey was soon upon the look out for another wife for John, and told him to don the suit of clothes which he had already worn at his birth-day, in order to be prepared to receive his bride. Mr. Bull did not much like being reminded of his birth-day, which had not gone off quite to his liking. Before Grey became steward he had always kept it in great state, went to church in his best clothes, said his belief aloud before all the family, and afterwards all the old folks had a noble feast in the great hall, where the table was covered with roast beef and plum pudding, and cans of stingo, which it did their hearts good to look at, and still more to swallow. But Grey said there was not a fat ox, or a bushel of malt on the farm, which could be spared for such doings, they must all be sent to market to turn a pennysworth; that as to going to church, he would let the horses out of the plough for a few hours, to draw the old family coach, but he would have no junketings in the hall. Now John had always thought the feast in the hall the cream of the jest; but as Grey wouldn't hear of it, he said at all events he would have a few friends to eat bread and cheese and drink small beer with him in his own room. The day went off flat enough, and folks neither liked John's dinner nor his dress. It must be confessed that John cut but a queer figure in it. His head was covered with an old gray whig, which he had discarded upwards of twenty years before, as unfit for use. His body was buttoned up in a second-hand spencer, and his nether parts were covered with patch work. Grey soon introduced the beldame he had selected for John's second wife, and if his dress was not in the best taste, his intended's was a match for it. She stalked into the hall in her pattens and black worsted stockings, and when the trustees stared at her for appearing in such guise, she told them that if they had been obliged to travel to the hall through such dirty ways as she had passed, they would not be sporting their pumps and silk stockings, any more than herself. The marriage was celebrated much in the usual way; but it was observed that John shut his eyes when he kissed the bride; but the poor man's other senses were unclosed, and she gave him such a pestilent whiff of Hollands, that he perceived she had not omitted her dream of blue ruin on the wedding morning. Grey soon found his *protege* but an ungrateful vixen. Instead of thanking him for bringing about the match, and placing her at the head of the family, she rated him so sorely, whenever he failed to comply with any of her whims, however unreasonable, that he soon found himself obliged to quit his place, and John was at his wit's end to get another steward; for few would undertake to manage the farm, under his new madam. For want of a better, he was feign to take one Lamb, a man he knew but little about, except that he had served under Grey.

Mr. Bull, though a sturdy well-built man, was by no means so stout and bulky as most of his neighbours; but in former days he had increased the stateliness of his appearance very much by a long train which he continually wore,—and many folks thought that John would never have been able to carry his head so high at parish meetings, if it were not for the richness of this train. He has long been very careful of it, and mighty testy if any one touched it without his leave.

Grey and some of his friends began to complain of the expense of this train, and said that it cost more than it was worth, but they found John not at all inclined to part with it, and to please the old gentleman, Grey had covered it with good-rich stuff, which looked well enough at first, but it was soon torn off in a scuffle, at the Church door, where Batterdown and his Ragamuffins were trying to break in to steal the plate. Grey wrapt up John's train in a handsome piece of Derbyshire ware, but that was shortly cracked in a scuffle of the same kind, and nothing remained but to cover it with a mat of Spring Rice, which Paddy Bull had lately raised. How this would have worn cannot be ascertained. for it was scarcely fitted on before the Trustees discovered that they had become entitled to John's spencer; and the poor man was left without a rag to his back.

John forthwith desired Lamb to provide him with some covering or other. Lamb mustered the only patterns he could get credit for at the tailor's, and sub-

11

mitted them for John's choice. The first was from
the little town manufactory. As soon as Lamb unfolded
it, he saw John fix his eyes upon some ugly spots; he
explained that one Dan Cowhell, who soiled everything
that he touched, had handled the piece at Donnybrook
fair; but he didn't doubt the stains might be scoured
out, and if not, folks were not so particular about appearances now-a-days, as they once were. But John
plumply said it was too dirty for a gentleman to wear,
and was about throwing it out of the window, when
Lamb proposed taking the mat of Spring Rice from his
train, and working it up, with a close-bodied jacket.

John didn't seem to relish this mode of robbing Peter
to pay Paul, and asked what was to become of his
train; but without waiting for an answer, he wished to
know what tailor Lamb could employ to alter it.
" You know," said he, " that you are in mighty bad
credit with the fellow in Cambridge street, who fitted it
on to my train, and I doubt if he will do another stitch
for you." Lamb looked very woe-begone, and said he
feared that was too true; nor did he know another
tailor in the whole parish, who would do the job for
him; " in short, Mr. Bull," said he, " the fellows are
grown so saucy, and spend so much of their time at the
Split Crown, that I can never be sure of getting a new
garment, or altering an old one for you, when it is
wanted." " Aye, aye, Mr. Lamb," said Bull, " if you
and your friends had not put an end to old Sam and his
family, we shouldn't have been reduced to this straight;
they were poor, it is true, and couldn't afford carousing
at the Split Crown, but they could turn their hands to
anything, and were always ready to work for their
money. If you cast a shoe on the road, there were they,
with their hammer and nails, to set you all to rights
again, without five minutes loss of time; and, when required, they could make or alter a garment for you in a
jiffee." Lamb drew a heavy sigh, but said not a word
in reply. When the old gentleman, who began to

shiver with the cold, placed his arms a-kimbo, and looking Lamb full in the face, said, in a loud voice, "Look ye, Mr. Lamb, I'll not stand here any longer, half naked, and if you can't provide me with decent covering, I'll send for my old friend Wellslay again, and see what he can do for me." John expected that Lamb would have roared like a lion, when he talked of sending for Wellslay; but, to his utter surprise, he replied, in the mildest voice possible, "Really, Mr. Bull, I think you cannot do better, and as I shall pass his door on my way home, I'll drop a note there for you, with all my heart." The truth was, Lamb knew well enough that he was not provided with any measures that would suit the posture in which John stood, and felt sure, that John must either employ Wellslay again, or that madcap Lamp-black, the coal-heaver, who was a fast friend of Batterdown.

Now, he and his wise-acres had found, that their cursed attempts to improve the family mansion, had nearly brought the house about their ears; he knew that Wellslay was the only man who had a chance of propping it up; but if Lamp-black once got to work upon it, the roof would soon be in the cellar; and he therefore willingly undertook to carry John's note to Wellslay. John's eyes overran with tears of joy, at the thoughts of getting his old friend Wellslay to manage the farm again, and although he was reckoning without his hostess (for madam was out visiting), he ventured at once to write the note, and Lamb promised to deliver it without delay. Wellslay was not long in coming, and seeing the plight in which the old gentleman was, he covered him at once from head to foot in a long cloak of his own, and told him he would arrange his dress, and provide him with his usual garments, as soon as Bob of Tamsworth came home. He's a clever lad, that Bob of Tamsworth, said Wellslay, and if you'll take my advice, you'll employ him as steward. He'll probably manage matters better with madam than I

can, as she knows I was such a fast friend to the old
lady that's gone. Bob stood well with her, too, but
then he's a smooth-tongued fellow, and may perhaps
persuade Mrs. Bull, that is, to hold up her head a little,
and keep good company. If we can once induce her to
break with that vile set at the Split Crown, she may yet
learn to live among gentle folks, and do the honors of
the house, so as not to bring disgrace upon the family;
though I fear, said he, sighing, that we shall miss old
Sam's folks sadly. But there is no raising the dead, my
good father, in this world.

John was rather anxious that Wellslay should manage the farm himself, but he stuck to it, that Bob was
the man. "It will be all one, father," said he, "I can
persuade him to anything. Why, don't you remember,
that night when we prevailed upon you, and the trustees, and old madam, to take down the bar, which we
had both helped so long to hold up, and let Pat in to
supper to keep him quiet, how nicely Bob managed
things? We had breakfasted together that morning in
our old orange-colored clothes; but we knew Pat always
grew sick at the sight of them, and as we didn't like to
throw them off altogether, Bob set to work to sponge,
and scour, and dye them, and did it so cleverly that
what you would have sworn looked like Orange Peel at
breakfast, was more like Potatoe Peel when we sat down
to supper." "Well, well, Master Wellslay," said John,
"I think you needn't boast much of that trick. Pat's not
much more peaceable, I trow, than he was before you
let him in to supper, and I don't much like the changes
of your slight-of-hand folks." "Why as to Pat" says
Wellslay, "there's no making him peaceable, unless you
set him fighting. Now in that affray with the frogs,
why he was among the best fellows that followed me,
and knocked them down with so much spirit and good
humour, that it did one's heart good to look at him; but
when he gets home, there's no keeping him quiet. I
only mentioned the matter to remind you what a clever

fellow Bob is, and how he can suit himself to the times; and as to his slight-of-hand, why he is a dexterous lad, that's true, but then he scorns to play foul with any body, and depend on't, if any one can persuade madam to behave herself decently, he's the man." John seated himself by the fire, and remained for a short time comfortably wrapt up in Wellslay's cloak; luckily Bob o' Tamsworth arrived before Mrs. Bull returned home, and John at once appointed him steward. He immediately provided John with a full suit of good honest true blue, and covered his train with a substantial piece of Scotch Plaid, which, from all appearances will wear well.

All John's old friends say that he looks more like himself than he has done for these four years past; instead of appearing half-clown, half-harlequin, as he did in his second-hand Spencer and Patchwork pantaloons, you would take him now for a respectable old English gentleman; but how madam will like him in his new dress is not yet known. If she gives herself any airs, however, it is thought Wellslay will persuade John to pack her off to the country for a short time; and as the conservators of the peace have renewed old Holdfast Bull's license at the King's Arms, on Constitution Hill, it is hoped the old lady will put up there, instead of going down to that dirty hole, the Split Crown.

Old Holdfast keeps an orderly house, in a quiet neighbourhood, and Constitution Hill presents a delightful prospect, extending for some distance over a peaceful valley. All the decent, substantial farmers, and tradesmen in the neighbourhood, frequent the King's Arms, and the good woman will learn different habits there from those of the dissolute set at the Split Crown. If she goes to old Holdfast's, therefore, all will be safe; but if she takes up with Batterdown and his gang again, why then, heaven help poor John Bull.

CHAPTER V.

For twenty-six years Mr. Justice Halliburton sat upon the Bench of Nova Scotia, as Assistant Judge. During this long period, of more than a quarter of a century, he had discharged his onerous duties with the most marked ability, and with great impartiality; in the language of the sixteenth century, he had "truly and indifferently ministered justice to the punishment of wickedness and vice, and to the maintenance of true religion and virtue." It was in the year 1816 that he had been appointed to a seat in the Council, then consisting of twelve members, and discharging both Executive and Legislative functions. The combination of judicial and political duties thus thrown upon him, formed a task no less difficult than toilsome; for it was the necessary consequence of this two-fold position, that the course which his sense of duty pointed out, and which he unswervingly followed, could not always be in accordance with the judgment or wishes of some portion of the inhabitants of the province.

But we can ask for no better proof of the wisdom and judgment which guided him, than the universal respect in which he was held throughout the country. He lived down all opposition. Not only did he outlive it, but he conquered and dispersed it, soon after it arose. In 1833 he was appointed Chief Justice of the Province, and became *ex officio* President of the Council, which

latter situation he held until the year 1837, when the
Council was remodelled, and the Executive department
separated from the Legislative, and the Chief Justice
and Judges ceased to be members of either.

There is something very pleasing in the tone of the
numerous addresses which were presented to him,
upon his elevation to the highest seat upon the Bench.
At these tokens of respect, which were shown to him
wherever he went in the performance of his judicial
duties, he must have been highly gratified. They were
not the offspring of strong political partizanship, but the
spontaneous and hearty expression of esteem and respect for a man who had presided in the courts of law
for a long period of time, with great ability, and marked
singleness of purpose. Immediately upon the announce-
ment of his well-earned promotion, the members of the
Bar, residing in Halifax, waited upon him with the following address, to which is subjoined his reply. Both
documents are worthy of being read, as they throw
some light upon his character, the esteem in which he
was held by others, and the spirit with which he received their congratulations.

" *To the Honourable* BRENTON HALLIBURTON, *Chief Justice*
of the Province of Nova Scotia:

" WE, the undersigned members of the Bar of Nova
Scotia, beg leave to offer you our most cordial and sincere congratulations, on your recent appointment to the
important station of Chief Justice of this Province.

" That the highest office connected with the administration of Justice, should be intrusted to one competent
to fulfil its duties, is an object of the greatest moment to
all interested in the welfare of the country. And we
rejoice that in the selection of a Judge, whose talent,

integrity, and zeal, already long known and justly appreciated, afford the most unequivocal testimony of his eminent qualifications for that office, his Majesty's Government have made a choice, from which all can most confidently anticipate the happiest results to the community. While your laborious exertions, for a long series of years, in the judicature of this Province, your experience and intimate acquaintance with the local circumstances of the country, your legal acquirements, and the strict impartiality which has characterized your conduct on the Bench, have commanded universal respect and confidence ; the unwearied patience, and invariable courtesy and kindness, displayed both in public and private, in your intercourse with the Bar, have secured our sincere esteem, and demand our most grateful acknowledgements.

"In the experience of the past we can perceive the most pleasing prospects for the future, and while we tender the most respectful assurance of our undiminished and increased regard, confidence, respect and esteem, we most earnestly desire that you may live many years to enjoy the dignity and honors you have so justly merited, and which have been so deservedly bestowed, and that your continued health will secure to this Province, in a more exalted situation, the exercise of those abilities, which you have already so often conspicuously employed in the public service."

To this the Chief Justice thus replied :—

"*Gentlemen*,—I should do myself injustice, if I did not assure you that the kind address you have presented to me, has excited feelings which I find myself unable to express.

"My professional career has passed under your immediate observation, and as it has ever been my anxious desire to discharge the duties of my office with diligence and impartiality, it affords me great gratification to learn that those who are so capable of forming a judgment upon my judicial conduct, entertain opinions so favourable and so flattering to me.

"I thank you, gentlemen, for the indulgent review which you have taken of the past, and so long as it may please my merciful Creator to bless me with health and strength, I shall endeavour to prevent your kind anticipations of the future from being altogether disappointed.

"When the period shall arrive in which I feel my strength unequal to the discharge of the laborious duties of my office, it will be a great solace to me if I find that I still retain the good opinion of my brethren of the Bar, and happy shall I be if I can retire with a portion of that respect and affection which has followed my venerable predecessor. Permit me now, gentlemen, to express my best wishes for the welfare of each of you. I assure you that it will give me great pleasure to see success attend all your honourable efforts to advance yourselves in your profession. We shall have much communication with each other, and I am sure you will unite with me in hoping that it may always be marked by that courtesy which regulates the intercourse of gentlemen, and by that kindness which it is so desirable to cultivate among members of the same profession."

It would be tedious to read one half of the addresses which the newly appointed Chief Justice received, during the course of his first circuit. Their reproduction would prove, indeed, that the regard in which he was held was universal; while to those who know anything of the history of the settlement of the Province, especially the different countries whence the immigrants to the several counties came, they would afford quite an interesting study, since each would be found very characteristic of the several national elements of which our heterogeneous population is composed. One only is selected—that handed to the Chief Justice upon his

arrival at Queen's county—as a specimen of straight-
forward and independent expression of feeling.

" *To the Honble.* BRENTON HALLIBURTON, *Chief Justice of*
  the Province of Nova Scotia :

" THE ADDRESS OF THE MAGISTRATES OF QUEEN'S COUNTY.

" *Honorable Sir*, — The magistrates of this county
have great pleasure in following the example of the rest
of the Province, on their own, and in behalf of the inhabitants of Queen's county, generally, in congratulating
your honor on your elevation to the Chief Justiceship.

" We believe that to a person of real worth and good
understanding, the fulsome language of flattery cannot
be pleasing ; we shall not offend you, sir, in that way,
on this occasion.

" We must, however, be allowed to express our gratification, that it has pleased our gracious Sovereign to
exalt to the station, a person whose unshaken integrity,
and long and faithful services in a judicial capacity, has
commanded general confidence, and entitled him to the
high situation.

" We have only to add, honourable sir, that should
it please a gracious Providence to prolong your life to
the late period which marked the retirement of your
venerable and most worthy predecessor, we trust it will
be with equal honour to yourself, and approbation of
the province.

"   We have the honor, &c., &c.

" LIVERPOOL, QUEEN'S Co., July, 1833."

It would not be within my province, nor come within
the scope of my purpose, even were I competent to the
task, to discuss the part which he took in politics. Yet
there is nothing more remarkable in his career than the
immense amount of labor which he performed at the
Council Board. By a reference to the minutes of that

body, it will be seen that his name recurs with an astonishing frequency. On every important question he was prepared to give his opinion, and on the majority of important questions he took the decided lead.

In a very sensible and dignified review of his life, published in the "Acadian" newspaper at Digby, N. S., 1860, the writer, in adverting to this period of his course, made the following pertinent observations. "In days gone by, when he occupied a prominent position in both the upper branch of the legislature and the Executive, and when he dispensed to a great extent, the governmental patronage of the country, it may be that a few disappointed aspirants for administration favors regarded some of his official acts with feelings of disapproval. But now that years have elapsed since he withdrew from the arena of politics, all parties concur in testifying to his capacity and uprightness as a Judge,— uniform deportment as a gentleman,—and unostentatious piety as a Christian."

In 1837 the old Council was dissolved, and a new one constructed on different principles. By the adoption of these new measures on the part of the government the Chief Justice no longer had a seat in the Council Chamber. At this juncture he was waited upon with the following address from the members of the old Council.

"To the Hon. BRENTON HALLIBURTON, late President of Her Majesty's Council, and Chief Justice of the Province of Nova Scotia, &c. &c. &c.

"We, the members of her Majesty's late Council, whose official intercourse with you is now terminated, beg to offer you the assurance of our affection, esteem and respect.

"The abilities, zeal, and high legal and parliamentary knowledge, with which you have at all times aided the Council in the performance of their duties, and the dignified and impartial manner in which you have presided over their deliberations since the retirement of your venerable predecessor, give you the strongest claim to the approbation of your Sovereign, and the respect and thanks of her Majesty's subjects in this Province; and we should not do justice to our feelings, were we to omit the expression of our regret at an event which has deprived the people of this colony of your valuable services in the councils of their country.

"In taking leave of you we shall carry with us, and always retain, a gratifying recollection of the kindness which has distinguished your conduct and intercourse with the Council, and although you no longer fill the situation which has enabled you to contribute so essentially to the good of the Province, we hope it may long enjoy the benefit of your talents and knowledge in the high judicial office you now hold; and with earnest prayers that you may long possess health and strength to enable you to discharge the duties of that important trust, we tender you our affectionate and respectful farewell."

" *To the Honorable Members of Her Majesty's late Council in Nova Scotia:*

" "Gentlemen,—Few things have occurred to me in the course of a long life, so truly gratifying as the address with which you have this day honored me.

"During the period that I have had a share in the Councils of this Colony, I have ever had an earnest desire to perform with fidelity, my duty to my Sovereign and to my fellow subjects.

"I feel amply compensated for all the care and anxiety inseparable from such desire, by the flattering testimonial which you have now presented to me.

"That my colleagues, who have witnessed my conduct should entertain and express such sentiments respecting it, as this address contains, affords me the highest satisfaction, and I shall carefully preserve it, as one of the most valuable records I possess.

"We live, gentlemen, in days of political experiments. Should the result prove that those who have made them have acted wisely, I am confident that, however they may affect us individually, we shall all not only cheerfully acquiesce, but sincerely rejoice in any changes which will eventually improve the institutions of the country, and promote the welfare of its inhabitants.

"But whatever the future may unfold, the present moment is saddened to me by the recollection that my connexion is terminated with a body of gentlemen whom I respect so highly, with some of whom I have been associated in public life for upwards of twenty years; whose strenuous efforts to advance the best interests of the Province, I have so often witnessed, and whose uniform kindness to myself I shall never forget.

"I beg, gentlemen, that each of you will accept of my best wishes for your future happiness, and whether you again embark in public or retire into private life, may you carry with you what you so fully deserve—the gratitude of the people of Nova Scotia.

"Believe me it is with no ordinary emotions that I now reciprocate your kind and affectionate farewell.

"BRENTON HALLIBURTON,

"Late President of Her Majesty's Council, in Nova Scotia.

"HALIFAX, Dec. 23, 1837."

Thus he stepped out from the political world, and thenceforward was left free from the anxieties which it produces, and the annoyances which are almost sure to be endured while in it. To a certain extent the Chief Justice must have felt relief on being severed from the cares incident to the party politics of the province, although his active mind must occasionally have felt a species of blank, so long and so deeply had he been interested in public affairs. Yet in some measure the scene had changed; there were new actors to contend with, and new plays brought upon the stage. It was no longer that to which for many years, he had been accustomed, and he soon decided that he was better out of than in the political world.

Sir Brenton was fond, in a leisure half-hour, of writing humorous pieces, evidently thrown off in a lively moment, and generally mingling some grave sentiment with some pungent wit. On the occasion just referred to he wrote the subjoined piece of pleasantry. None will probably enjoy it more than those who took part in effecting the change in the Council.

"DEATH OF THE OLD COUNCIL."

"Died, suddenly, at the Government House, on Tuesday last, in the eighty-eighth year of her age, Mrs. Majesty's Council.

"The sudden death of this venerable old lady, has excited some sensation in the community of which she had long been an influential member. We do not subscribe to the maxim, *de mortuis nil &c.*, but we feel it unnecessary to make any comments upon the character of the deceased. She did not live in a corner, and as her conduct is before the public, every individual is entitled to form his own judgment upon it.

"Some rumours of an unpleasant nature are afloat, occasioned we suppose by her expiring so suddenly. From various symptoms that had recently displayed themselves, her friends were apprehensive that some change in her constitution was about to take place, but none of them anticipated her immediate dissolution. We, ourselves, firmly believe, that if the good lady had not fallen into the hands of quacks, she would have long lived to exercise her usual and useful functions. On the morning of her decease, she walked to the Government House, as she was wont to do, whenever she understood that his Excellency was desirous of availing himself of her knowledge and experience in the management of the affairs of this little community. But she had scarcely taken her seat, when a dose, which had been prescribed by a practitioner in Printer's Square, and prepared by an apothecary in Downing Street, was administered to her. How it was concocted, we say not: many say they do know How,—but we say nothing !

"The old lady swallowed it with great reluctance, and we regret to state that it proved almost instantly fatal. She never spoke afterwards. She immediately lost the use of all her members, and her head actually dropt from her body. We have no doubt that her loss will be sincerely deplored by many intelligent and respectable members of the community.

"As the good lady died without a will, and has left no lawful heirs, her large possessions in Actingville and Plannington will revert to the Crown. As the public are much interested in the produce of these estates, we trust that they will be committed to the management of persons who will render them at least as productive as they were when in the hands of the late possessor. Report says that they will not be again united. From the nature of the property, we ourselves doubt whether they can be well cultivated, if entirely severed from each other.

"It is pretty confidently asserted, that a younger sister of the deceased (Mrs. Botherall, of Howling Hall) was instrumental in procuring the administering of this fatal dose. The two sisters lived formerly upon very friendly terms, but there has latterly been much bickering between them, and it is surmised that Mrs. Botherall has for some time cast a longing eye upon Actingville. She was servant in common of Planinngtown, but it is said she has been anxious to have the sole con-

trol of that estate. We trust that she will be disappointed. She has not managed her property so well,
as to induce us to wish for an extension of it. We
would like to see Howling Hall in better order, before
any addition is made to the estate of Mrs. Botherall."

The Chief Justice proved himself, during the years
which followed his separation from the Council, a most
painstaking, laborious Judge. He never trifled with a
cause, but made it a matter of serious study. His great
anxiety to do right, to deal impartially, to show no
respect of persons, was manifest throughout his career.

When his life had drawn to its close, men looked
back upon his judicial career with admiration. The
integrity, legal ability, and firmness, which he displayed
at different times, and under different circumstances,
called forth justly merited eulogies. One evidently
written by a lawyer, and already alluded to, is worthy
of being read, as containing a truthful estimate of his
powers, without being fulsome.

" With an intellect sufficiently profound to compre-
hend the general principles of law and equity, and with
powers of acute analytical discrimination, he was well
fitted to grapple with matters of legal intricacy, which
were frequently submitted to him for judicial decision.
As a Judge, towards his brothers on the Bench, he was
deferential, urbane, and dignified ; and towards the Bar,
he was courteous, patronizing, patient and forbearing.
To young lawyers in whom he recognized indications of
undeveloped talent, he extended the friendly smile of
encouragement. He had the happy faculty of being
familiar with persons in an inferior position, without
compromising his dignity, or impairing the respect that
was due to his elevated station. Indeed, respect was as
much accorded to his *person* as to the high office he
filled.

"It is said that he was an industrious and thorough legal student, even in advanced life ; and that he brought to the difficult and responsible duties of the Bench, an amount of legal knowledge, of which few of his Colonial contemporaries could boast. He made himself perfectly conversant with every new treatise of value upon law; and he was familiar with the improving practice and accumulating decisions of the English Courts.

"His mind was well disciplined, and enriched with the treasures of legal lore ; and his lucidly vigorous understanding was thus prepared for the complicated questions upon which it was his duty to adjudicate. In short, it is universally admitted that he was an able and upright Judge. During his long judicial life, it was sometimes his duty to pronounce upon convicted criminals the extreme penalty of the law. They who heard him on such occasions, remember the pathetically impressive tones of his voice, while he vindicated the righteousness and prerogatives of the law ; and at the same time, addressed the condemned culprit in the language of Christian charity and commiseration. He blended the stern rigour of the Judge with the compassionate spirit of an Evangelist. The man that was sentenced to the gallows, was directed to the cross ; and an effort was made to arouse the conscience—to awaken repentance—and to inspire faith in the soul of the guilty individual, who was soon to be arraigned before a holier and more august tribunal. In Judge Halliburton's language at such times there was nothing harsh or reproachful. His pious exhortations—often accompanied with tears, which bespoke the Christian sympathy of his heart—were always as earnest, solemn, and impressive as any that were ever uttered by the most devoted clergyman."

Judge Halliburton took a very deep interest in the cause of Education. On this subject he held most enlightened and liberal views. His whole course of conduct relative to the Pictou Academy, sufficiently shows
12

the value which he set on a sound and thorough system
of instruction, and at the same time his own freedom
from the trammels of a narrow-minded bigotry.   It was
by no means in accordance with the judgment of some
of his most highly esteemed personal friends, that he
acted in the beginning of that exciting contest, but rather
in direct antagonism to their wishes.   The same difficulty
presented itself then, as now meets the country—that
of providing Common School education for every section
of the Province,—and of appropriating on sound principles, a share of public money towards the establishment
and maintenance of institutions in which the higher
branches of learning should be taught.   It would have
been a great boon to the colony, if this great question
had been fairly grappled with and settled, before the
population had increased to its present size ; but there
were obstacles in the way, especially in reference to the
founding of a system of Collegiate instruction, and chief
amongst them, a jealousy of the predominant influence
of the Church of England.   .The number adhering to the
Church, throughout the Province, was comparatively
small ; but in Halifax, the centre of power, it was comparatively large, and many held places of trust and influence in the Government.   There, possibly, was some
cause for this feeling, to be found in the opinions and
conduct of the Churchmen of the day.   They had a
College of their own, whose foundations had been laid
under the auspices and through the exertions of the first
Bishop ; it had been fostered with care by him and his
successors ; large sums of money had been brought from
England and expended upon its erection and maintenance ; it was the first College in a British colony which

had received a Royal charter; it was modelled, as to its
curriculum of study, after the most famous University in
the world; it had served the Province well in sending
from its Halls, even in its earliest days, men who graced
the Senate and the Bar,—who discharged the duties of a
minister with ability and devotion,—of a physician with
skill and success.   It was natural that Churchmen should
cherish an institution with which they were so intimately
blended; and we can scarcely wonder that they, on their
part, should have been anxious to give pre-eminence to
King's College at Windsor, whenever the question of
University education was discussed.   With this jealousy
on either side, we can scarcely wonder that no better
system of providing instruction of a higher order was
adopted.   But it may be doubted whether time has improved, though it may have changed, the aspect of the
question, or in any degree lessened the difficulties.   As
regards the Common School education of the country, it
could not be much worse than at present; the theory
and practice are equally bad.

As respects the higher schools and Colleges, the
principle adopted by the Legislature of the country, of
giving a like sum to each denomination of Christians, for
the support of institutions which should be under their
own management, is thoroughly unsound; and its practical working proves it to be a failure.   It tends to create
a spirit of religious rivalry which is far from wholesome
in itself, and by no means conducive towards that much
to be desired end, in any country, but especially in a
young colony—a unity of feeling and interests amongst
the inhabitants.   Separate interests are sustained, and
even called out, by these different communities, and

youths educated within them are so completely moulded
after the pattern of each, that they go forth into the
world, with a species of conviction that it is their first
and chief duty to promote the necessarily limited aims
and objects of those with whom they have been associated for years.   So to train the pupils is not intentional
on the part of the several Faculties at the head of these
Colleges, except in so far as regards the students of
Theology; these, of course, are specially taught the
doctrines peculiar to the body of Christians to whom the
College belongs, and conscientiously are impressed with
the superior value and soundness of that system of
doctrine and government to all others.   With this no
fault can be found, but unhappily the particular interest
of the religious denomination, as such, imperceptibly
insinuates itself into the minds of the taught, through
various channels, such as the class of books in general
circulation within the walls of the College, and the ordinary tone of sentiment, feeling, and conversation.   As
an almost necessary consequence, every year finds a fresh
set of young men ushered into the Province, who have
just passed their examination, and are about to take
their places as students in the several professions, or
clerks in the merchants counting house; yet who are
disunited; who have come from four or five different
Colleges; who form as many separate companies; who
have, many perhaps unconsciously, though not less
surely, separate public interests; who have each been
living with those of their own way of thinking, and
meeting no opposition, deem themselves and the class
with which they are linked, to be right, and all the rest
of the world wrong; who know comparatively nothing

of the great world outside of their own narrow circum-
ference, and are resolved that they and theirs must be
upheld politically as well as religiously at any cost.
For the good of the Province at large, it would be a
marvel, if men brought up under such influences could
as a rule, coalesce ; as says Sir William Temple, " Divisions hinder the common interest and public good."
Great public measures, tending to the welfare of the
colony, are lost sight of in the resolve to push forward
the interests and increase the influence of the various
religious bodies.

There can also be little doubt, that our strength is
sadly weakened by the division of public money, now
granted by the House of Assembly, for the promotion
of a Collegiate education.　At present it is frittered
away in small sums, too trifling in amount to be of any
great value to each, and merely enabling the several
Governors to eke out a small, and in most instances,
pitiably deficient support to their Professors and Tutors.
It is true that none could well continue without this
little aid, for the respective endowments are, in all cases,
far too small for the respectable support of the several
Colleges ; but it may be questioned whether this aid,
thus bestowed, is for the real welfare of the Province,
when the various sums combined, together with an additional grant, would support one good University.
Let the country prosper as it may, for many years to
come the Denominational Colleges must continue to be
very small and insignificant institutions ; while their
funds must ever be kept up, and when lost, renewed, by
evoking the feelings of the Denominations whose cherished care they are : a practice which may indeed " pro-

voke to good " works," but not necessarily to "love."
In addition to all, it is clear that the leading object
of a University is wholly unattained by this division of
labour and separation of students.   A University gathers
from the wide universe of knowledge, men versed in all
branches of learning; brings to one centre, men who are
masters in some special subject; culls them out of each
department of learning, and by uniting them, concen-
trates their light, intensifies their power, and by mutual
reflection increases the knowledge each of the other.   It
attracts by its own intrinsic excellence students from all
parts of a country, who have been brought up under
different influences, and innoculated with various opinions, and mingling them with each other, rubs off
their rough edges of thought, and gives them a general
insight into the human mind in all its phases.   It must
be regretted that some one central University had not, in
the early stage of the colony, been established; and had
all the leading men looked wisely forward to the future
of the Province, they might have so arranged as to have
effected this object with perhaps even less difficulty than
at present, or at any time hereafter.   King's College,
at Windsor, had a Royal charter, a small endowment,
and a staff of Professors; a little kindly consultation,
would have removed, as it long since has done, the ob-
noxious test of subscription to the thirty-nine articles.
The foundation was already laid; nor need the selection
of this, the oldest chartered College in the British Colonies, in any way have interfered with the establishment
of Theological schools by each denomination for the
especial benefit of their own students in Divinity.   These
Halls, which might easily have been maintained as to

the staff required by each body of Christians, could either have been so situated as that the religious instruction should have been imparted simultaneously with the secular, or students in that Faculty been drafted into them at the close of their University career. Possibly the day is not far distant when this will be accomplished and a central University be established. Judge Halliburton no doubt would gladly have lent his aid to the furtherance of any good scheme, which might have been prepared for this end; and deeply as he was interested in the welfare of King's College he naturally would have desired that it should have been the mother University, with which all Denominational Colleges for instruction in Theology should be affiliated. In advocating the claims of the Pictou Academy, as he at first did, he took high ground, and wished that its supporters should have the privilege of educating their children in their own principles of religion, as then it seemed impracticable to arrange any one plan by which all could be taught within the same walls and their various forms of creed not interfered with. It is true that for a reason already mentioned he finally refused to unite with the advocates of the grant; the question was settled after many warm debates, and the principle adopted of giving like sums to each denomination which should establish a College in their own interests. A few years will tell us or our children whether all will not unite to have one University, in which literature, art, and science shall be imparted to the youth of the country; and while God is honored and worshipped daily in its chapels, the special study of Theology is conducted in Halls and Colleges connected with it. A Faculty of five and twenty or

thirty professors and lecturers; a Library of some thirty
thousand volumes; philosophical apparatus of every
kind; collections of specimens in all the branches of
science where they may be gathered; and two or three
hundred students—would form a University in reality as
in name, from which it would be an honor to carry out
a degree.   These views are thrown out as those of the
writer rather than the subject of this memoir; and have
been introduced as reflections arising from the debate on
the question alluded to.   The principle of assessment
for the support of schools has within a short time been
most wisely adopted by the Legislature of the land; and
although some difficulties of detail may cause it to be
unfavorably received by a few, these will very soon
vanish, and the course taken be universally pronounced a
blessing.   Should the weighty question of a central University be brought before the public at a future period,
the inhabitants of the Province, it is hoped, will consider it in a frank and liberal spirit, and bend their
energies towards the attainment of that which would
tend more to keep down petty prejudices and create a
bond of union amongst the men who, as a rule, must
ever be leading in the land, than any other means which
could be devised.

The Judge's intimate connection with King's College
has been stated already.   As in his youthful days, so to
the end of his long life he displayed a warm interest in
its welfare.   From the meetings of the Board of Governors he was seldom absent.   For many years he made it
a matter of duty to drive to Windsor for the purpose of
attending the most important—the annual—meeting held
in the month of September in the Library of the College,

and when there was always treated with that deep respect which met him every where else.   Indeed he
seemed to be so integral an element of the Institution
that it would have scarcely appeared like a meeting
without him.   As he grew older, and his always fragile
frame became weak, so highly esteemed were his wise
counsels, that rather than lose them the Board of
Governors proposed meeting at his house, to which he
willingly acceded; and they accordingly did so until
his last illness.   It would not engage the interest of the
provincial public in general, to have a relation of his
sentiments on those various questions of detail which
came before the Board of Governors; but as a public
man they are entitled to know of him, that he ever desired to legislate when sitting there, as would best sub-
serve the interest of the whole body of people.   While
he ever defended the rights of King's-College with zeal
and ability, he never forgot to be just and liberal towards all.

When the Encænia next succeeding his death took
place, the President of the College from his place on the
dais in the public hall alluded to him in terms of great
respect.

"In all our difficulties he was a firm and constant
friend.   In the Provincial Councils he was ever a most
prompt, energetic and judicious benefactor.   When at
the bidding of that Lord whose *cancrine and palindromic*
name reads as harshly backwards as forwards—*nomen et
omen habes*—well betokening his retrograde measures—
when Lord Glenelg, I mean, called upon us (in his
notorious No. 1 Despatch, dated April 30th, 1835) to
surrender our Royal Charter, the firm but characteris-
tically playful reply of this old soldier to Sir Colin

Campbell was "*No surrender*, your Excellency! our
Royal Charter has never been *violated* and shall not be
surrendered—it will survive even this Despatch!" When
the *Imperial Grant* was withdrawn he was among the
first to aid us by a liberal donation, and joined by other
friends a new Professorship was added to our Staff.
This example was soon nobly followed by our Alumni,
so that when the *Provincial Grant* was reduced two
more Professorships were immediately founded.   It
seemed a pity we had no more to lose, or who can tell
how many learned Professors would be gracing our halls
on this happy occasion, and swelling the already goodly
number of my valued confreres?   It was a crisis tending to remind us of the sweet lines from his *own* pen:

> 'Deep feels my heart, God's providence can still
> Surpassing good produce from passing ill.'

"Time would fail me were I to attempt his eulogy.
Honored by his Sovereign—happily panegyrized as you
may remember in this Hall, by Lord Mulgrave—venerated by his Brother Judges and by all the numerous
and brilliant ornaments of his Profession, as well as re-
vered by all orders of men in the Province—eulogised
on his decease by the eloquent and friendly pen of one
who knew him well—a graceful tribute whose touching
power stirred the depths of many an heart—I feel were
I to add a word I should be guilty of the folly of attempting "*Iliada post Homerum scribere.*"
"The last Encænia I remember him to have attended,
Judge Parker and Judge Haliburton, our honored sons,
were both present.   "The good old Chief,"—such the
phrase universally applied,—"the old man eloquent"
drew a simultaneous burst of especial applause from
them, and from the whole assembly, by an impromptu
address of genuine and glowing eloquence, pathos and
burning vigor, which, while it charmed every heart,
evinced the deepest interest in our College, and was
pronounced to be a spontaneous effort worthy of the

best days of his prime. He honored me with his friendship and occasional correspondence. He wrote for me
a short but most interesting biography, and a year or
two before his death sent me in manuscript for perusal
(afterwards privately printed) a poem on the passing
events of that exciting period, containing paragraphs
almost prophetically describing as the natural consequence of their system the present internecine struggle
in the *then United* States."

It was well said in the closing paragraph of the resolution afterward passed at the Board of Governors :
" As in the profession of which he was at the head, and
in the society of which he occupied the highest place,
so at this Board he was venerated by all, the oldest as
well as the youngest, in the light of a parent ; and his
counsels were received with additional respect, because
his wisdom was always tempered by kindness."

Sir Brenton was a member of the Church of England,
and as such very devoted to its interests. He was convinced of the Scriptural basis on which its government,
doctrine and discipline were built, and zealously advocated its claims whenever opportunity offered. When
the Diocesan Church Society was formed, in 1837,
under the joint auspices of the late Bishop Inglis and
the Reverend William Cogswell, the Chief Justice lent
his valuable aid. As a member of the executive committee, he worked with as much zeal and interest as
any of the clergy. Whenever he was not absent from
town, on circuit or other business, he was almost sure
to be seen on the afternoons of meeting making his way
up to the National School in which the committee met.
It was remarkable also, how very attentive he was to
the proceedings, which oftentimes were necessarily dry

enough.   But whatever they were he was never inat-
tentive.   It may be doubted whether any one can remember his sitting listlessly, as the business was trans-
*acted, in any one instance.   When anything was said
which he did not distinctly hear, as was sometimes the
case in his later years, he would lean forward in a way
peculiarly his own for a minute and then resume his
position.   If he was much interested in what was going
on, he would do this frequently while the speaker was
addressing the meeting, and as would be proved by
what he himself would afterward say, had listened to
and mastered the whole speech.   One might have supposed that with his accumulated experience and native
wisdom, he would have felt it very wearisome to hear
the remarks of quite young men, and scarcely have
listened to them ; but if no one else in the room paid
attention to the crude ideas, and badly expressed
thoughts of an inexperienced youth, he did.   The truth
was, he obeyed the apostolic precept,—" he honored all
men," and instead of discouraging a young man in his
first attempts, by inattention, or an evident disregard to
what he was saying, he patiently listened through it all.

At the annual public meetings of the Society, his
speech was anticipated with the greatest pleasure.   He
usually moved the adoption and publishing of the report
of the executive committee, which gave him an opportunity of reviewing the progress made during the past
year ; and such was his familiar acquaintance with every
part of the Province, that he spoke with a fluency and
clearness of the work of the missionaries and the state
of the churches, as to afford information while he gave
pleasure to his audience.   It will be long remembered

by those who were present how touchingly and how usefully he adverted one night in Temperance Hall, to the mutineers of the *Saladin,* who were tried and executed at Halifax. He was speaking of the influence which education exerted over a community; and in referring more particularly to reading he stated the vast importance of circulating books and periodicals that contained sound principles. Suddenly stopping he stooped down, and reaching a book, held it up before the assembly: " This," said he " is a book which belonged to the unhappy men who committed murder in the *Saladin;* it contains many a valuable treatise; it is widely known and very justly is it highly prized; it is Chambers' Journal. You may perceive that certain pages are turned down at the corners. The book in general has scarcely been read at all; these have evidently been re-read many times; they bear marks of thorough study; and what is written in these pages? *The story of a successful mutiny!* Who can tell but that the thought was first suggested, to a mind hitherto untainted with such diabolical designs, by a perusal of the injudicious tale? The well-thumbed leaves bear painful testimony, that if not planted, the thought was fostered by the high wrought story. When men are influenced by others thoughts, what Christian will not wish to avoid sending forth what may lead to evil, and use every effort to spread abroad only such works as may tend to good?" None will forget the earnest tones of voice with which these sentiments were uttered, or the nerve and vigour which animated the frame of the eloquent old man.

But Sir Brenton was no narrow minded zealot.

True, he loved most dearly the Church of England.
But he loved all, who loved his Lord.   In every respect he thought the Church stood pre-eminently high ;
as to its administration, its forms of worship, and the
doctrines which it drew from Scripture.   As an instrument in God's hands for building up believers in their
faith, and as a means of extending a knowledge of our
Lord and Saviour Jesus Christ to fallen man, he believed
it the purest, and the means best adapted to the end.
Yet he hailed gladly every servant of Christ and bid
God-speed to all who maintained the essential truths of
the Christian religion.   The Bible in these matters was
his text book.   Whatever in it was plainly, unequivocally
stated, he received with deepest reverence ; but on
points upon which it was silent, he accepted no dictum
from other sources.   His mind and heart equally were
far above adopting contracted notions on the grand
question, What is Truth?   He was one of those who
knew that the great, comprehensive, absorbing doctrine
taught in Holy Writ, was the *Union of the Soul with
God through Christ by the operation of the Spirit.*   This is
the truth in which every man on earth is personally in·
terested.   A wonderful being, who came originally from
God, he has derived his light, moral and intellectual, as
well as his life, from the Divine Being.   He knows by in-
tuition and experience, that as a link of the human family, as a link in the one long chain of human life, he is
alienated, estranged and separated from his Creator and
God.   The Bible tells him how he may return and be
re-united to Him ; and how when this lower stage of his
existence is over, he may be admitted into His immediate presence, and, dwelling in the atmosphere

which is round about Him, live, as He lives, for ever and for ever. Redemption by Christ, and Sanctification by the Holy Spirit, or dropping these theological expressions, the atonement which the Lord Jesus, "God manifest in the flesh," has made for sin, and the blessed influence of the Holy Spirit, which though as unseen as the wind, is as surely felt, are the foundations on which alone man can rest his hope. Doubtless, there are many truths beside these clearly expressed in the inspired volume; but to these they may all be traced back, that Christ may be "all in all."

For the better preservation of these truths, and their better promulgation, through the world, Christ and His apostles have laid down broad rules and plain principles—but they have entered into no detail. The grand criteria by which we are to know the people of God, are as few as they are clear. Whoever he be who believes in, and loves the Lord Jesus Christ in sincerity and in truth, and who brings forth the fruits of the Spirit in his walk through the world—that man has apprehended the truth, and has found access by Christ through the Spirit with the Father. Such, we believe, as might be gathered from his conduct and conversation, were the broad and enlightened views of Sir Brenton. He liked the walls and bulwarks that were round about the Church of England. The government, the liturgy, the rites and ceremonies, he deemed more than expedient, he set a very high value upon them; but he did not think it necessary that every man should be within the walls which surrounded the Church of England, with whatever wisdom they were built, before he could hail him as a companion and fellow-laborer in God's vineyard. Having a brotherly esteem for all Christians, he gladly united with them in the furtherance of any good object. As a member of the Bible Society, and of the Sabbath Alliance, and such associations, he joined most cordially with men of other denominations. The last public meeting at which he was present was one held for united prayer. His appearance on that occasion was welcomed by Christians with great warmth of feeling. It was a fine scene in every way. The public hall was crowded with worshippers; it was wholly unlike the ordinary gatherings within those walls; the time was mid-day; the attendants were not merely or mostly the curious and idle. Men of business had left their counting houses, and offices and shops, to wait upon God, and present their supplications and prayers, and intercessions before Him; the aged as well as the young were amongst the throng. On the raised platform were the ministers, and many of the older members, of each denomination. In their midst sat the venerable Chief-Justice. With a few solemn words he opened the meeting, and the worship began. After the reading of God's Word, the offering up of prayer, and an address from one or two of the clergymen present, he began to feel the effect of his unwonted exertion, and fatigue compelled him to retire. Without notice he rose from his seat; in a few well-chosen words, he said to the immense audience, that a weary frame warned him to depart; and then the honored patriarch, looking over the vast assemblage, uttered in those tremulous tones which made the heart swell with feeling : " God bless you." The whole assembly, as by common consent, remained in solemn silence, as leaning on the arm of a friend he slowly passed with feeble step through their midst: the door closed, and he was gone.

His seat in St. Paul's Church was seldom vacant. Even when he had become very infirm, and might have deemed himself unequal to the effort, he so enjoyed public worship that he could not lose the opportunity whenever it offered. There was no individual in the congregation more devout than he, nor more attentive to the sermon. He did not consider himself so wise but that he might hear something of which he had not thought before, or some old thought put in a new form. His whole manner from the time he entered the house of God until he left it, was an example of all that could be supposed reverential or devotional. His voice was heard in the immediate vicinity of his pew as that of one who had wholly lost sight of those who were about him, and was in earnest in seeking grace for himself, and God's blessing upon others. When he took his accustomed seat in the church, it seemed natural that he should be there, and gave a look of familiarity to that venerable place of worship. When his well-known form was absent, there was a blank which for long was felt.

Towards the immediate close of life the Chief-Justice's hearing had become slightly impaired, and in conse- quence, he had some difficulty in catching the voice of the officiating minister, as his pew was on the ground floor. To remedy in some measure the evil, he resolved to obtain, if possible, a sitting which would bring him nearer to the pulpit; and he therefore paid a visit to his Parish church on a week day for the purpose of select- ing a seat in which he could better hear the sermon.

13

At his time of life, and feeble in limb as he had then
become, the ascending of the long flight of stairs was a
serious effort; he, nevertheless, mounted the steps to the
gallery, and after looking at the various pews in the
proximity of the pulpit, he decided on one in which he
thought he might hear the clergyman's voice; and when
a friend who accompanied him read aloud in the pulpit,
and he distinctly caught the words, he felt and manifested great delight.　An effort was made to negotiate with
the occupiers of this pew for permission to the Chief-
Justice to have a seat in it; but, strange to say, the application was unsuccessful, and when this result to the
attempt was communicated to him, he felt the disap-
pointment to which it subjected him most keenly.　As
in the Providence of God it so occurred, he might have
been spared the pain of a denial, for this was his last
visit to that sacred place whose hallowed courts he had
trodden for fourscore years.

　The Chief-Justice in private life was one of the most
kind, amiable and cheerful of men; while a retentive
memory, and a great fund of humor, rendered him a
most delightful companion.　"Given to hospitality," he
frequently entertained his personal friends, and any
leading men who might have come to the Province in
an official capacity, or were paying Halifax a passing
visit.　He charmed his guests with a constant flow of
lively conversation; sometimes he instructed by grave
discussion on the leading topics of the day; at others he
amused by his anecdotes.　He was especially familiar
with the lives and characters of the most able and influential men, who at any time had held high places in
the Province, and of these he often spake; now relating

some incident of interest which had occurred to them, during some part of their career,—and now recalling some happy remark or quick retort or witticism. So playful was his mind on all occasions when it was right to yield to its bent, that one could scarcely avoid recalling the proverb of the wise king : " He that is of a merry heart has a continual feast;" and as to its influence upon others, " a merry heart doeth good like a medicine."

Blended as he was for so many years with the history of Nova Scotia, and a very prominent actor in all the important events which occurred within its limits, the Chief-Justice was seldom or never the hero of his own stories; and, as a consequence, but few of the facts of his own life could be gleaned from his conversation. Thus many an instructive and interesting passage of his career has passed into oblivion. In his own house, and amongst the members of his own family, he was uniformly most kind, considerate and indulgent. His cheerfulness and readiness to please were always at hand, and always in action. They cost him no effort, but manifested themselves spontaneously. Alike to those who were daily with him, and those who visited his house, he displayed an even gentleness of disposition and urbanity of manner. To the poor and distressed he exhibited not mere sympathy of feeling, but proved it by generous dealing ; the value of the latter was enhanced by the former—while he was beneficent he was also benevolent. Numbered amongst his pleasant ways at home was one which afforded a good deal of pleasure to others. It was that of putting some thought into metre ; sometimes he would concoct a

riddle, at others indite a poetical epistle, or again clothe
some scene in which he had taken part in verse, and send
the production to his friend. Such was the agreeable
turn of his disposition ; happy himself, he endeavoured
by little as well as great things to make those around
him happy also. In that sweet little poem of which he
was very fond, " The Deserted Village," there are lines
which could be most truthfully applied to him, as the
venerable old man, surrounded by his family and
friends, passed the evening of his life :—

His ready smile a parent's warmth exprest ;
Their welfare pleased him, and their cares distrest ;
To them his heart, his love, his griefs were given,
But all his serious thoughts had rest in Heaven :
As some tall cliff that lifts its awful form,
Swells from the vale, and midway leaves the storm ;
Though round its breast, the rolling clouds are spread,
Eternal sunshine settles on its head.

The Chief-Justice was during the progress of his
career the recipient of numerous testimonials of the high
esteem in which he was held. It was not only after his
life had closed, as so often is the case, that men began
to discern his worth, and pronounce eulogies upon his
character ; but while he was still living and taking
an active part in public affairs. This fact imparts
significance to those documents in which his course of
conduct is lauded and his character admired.

Amongst many other tokens of respect and esteem
shown to him was one on which he must have set a
high value, because of the persons from whom it
emanated, and the high honor which it conferred on
him. The members of the Bar resolved on asking his
permission to have his portrait taken, and hung in that

Council Chamber in which he had so long sat as a member, and afterward as President. He acceded to the wish : an admirable likeness was executed by the artist, and placed beside those of royalty and some of his predecessors. It is needless, in looking at this memorial, and the distinguished position which it occupies, to speak of the estimation in which he was held by those who saw him most and knew him best as a public man.

A pleasing custom was introduced by the members of the Bench and Bar, during the latter years of the Chief-Justice's life, of their waiting upon him on his successive birth days to congratulate him on his continued health, and the unimpaired state of his faculties. On these occasions he ever received his brethren, and the Barristers who accompanied them in a body, with courtesy and dignity ; while his lively disposition, the ready wit, and the appropriate anecdote at his command, rendered these visits most pleasant to his friends. They usually spent an hour or two with him as guests, and in his cheerful society renewed their feeling of affectionate regard for him. His replies to the congratulations offered to him at these times were often in a touching strain. As he grew older he felt that these yearly gatherings could not be long repeated ; and the venerable man, when he referred to the past and glanced at the future, generally touched a tender chord at once by the deep pathos of his sentiments and the earnest tones of his familiar voice.

He was drawing very near the end of his course, when once more he was to receive tokens of respect and honor from his fellow-men. This time it was from the

fountain from which alone all earthly dignities and
positions of rank in the British dominions, can legiti-
mately flow.   Her Majesty conferred on him the honor
of knighthood.   It was a fitting climax to all his
testimonials.   The greatest was reserved for the last.
Nor could the Sovereign have granted the honor either
to one more worthy to receive it in consideration of his
long and faithful services, or to one in whom there beat
a more thoroughly loyal heart.   Many a year before
her Majesty was born, he had served under her royal
father.   As we have seen, he "knew and loved him
well."   He had seen him much in private as well as
public; and now in the same town in which he had
known the Duke of Kent, some sixty years before, the
aged man was to receive at the hands of his royal
daughter, a distinguishing mark of her approbation.
At the close of the last century, the Duke had given
him a commission in the regiment.   When more than
half the present century had passed away, the Queen
enrolled him amongst her knights.

His friends, the Profession, the Province at large,
expressed pleasure at the act.   The Bench and Bar
once more approached him in the language of congra-
tulation :—

"On Monday the 9th of May (1859) the members of
the Bench and Bar, resident at Halifax, waited on Sir
Brenton Halliburton, at his residence, where the Honble.
Mr. Justice Bliss, after a few very appropriate remarks,
presented and read the following address :—

'To the Honorable Sir Brenton Halliburton, Chief-
    Justice of Nova Scotia :

    'It has afforded all the members of the Bench and Bar of

the Supreme Court over which you have so long presided, great gratification to learn that your lengthened term of judicial labors, extending over a period of more than half a century, and your great ability and rectitude in the discharge of the duties of your office, which have long secured to you the respect and esteem of the inhabitants of this Province, have been recognized by the Imperial Government, and that her most gracious Majesty has been pleased to confer upon you the dignity of a Knight of the United Kingdom of Great Britain and Ireland.

'While, as admirers of your public and private virtues, we are much gratified by this event, we also feel grateful that this mark of her Royal favor has been bestowed upon the head of the profession to which we have the honor to belong, and that her most gracious Majesty has been pleased to approve of your valuable public services in the high office which you have so long occupied and adorned.

'Her Majesty could not have adopted a more effective mode of retaining the affections of her loyal subjects in this Province, and of making them feel that it forms a component part of her empire, than by thus conferring her Royal favor upon one whom they so much honor and esteem.

'Few of us are old enough to recall the time when you first assumed your judicial duties : but though providence has blessed you with many more years than are usually allotted to man, age, we are happy to know, has not impaired those qualities of mind and heart for which you have been so conspicuous, nor weakened those generous and social virtues which have so endeared you to us. That you may long be spared to enjoy the honor which her Majesty has conferred upon you is our sincere and heartfelt wish.'

"To which Sir Brenton Halliburton read the following reply :—

'My Brethren of the Bench and of the Bar :

'Accept my heartfelt thanks for the kind and affectionate address which you have given to me upon her most gracious Majesty's conferring upon me the dignity of a Knight of the United Kingdom of Great Britain and Ireland.

'Although at my age I ought to be, and I humbly trust I am, more solicitous to obtain the blessed promises which our gracious Saviour has made to all believers in his Holy Gos-

pel. than any earthly honors, yet I value highly the approbation of a Sovereign, esteemed and beloved by her subjects
for her public and private virtues.

'To our respected Governor his excellency the Earl of
Mulgrave I feel great gratitude for having totally unsolicited
by me, brought my services under her Royal consideration.
to which I attribute the honor that has been conferred upon
me.

'I consider this honor as paid to the profession to which I
belong, and it greatly increases my gratification so to consider it.

'I am much indebted to my brethren of the Bench for the
satisfaction which I learn my judgments have given, for.
generally speaking, it is with their concurrence and approval
that those judgments have been pronounced; and I am sure
they will join with me in declaring that the labors of the
Bench have frequently been greatly diminished by the industry and talent of the Bar.

'And now, gentlemen, accept of an old man's affectionate
prayer for your welfare. May you at the close of life feel
the great comfort of having made your peace with God
through the merits of your Saviour. God bless you all.

    '(Signed)   BRENTON HALLIBURTON.
'May 9th, 1859.'

"The members of the Bench and Bar then partook of
the hospitalities of the Venerable Chief-Justice, who
seemed much gratified by the very cordial and unanimous feeling of respect and esteem evinced towards him
by the profession over which he has so long presided.

        "ROBT. HALIBURTON,
    "*Secretary of N. S. Barristers' Society.*"

Notwithstanding all the homage that was paid him
through a long life,—the continual prosperity which
attended him,—the expressions of approbation which
were constantly offered to him—he remained humble
and affable in his manners. He was not spoiled by
these testimonials. The effect was for good, and not for
evil to his character. He seemed to grow in kindliness

of feeling toward the young,—in benevolence towards
the poor and needy.   Known throughout the Province
for a longer period than any other man who ever held
a public office in it,—revisiting each circuit year after
year, and deciding upon all manner of cases brought
into Court by contending people—deciding as he must
do, in favor of one and against another—instead of
alienating gradually from himself the people of the
country, their voices were raised almost as the voice of
one man to welcome him when he approached, and at
last to mourn for him when he died.   In his connection
with the Bench, the feelings which had been manifested
to him all through his life, were again strongly called
forth at his death.   And although perhaps somewhat
anticipating the narrative, the course adopted by the
legal profession on hearing of his departure, can not be
introduced in a more appropriate place.

It was little more than a year after the last-named
event, that this same Profession once again met for the
special purpose of doing honor to him who had been
their head.   It was now to his memory.   When a meeting
was called upon hearing of his death, it was most
numerously attended.   The Judges specially were
deeply interested, and, as was proper, took the lead in
the solemn business of the day.   A resolution had been
prepared by the Honorable Mr. Justice Bliss, which
was moved by the Hon. Mr. Justice Wilkins, as
follows :—

" *Resolved*, That the Bench and Bar receive with feelings
of the deepest sorrow and regret the intelligence of the death
of their VENERABLE CHIEF-JUSTICE.   Occupying a seat on
the Bench for 53 years—a tenure of office, unexampled in
judicial annals—and for more than half of that period Chief-

Justice of the Province, he was distinguished by great
ability, a sound discriminating judgment, unwearied patience
and industry,—a strong inherent love of justice, and an
earnest, anxious, faithful attention to the discharge of every
duty. Conscientious, upright and impartial, firm in the
administration of the Law, and ever kind and courteous in
demeanor, he presided over the Court with dignity, and won
the reverential esteem and affection alike of the Bench, of
the Bar, and of all classes of the community. So extended
had been his term of service on the Bench that there is not
now a member of the Bar who did not enter the Profession
since the commencement of his judicial career; but the
experience of all, whatever their standing, enables them to
bear willing testimony to his eminent qualifications, his
public worth and private virtues. These have endeared him
to their hearts, and will long be retained in their memories.
They have called forth one universal regret for the loss of a
good man, an honest valuable public servant. While the
Bench and the Bar pay this imperfect tribute of their love
and veneration to him who so long and so ably presided
over them, they beg to offer their very sincere condolence on
this mournful occasion to his sorrowing and afflicted family.

For many years of his life the Chief-Justice and his
family spent some portion of the summer at a country
seat of his own, which was called Margaretville, situated
in the county of Annapolis. In this neighbourhood the
first Bishop of the Diocese, already alluded to, had
purchased a property to which he resorted much in the
latter period of his life. His son, when he succeeded
to the Diocese, and also to his father's private estate,
retained Clermont (as the place was called) as a summer retreat for himself and family. This made it pleasant for the Chief-Justice and his friends to visit the
country ; they were not altogether without companion-
ship for the two or three months which they spent in
the comparatively quiet abode. To one who led so
busy and anxious a life as he, the quiet and rest which

he there enjoyed must have been at once delightful and healthful. The total change of air, scenery, and employment, contributed, no doubt, to that cheerfulness of spirit and vigour of mind, which were characteristic of him to the end. These pleasant visits were, however, brought to a close some years previous to his death. The journey was a long one, and old age rendered it more prudent and more conducive to the Chief-Justice's health, to take a less wearisome drive. Thus, for the remainder of his life he spent the summer season at his well known residence near the North West Arm, called " The Bower" ; and it was here that he closed his long career.

Early in the year 1860 he was warned by various symptoms that his time of departure was drawing near. Nature was well-nigh exhausted. He was gradually losing strength ; however pleasing for his friends his continuance in their midst might be, for himself it was but " labor and sorrow." Feeling that the day was far spent, and that he should soon leave the tabernacle, in which he had dwelt, and soar into another region of light and life, he looked forward with joy to the grand event. As he lay upon the sofa, and listened to the word of God, when quoted or read, his whole expression was that of one who drank in of the river of pleasures which flowed from the Throne of God. When he joined in the prayers which were offered at his side, the intense earnestness which he threw into his own utterances at the close of each petition was most marked.

There was something particularly pleasing in the simplicity of his faith. The promises were, as St. Paul expresses it, "all yea and Amen in Christ Jesus." He heard them with gladness; he laid hold of them with strength; he could say, " I know whom I have believed, and am persuaded that he is able to keep that which I have committed unto Him till that day."

When the weather had become sufficiently warm, and nature had again adorned the trees and shrubs abounding in that sequestered place with fresh leaves, and the fields with new verdure, the family determined to make their accustomed move. Sir Brenton, however, did not at first readily acquiesce, and dreaded the effort. No doubt he did not feel equal to the exertion and bustle consequent upon the removal. For, previous to this he had been very ill; so much so, indeed, that he thought himself during one night to be dying. To this impression he alluded on the following morning when in conversation with his physician, adding that such had been his happiness in resting on his Saviour's merits, and such the joys which he had experienced, he would not barter them for the most robust health.

The urgent wish of his family, and the advice of his physician, prevailed upon Sir Brenton to try the fresh air and the quiet of "The Bower." On the 2nd June the move was accomplished; and on that day he rallied his old genial disposition, and joined with lively interest in the little incidents of the day. The weather was very fine, and for the first few days he seemed rather to improve, and apparently to gain strength, and so to enjoy being in his accustomed retreat as much as ever.

This respite, however, was of short duration. On Saturday the 30th of June he felt himself to be ill, and unable to go to Church. Had his strength been equal to it he would no doubt have attended divine service as usual, but it would have been with somewhat disappointed feelings, in consequence of the circumstance already mentioned in reference to his efforts to obtain the seat he desired. This pain he was spared. But he had two full services at home, and was—as indeed he always was—most fervent in the utterance of the responses; while he listened with apparent enjoyment, exhausted though he was, to a sermon by the late John Angell James, on "Faith in relation to Sanctification."

On Monday he was no better, but yet was able to see a few friends who called to inquire for him; and though he did not leave the sofa much through the day, toward evening he joined his family in the dining room, and remained for some little time. During the night he awoke and calling his son advised him what to do in case of his death. After a few words of hopeful reply, Sir Brenton lay down and slept as usual. On the following morning he rose for the last time, at his accustomed hour, and went to the breakfast table; but he was evidently weaker and unable to endure as much exertion as the day before. It was on the evening of this day that he was struck with paralysis, and from this attack he never recovered. On retiring for the night, and doubtless now feeling his helplessness increasing, he alluded to the paralytic stroke, saying in a very mournful though resigned tone, as he pointed to his right side: "This side dead!" then to the left: "This side alive!" This circumstance brought to his recollection an aged friend who had lingered for some months in this same state; and he felt somewhat fearful lest he should become impatient to die instead of waiting

in meek submission the divine will. Hence it was his
constant prayer that he might be patient, and wonderfully he was strengthened and supported throughout,
and not a murmur escaped his lips. His implicit trust
in his Saviour was never broken, and not for a moment
was he suffered to feel a doubt of his pardon and acceptance through the merits of his Redeemer. He was a
remarkable instance of that firm assurance which knows
no wavering. He knew practically the meaning of
those comforting words: "Thou wilt keep him in perfect peace whose mind is stayed on Thee, because he
trusteth in Thee." The Holy Spirit bore constant
witness with his spirit that he was the heir of God
and the joint heir with Christ.

Whenever he was able to see a Christian friend, it
afforded him sincere delight; and oftentimes, when
weary and weak, he was visibly refreshed as he listened
to some consoling truths from the Word of Life, or
united in the prayer offered beside his couch. Day by
day he grew more feeble; the light flickered, the lamp
was burning out; and as he realised it, he was humble
as a little child; he bowed with meekness before his
Father's will, and as he neared his journey's end, although he grew not impatient of the delay, he longed
to reach his Father's House.

The hour came at last. On the 16th July the old
pilgrim finished his course and laid down his staff; the
soldier had fought the fight and received the crown;
the servant had done his work and lay down to rest.

Thus imperfectly has the writer sketched a brief
memoir of one whose name was a household word in
Nova Scotia; and he trusts that those who have read

thus far will do him the justice to read that which follows. He had intended to have written at some length the "Life and Times" of Sir Brenton Halliburton; and for this purpose a rough outline was conceived of the internal history of the Province, from the year of the "Declaration of Independence," until the middle of the present century. It was purposed to write the various chapters, which would constitute such a book, in "leisure hours." These, however, gradually became so few, that he was compelled to abandon the first project, and content himself with compiling a short running memoir, linking together some of the chief events of his life, though omitting many that might have been made very interesting to those who know anything of Colonial life in general, and of this Province in particular. A lawyer might have entered largely into his career as a Judge,—analysed his legal knowledge,—discussed his judgments pronounced upon the Bench,—and following him through his circuits, lightened it all with many an amusing anecdote, and many a witty saying which he uttered. There were scenes, adventures, and conversations in which he was an important element, that would have rendered a sketch of his life an object of interest to many who would without them deem it dull and wearisome. A politician might have scrutinized the opinions which he held,—and examined at length the principles he maintained,—or have gone fully into the questions affecting local interests. The compiler had not the power to do this, and certainly had not the wish. Even the point towards which he aimed he was obliged to change—and rest satisfied with a very superficial narrative, and the rescue of some of the productions of Sir Brenton's mind from oblivion.

It is due to the writer himself to add that the few pages which compose this memoir, have been written for the most part in the midst of many and pressing avocations, which left but little time for a recreation of the kind. The high and holy duties of the ministry are paramount to all others; and he who is entrusted with the message of salvation to his fellow-men feels that though, when he requires rest, he may perhaps thus best unbend the bow, yet that the occupation must never infringe on the time that ought to be directly given to God, — or interfere with the special obligations of his sacred calling. And such has been the constant pressure for the last eighteen months upon his thoughts and time, that had it not been for the fact that he had already gathered some information on the subject,—possessed some papers most kindly entrusted, to him — he would have thrown it aside altogether, when, perhaps, some abler hand would have written a more worthy memoir of Sir Brenton Halliburton.

APPENDIX.

A day or two previous to my delivering in Halifax a lecture, entitled "The Life and Times of the late Sir Brenton Halliburton," I received a highly interesting letter from Mr. Robert G. Haliburton, F. S. A. It was too late to make use of it on that occasion, but I carefully put it by for reference, so that if at any future day I should publish a pamphlet containing a sketch of Sir Brenton's life, I might be enabled to draw from its resources.

Having some months since, as stated in my Preface, been requested by the Messrs. Bowes, to allow them to publish the manuscript read by me at the Temperance Hall, together with any addition I might see fit to make, and having acceded to their wish, I determined to ask leave of Mr. Haliburton to publish entire the greater part of his letter, rather than mar it by making extracts. The author of "The Festival of the Dead," is so well known in the Literary world as an accomplished scholar, and his research into all matters of history is so thorough, and his information so accurate, that any annotations of his on such a subject are invested with a value proportioned to his acknowledged attainments.

"JANUARY 15th, 1862.

"DEAR MR. HILL,—

" As you are going to give a lecture on Sir Brenton Halliburton's Life, &c., which you may at some future time put into a more permanent form, the following remarks concerning his family history, may not be uninteresting to you, though they will hardly serve you in your present undertaking. These facts were, I believe, unknown to Sir Brenton himself.

14

" There was a work published privately by Sir Walter Scott, entitled, ' Memorials of the Haliburtons.' Sir Walter was connected with that family, through his grandmother. As none of the name survived in Scotland in his time, he claimed to represent it by right of his grandmother; and was ' duly served heritor of St. Mary's Aisle in Dryburgh Abbey,' the burial place of the Haliburton family. His wife was buried there, and subsequently Sir Walter, as well as his son-in-law Lockhart, and the last Baronet, Sir Walter. There is a Latin inscription in the aisle, which I remember reading, which says that as the heir of that family Sir Walter Scott became possessed of the aisle.

" ' The Memorials' were commenced (Sir Walter says) by his father, in reply to some inquiries made by Mr. W. Haliburton, of Halifax, N. S., (my great grandfather) about the year 1793. I had in my possession all the original correspondence, relating to a claim to property made by Mr. W. Haliburton, as the nearest heir to his uncle. A person named Robertson from near Melrose, who was then living at Windsor, N.S., advised Mr. W. Haliburton to write to Mr. Brown of Melrose, (who is mentioned in the ' Memorials,') and also suggested that he had better write to ' Mr. Walter Scott, *a very respectable writer of the Signet*, whose mother he thought was a Haliburton.' This Walter Scott was the father of the immortal Sir Walter Scott. Old Walter Scott in his portion of the ' Memorials' (which were afterwards enlarged for publication by Sir Walter, his son,) mentions all of the name (1793 -- 1796) who were then living in Scotland. Among the rest he mentions ' a very worthy gentleman, Dr. John Haliburton, of Haddington.' Now Sir Brenton's father was Dr. John Haliburton, who came from that place. We may, therefore, conclude, that he was a son, or at least a near relative of the gentleman referred to in the ' Memorials.' I am very sorry that my copy of the ' Memorials' and all the original correspondence were burned. Mr. Robert Chambers told me the work could not be bought, but that he might get me a MS. copy of it: but I have delayed writing to him, as I have been in hopes that I shall be able to procure a copy without troubling him.

" Walter Scott, senr., mentions among others, the Rev. Simon Haliburton, minister of Ashkirk. I have found out, that the late Mrs. Forrester, who was a Davidson, was a grand-daughter of his. The Rev. Dr. Forrester has now the Bible of old Mr. Simon Haliburton in his possession. The Davidsons were connected with the Scotts, as well as with the Haliburtons; and I can remember that the title to the property claimed turned upon a dispute as to an Elizabeth Davidson, who had been in possession of property claimed by Mr. W. Haliburton, somewhere on 'the Borders.' Sir Walter sent a copy of the 'Memorials' to Mr. Alexander Haliburton, the father of my brother-in-law, Alexander F. Haliburton; and some old relatives of theirs pointed out that there was some mistake as to the account of Elizabeth Davidson. They were not aware that she had been a subject of controversy between old Walter Scott and my great grandfather—and of a correspondence which led to the commencement of the 'Memorials.' This work of Sir Walter Scott is referred to by Lockhart, in his life of Sir Walter; and is constantly quoted from, in a little work I have by Sir Davis Erskine, called 'Memorials of Dryburgh Abbey.'

" Sir Brenton's family crest, as well as that of my brother-in-law's family, is a *Moor's head*. Sir Walter mentions that the Border family of Haliburtons, were strong allies of the great Earls of Douglas: one of the family was the favorite companion and Standard-bearer of the Earl of Douglas.*

" You remember the historical death of the friend of Robert Bruce. He was entrusted by the Bruce, as he was dying, with the duty of having the heart of his King buried in the Holy Land. With a large concourse of Knights and retainers he left

---

* Lockhart in his Life of Sir Walter Scott, I. ch. 2, says: " From the genealogical deduction in the Memorials, it appears that the Haliburtons of Newmains were descended from and represented the ancient and once powerful family of Haliburton of Mertoun, which became extinct in the beginning of the eighteenth century. The first of this latter family possessed the lands and barony of Mertoun by a charter granted by the Earl of Douglas and Lord of Galloway (one of those tremendous lords whose coronets counterpoised the Scottish crown) to Henry de Haliburton, whom he designates as his standard-bearer, on account of his service to the earl in England. On this account the Haliburtons of Mertoun and those of Newmains, in addition to the arms borne by the Haliburtons of Dirleton (the ancient chiefs of that once great and powerful, but now almost extinguished name)—viz. or, on a bend *azure*, three mascles of the first—gave the distinctive bearing of a buckle of the second in the sinister canton. These arms still appear on various old tombs in the abbeys of Melrose and Dryburgh, as well as on their house at Dryburgh, which was built in 1572."—*MS. Memorandum*, 1820. Sir Walter was served heir to these Haliburtons soon after the date of this Memorandum, and thenceforth quartered the arms above described with those of his paternal family.

Scotland for Palestine; but unfortunately, while in Spain, on his way, he was tempted to join in a battle between the Moors and Christians; and being surrounded, he flung the heart of the Bruce, which was in a golden casket, among the enemy, exclaiming, 'lead on thou gallant heart, as thou wert wont!' The Douglas was killed, but his companions recovered the heart of the Bruce, and carried it to Palestine. We cannot doubt that the favorite knight, and Standard-bearer of the Douglas accompanied him: and I think we may conclude that the *Moor's head*, used as a crest by some branches of the family, is in some way connected with an event that is the most noted occurrence in the history of Scottish chivalry.

"In an Army list for 1801, I find Sir Brenton's name entered among the Captains of the 7th Fusileers, as follows: 'B. Haliburton, 25th Ja. '98.' Has that family changed the mode of spelling their names? Sir Walter Scott says that members of the same family frequently spelled the name differently: 'Haliburton, Halliburton, Halyburton, and Hallyburton.' I have an ancient silver spoon that belonged to some of my ancestors, which has the name spelled *Hallyburton*, which is decidedly an improvement on the present mode. Mr. Walter Scott spells Dr. John Haliburton's name with *one l*, which, however, does not conflict with my inferences.

"In looking over my note to you, I find nothing to add except an odd occurrence that recently took place, which may interest persons of the name. Sir Walter mentions that the Border family which have resided near Dryburgh since 1250, were younger cadets of the Earl of Dirleton's family, a title that has been extinct since the time of the Reformation in Scotland.

"Sir Walter supposed that the well known Earl of Gowrie, was the last representative of the Dirleton branch.* There is, however, in Scottish history an account of several noble families, among whom were the Haliburtons, who in consequence

---

* In Constable's Miscellany, vol. I., History of Remarkable Conspiracies, by John Parker Lawson, M.A., p. 228, the following passage occurs: "The first Earl of Gowrie was, however, connected with the Royal family without that alliance. His grandfather William, second Lord Ruthven, married Janet Haliburton, eldest daughter and co heiress of Patrick Lord Haliburton, of Dirleton, in East Lothian, by which he obtained that Barony. This lady was of royal abstraction, as Lord Haliburton's ancestor, Sir Walter Haliburton, married Lady Isabel Stuart, eldest daughter of Robert Duke of Albany, Regent of Scotland, and third son of King Robert II.

of the Reformation, emigrated to Poland. Nothing further concerning this fact has hitherto been known. Recently, my father received a letter from a Polish gentleman named Joseph Haliburton, mentioning that his family at the time of the Reformation emigrated to Poland, where the head of the family owns several villages, and is one of the Polish nobility. The family archives brought from Scotland are still in possession of the head of the Polish branch. He wished to make inquiries in Scotland as to his family history prior to the Reformation.

"Besides the Polish branch and the two families in Nova Scotia, there are only three others that I have ever heard of, which are represented respectively by the Honourable James D. Halyburton of Virginia, de facto Chief-Justice of the Confederate States; by my brother-in-law, A. F. Haliburton, Esq., of Whitly near Wigan, and of Grafton, Torquay; and by the Haliburtons (or Burtons) of St. Leonards on the Sea.

"In India the family has been strangely connected with the rise and fall of the Sepoy power. Mill, in his history of India, says that a gentleman of the name of Haliburton first organized the Sepoys. He was murdered by a native; but the name, Mill says, was long remembered by the Madras Sepoys. A century after, Major Haliburton, brother of A. F. Haliburton, was mortally wounded while commanding the 78th Highlanders when they led Havelock's army into Lucknow, an event from which we may date the downfall of the Sepoy power in India.

"If you wish to make use of any of these facts they are at your service. I have made this letter as full as possible, so that you may select such portions as you think will be interesting to the friends of Sir Brenton Halliburton.

> "Yours very truly,
>
> "ROBERT G. HALIBURTON."

There is no doubt that the original spelling of Sir Brenton's family surname was with one l; and the change, or additional letter l, came about as follows: When his father entered the Navy, his name was recorded in the official books *Halliburton*. On discovering this he determined to adopt that spelling, in order to avoid any trouble that possibly might arise, from his signature being different from that which was known at the Admiralty.

G. W. II.

Ext. History Rhode Island.

" William Brenton was a native of England, and previous to his removal, was a respectable merchant of Boston. He came to Rhode Island soon after the first settlement. He was Deputy Governor from 1640 to 1646; President of the Colony from 1660 to 1662, and Governor from 1665 to 1669. He was one of the largest proprietors of land on Rhode Island, and owned the whole of the land called Brenton's Neck. He died in 1674, at an advanced age, leaving three sons and four daughters."

" Jahleel Brenton, was the eldest son of Governor William Brenton, and inherited most of the estate. He was the first Collector appointed by the King. In 1699, in consequence of some personal difficulty with Sir William Phipps, the Governor of Massachussetts, he went to England, when he and others prepared charges against the Governor, who, in consequence, was summoned to Whitehall, to answer for his conduct. Governor Phipps died of fever soon after he had arrived in England, and before the trial could take place. Mr. Brenton was soon after appointed Agent for the Colony of Rhode Island, and as such remained in England several years. He returned from England with a commission from the King, appointing him Surveyor-General of the Customs of the American Colonies. He owned all the land in Newport, which is now known as Brenton's neck, where he had his residence; he also owned a large tract of land in Narragansett, being one of the original Pettoquamsett purchasers. He died in Newport, on the 8th of November, 1732, aged 77 years, without issue. He was buried on his own land, in that part which is now the site of Fort Adams. By his will he gave all his lands in the neck, known as the Hammersmith and Rocky Farms, to his nephew, the second Jahleel Brenton. In 1720, he built the house in Thames Street, now in the possession of Simmons S. Coe. Among his descendants, was the gallant Jahleel Brenton, Admiral of the British Navy, and the Hon. Brenton Halliburton, of the Supreme Court of Nova Scotia, both natives of Newport."

In addition to those writings of Sir Brenton, which are published in the foregoing memoir, there are several which it was thought would not prove uninteresting to some of his friends, and which are hereby printed in this, which is strictly a *private edition*. One is a humorous article written previous to the Canadian rebellion, with serious notes appended; another contains a few touching thoughts on the death of a Grandchild; and the third is a Poem on " Passing Events," written by him when over eighty years of age.

John Bull and his Calves.

(Written Previous to the Canadian Rebellion.)

ALL the world have heard of John Bull; some of his Calves have made a little noise too. John had a fine drove of thirteen of them in a large pasture to the westward of the Lake which divides his estate, and as he had been put to a great deal of trouble and expense in fencing the pasture and keeping Master Frog's folks from devouring the stock and destroying the herbage, he thought when the Calves had grown up, that he was entitled to a portion of their milk. The tenants on this part of the Farm did not absolutely deny the justice of the claim, but they insisted upon it that no one should milk the heifers but their own ribs, and that John should be satisfied with the portion of milk which they allotted to him. Whether John thought that these dames would give him nothing but skim milk or butter-milk, or perhaps if they got into their tantrums, no milk at all, he vowed that Mrs. Bull should milk them, and take as much milk as she thought reasonable: the upshot of which was that John Bull had a great row with his more than half-grown Calves, and though he knocked them head over heels whenever he got a fair run at them in the open field, yet they worried him so much from behind the trees with which the pasture was covered, bit his tail, gored his flanks, and were off in the woods again ere he could well turn round, that at last he gave a tremendous roar, dashed into the lake, swam home, and left them to themselves.

He had still, however, a few young Calves on the north side of the pasture, who had not taken part in the squabble. One of these was a queer creature; it was not of John's own breed: he had harried it from the

Frogs in one of his scuffles, but he treated it just as if it was one of his own begotten Calves, and often used to flatter himself that the poor thing would soon forget all about the Frogs, and feel himself a Bull from head to foot.   But these feelings flowed from John's heart rather than his head.   He might have known that the Frog blood would never mix well with the Bulls.   As it grew up, however, John did succeed in licking it a little into shape; the head began to look rather Bullish,* but the body, legs and feet were still Frog all over. It was really a curious looking animal, and was in fact more of a Bull-Frog than a Bull ; it made a tremendous noise, but that noise was more of a croak than a roar. It was, however, a great pet, and in process of time John proposed to Mrs. Bull to provide a wife for it. Some of the family thought that this might as well have been left alone, but wives were all the fashion about this time.†   Old Frog himself had just taken one who soon set all his family by the ears, and made the old gentle- man kick the bucket before the honey-moon was half over.

A wife, therefore, it was decided that young Bull- Frog should have.   Well, then, said those who thought he would do just as well without one, if he must have a wife let her be of the Bull breed, and not of the Frog: let her roar rather than croak, for mercy's sake.   But fashion decides every thing, and it was the fashion then for those who knew little to leave all matters to the decision of those who knew less ; and these wiseacres determined that Master Bull-Frog should choose a wife for himself.   Now, as I said before, although his head had begun to look a little Bullish, he was still more than three-fourths Frog, and it was therefore natural for him to cohabit more with the Frogs than the Bulls.   As might be supposed, then, he took unto himself a most thorough-going Frog

* British inhabitants in the towns.   † 1791.

for a wife, who soon set up such a croaking that there was no peace in the pasture.

John and Mrs. Bull had had the marriage articles drawn up under their own superintendance, and had taken every care, as they supposed, of that part of the estate. John's overseer still continued to superintend the farm, and he had trustees* to join with him and Mrs. Bull-Frog in the management of it.

There was enough to be done; it was a fine property to be sure, and if well cultivated would soon have enriched all who dwelt upon it; but when the overseer and trustees, wanted to drain off the stagnant pools† and render it wholesome and productive, like John's farm on the other side of the lake, Mrs. Bull-Frog set up such a croaking that not a word which the overseer or trustees said could be heard. She did not want the pools drained—not she—she wanted none of their Bullish improvements. Improvements indeed! She knew well enough what they meant. If the marshes and meadows were all drained, these lordly Bulls would stalk over them and crush her poor dear Frogs under their feet. She wanted no interference with nature, which had provided these delightful fens for the Frogs to luxuriate in; and if the Bulls did not like them, why let them leave them. Fair and softly, Mrs. Bull-Frog, replied the overseer and trustees, if the Bulls don't like them, why let them leave them, forsooth! do you forget that they belong to the Bulls? Did'nt they take them from old Frog after many a hard day's fighting? and did he not surrender all his right to them to old Mr. Bull; and are those who are thorough-bred Bulls to abandon what would soon become rich and beautiful meadows, merely that you and your tadpoles may have your dirty mud-holes to squeak and croak in? Had old Master Frog wrenched one of John Bull's

* Legislative Council.

† Wanted to introduce English Laws for the encouragement of Commerce.

farms from him, and been able to keep it, I'll be bound
he never would have given us the chance that we have
given you; and therefore if you wish to live in the land,
live in it and welcome—no one shall hurt you—but you
must live in it as our land, and not as yours.

This seemed to be reasonable enough, but not so
thought Mrs. Bull-Frog; she continued to croak, croak,
and as the marriage articles prohibited the overseers and
trustees from adopting any measure without her consent,
no improvement could be effected. But the mischief
did not end in merely preventing improvements. Mrs.
Bull-Frog soon began to assert that she was as great a
woman on this side of the Lake, as Mrs. Bull was on
the other, and that no one but herself should handle the
purse-strings. At first good old John Bull laughed at
her attempting to raise a storm in her puddle, and went
on paying for the performance of the ordinary work as
usual. But when the old gentleman became a little
hipped and thought himself too poor to pay the labourers
upon his out-farms, he offered to give up all the rents
and profits of this part of the estate to Mrs Bull-Frog,
provided she would engage to keep it in order, and pay
the overseer and workmen their accustomed wages.

Mrs. Bull-Frog joyfully assented to receive the rents
and profits for ever, and consented to pay the wages so
long, and in such proportions, as she pleased. John
was so much occupied with matters nearer home, that he
did not notice the difference between his offer and
Madame's acceptance of it; but rubbed his hands and
congratulated himself upon having got rid of that
troublesome concern.

In a short time, however, John, like most folks who
want to shove off their business upon others, instead of
attending to it themselves, found that matters had got
into a sad state on this part of his property. Madame
Bull-Frog having got hold of the key of the money-
chest, thrust it into her under-petticoat pocket, and
swore that neither overseer or labourers should have a

farthing to feed or clothe themselves, until they would just do her bidding. The overseer and trustees did all they could, to bring her to reason, but the more they coaxed, the more she croaked, and they found that the farm was going fast to ruin, and that those who worked it were on the verge of starvation.

John after rubbing his eyes a little, looked over the letters and accounts which the overseer sent to him, but he was so harassed and perplexed with the homestead, that he could not give much attention to affairs on the other side of the Lake; and as Madame Bull-Frog complained so much of his overseer, he thought, without enquiring further into the matter, that he might as well send her another, he therefore selected one Ramsay* who had managed a neighbouring farm to his heart's content, and that of all who lived on it also. Ramsay was an honest, noble fellow, whose heart was just in the right place; he would neither do nor suffer wrong. John thought he had hit on the very man to satisfy Madame Bull-Frog, let her be ever so capricious. But poor John knew little of Madame's freaks; he thought, poor simple soul, that she merely wished to be well governed. But Madame did not wish to be governed at all; and as she knew that Ramsay would do nothing that she could find fault with, unless she got his temper up, she set herself to work to insult him.

Mrs. Bull-Frog knowing that she had not an honest face to show, had long thought it politic to wear a mask—she had recently attached to it a hideous† *paper nose*, which being a very prominent feature, and attracting great attention from all who looked upon her, she soon acquired the habit of speaking through it in a most offensive manner. She had, however, no right to wear it, without the overseer's consent, and as she had, upon several occasions snuffled very abusive language through it against Ramsay, he twisted it off and threw it in her face. Oh! what an uproar the old woman made.

---

* The Earl of Dalhousie.   † L. J. Papineau, Speaker H. of A.

Ramsay told her to go to the —— and shake herself,
and as she did not know how to behave, and Mr. Bull
did not know how to make her, he left them to settle
the matter between them. Well, says John, when it
was told him that Ramsay had wrung the old woman's
nose off, I'll try her with another overseer; there is
Jemmy Thorough-work,* who has managed the farm
Ramsay had once in hand, so well, that all the tenants
were delighted with him. I'll send him to her. Away
went Jemmy to see how he could manage Madame ; but
there was a terrible difficulty in Jemmy's way upon the
very threshold : Ramsay had pulled off Madame's
paper nose. Now Madame contended that Ramsay
had no right to pull it off, and therefore she said that it
was not pulled off at all. Still there lay the paper nose ;
it was'nt on Madame's face, and as she had acquired
such a habit of speaking through it, that she could'nt
speak without it, how was she to say a single word to
Jemmy until this organ was replaced! this dilemma
perplexed them both sadly, for Jemmy was very
anxious to put matters to rights if he could, and that
was impossible without having some intercourse with
Mrs. Bull-Frog ; and she was equally anxious to
recommence her manœuvres, not caring much whether
she cajoled or abused Jemmy! but one or the other she
longed to do.

As both sides, therefore, were desirous to have the
paper nose replaced, after some consultation in the back
chamber, it was agreed that Madame should make it
adhere again with a little spittle, present herself to
Jemmy as if nothing had happened, and request his
leave to wear it—without taking any notice of Ramsay's
having wrung it off. Jemmy made her a neat little
bow, told her, it was very becoming to her, that he
admired it much, and gave his consent, as a matter
of course, in order to open a communication with her.

John next selected an honest, open-hearted son† of

* Sir James Kempt.   † Lord Aylmer.

Paddy Bull's, who told Madame at his first interview with her, that he could not sleep a wink for dreaming of doing her good ;* but it was not long before he discovered that whatever good he might be dreaming of she dreamt of nothing but evil. She had for some-time made a terrible uproar about the infringement of the marriage articles. The articles themselves, she said, were the best possible articles ;† all she wanted, poor woman, was the full benefit of them, which she insisted was most shamefully withheld from her. Mrs. Bull said this must be looked into, and directed Pat to enquire fully into the affair. Pat sent for Madame, and begged to know what infringements she complained of, and, " Come, my dear Madame Bull-Frog," said he, squeez-ing her hand, and giving her one of those kind glances with which Paddy's sons are in the habit of softening the hearts of the sex, " tell me frankly, now, who has abused you, and by the hand of my lady, my jewel, I'll be the man to right you wherever you've been wronged. Let us have the whole story, darlint, that we may put all to rights at once, and leave no old sores without a plaster."

But Mrs. Bull-Frog had no notion of this wholesale dealing; she was a retailer of grievances, and knew it would be the ruin of her to part with her whole stock in trade at once. Evading, therefore, Pat's kind offer of a panacea for all complaints, she fell to abusing the trustees, said John had appointed no one but Bulls, who trampled upon the Frogs most cruelly, and that the farm would never flourish until John dismissed the Bulls and appointed Frogs in their place.

By the powers, says Pat, this is a pretty story ; here are you Madame (without whose consent we cannot stir a step) Frog both head and heart, and yet my master, Mr.

---

* My first thought each morning, was, " What can I do for Canada?"

† See the first petitions, which lauded the Constitution conferred by the Act 31st Geo. 3rd and only complained of their not enjoying the full benefit of it.

16

Bull, is to be deemed guilty of a breach of the marriage articles because he appoints a few Bulls to take care of the interests of that part of the family. Appoint Frogs trustees, indeed! faith, he's appointed more than's good of them already, and if he appointed any more, it's my notion they'll be a greater curse than they were in Egypt of old, and make such a croaking that not a Bull will be able to enjoy any peace in the country. I tell you, Mrs. Bull-Frog, it's no infringement of the marriage articles; hasn't Mr. Bull a right to appoint trustees under the articles themselves?

Sacre, she exclaimed, with a horrible grin, then the marriage articles are cursed bad articles, and I will never rest contented until I and my dear Frogs have the appointment of the trustees ourselves!

Wheugh! whistled Pat, why you old ———; but stop, said he, drawing his breath, and endeavouring to regain his composure, did'nt you yourself say, my dear Madame, not five minutes ago, that the articles were the best of all possible articles, and that all you wanted was the fulfilment of them?

What if I did, you blathering blockhead! roared she, don't people grow wiser as they grow older! and I now think that the articles are the vilest articles that ever were drawn; and unless Mr. and Mrs. Bull consent to alter them, and let the Frogs choose the trustees, I'll— but I'm not going to tell you what I shall do; let old Bull remember how his other calves served him, that's all — that's all, Master Pat; and away she dashed.

Pat was at his wits' end to know how to deal with such a termagant; he had a real desire to improve the property, but Madame could not allow a penny to be expended upon it; and of course matters went from bad to worse. Now, though she would not give a farthing for the necessary expenses of the farm, she had the impudence to ask Pat to consent to her taking a large sum out of the chest to purchase coals, and candles, and brooms, and scrubbing brushes, for her own room. Pat thought that the beldame wanted fuel enough to set the town on fire from the sum she demanded; but in the hope of bringing her into good humour, he complied with her request, and soon after in the gentlest manner possible, he begged her to take into consideration the wants of the farm and the state of the workmen, who had been left so long without their wages.

Would you believe it, that the vixen not only turned a deaf ear to his kind suggestions, but refused even to give him a receipt for the money he had advanced to her; and flouncing out of the room in a rage, vowed she'd scratch the eyes out of any one who would venture to touch the chest in her absence. The poor workmen were left with freezing fingers and empty stomachs, and were altogether in such a piteous plight, that Mr. Bull, though his present wife hauled him over the coals whenever he expended an extra penny, consented, upon Pat's earnest entreaty, to advance thirty pounds to dole out among them, just to keep soul and body together.

At their very next meeting, with unparalleled effrontery, Madame applied to Pat for a much larger sum of money than before, to squander away on bad company, under the pretext that she wanted it merely to keep her room in order; but independent of the extravagant amount she demanded, and which he knew would be applied to the most mischeivous purposes, he reminded her of her refusal to give him a receipt for what he had advanced before, without which he could'nt settle his accounts, and he therefore civilly gave that as a reason for his non-compliance with her request. She dashed off in a furious passion, slammed the door behind her so that it nearly flew off the hinges, and swore that she would never speak a word more with Pat about the concerns of the farm.

John Bull might have seen with half an eye, if he had chosen to open either of them so far, that it was useless to yield any longer to such a capricious creature;

but, good easy man, he thought that concession would
at last bring her about, so he recalled Pat, and sent out
one Mr. Goose-Frog * as overseer, with two assistants
to oversee him, as some folks thought.

There was a great to do on both sides of the Lake
about sending out Mr. Goose-Frog and his assistants :
they were to set all matters to rights in a trice, and
make the Bulls and the Frogs dwell together like
brethren. How this was to be accomplished puzzled
folks not a little, for the Bulls liked to range in well
thoroughly drained meadows, which produced abundantly; while the Frogs preferred squatting themselves down in the dirty pools and fens, where the
Bulls would be mired if they came near them.

However, it was an age of wonders, John Bull had
within a few years made a great discovery at home that
the best way to keep his house in order was to allow all
the disorderly vagabonds in the country to send whoever they pleased into the parlour, to toss the fire about
the room, and then break the windows to let the wind
blow it out. In short, the political millenium had
commenced. The great lion Dan O'Hell, had already
lain down with John's Lamb, and in the warmth of his
love had twisted his tail so fast round the neck of the
innocent creature that he couldn't utter a bleat except
when Dan chose to ease off a little. John thought after
this miracle he might easily reduce the Bulls and the
Frogs to the same state of harmony.

Soon after Goose-Frog's arrival, Madame began to
poke her Paper nose about him, to smell out his plan
of proceeding and satisfied herself that the Frogs would
be left in full enjoyment of their fens, and that the
Bulls might roar away to their hearts content. Upon
the first intimation that he was ready to receive her,
she walked up to him in presence of the trustees, with
her mask on, and her prominent Paper nose, which he

---

* Lord Gosford, Sir —— Grey, and Sir George Gipps.

stroked as kindly as a friendly Esquimaux could have done, vowed that Slawkenburguis could never have found its equal in the whole promontory, and begged her to wear it for his sake.

Madame pretended to be quite delighted with this polite gentleman, and listened with apparent attention to a long speech which he addressed to her and the trustees. He assured them that Mr. Bull took the greatest interest in their welfare, and had commanded him to compel the Bulls and the Frogs to live together in peace and prosperity; that as to money for the fuel, and furniture, &c., &c., &c., which they might want for their respective rooms, Mr. Bull had desired him to give both the trustees and Madame whatever they might require, giving as he uttered this a significant glance to Madame Bull-Frog, as much as to say, I shall not investigate *your* items very strictly.

He then very feelingly deplored the distressed state of the workmen, trusted that their just claims would be attended to, and that all would unite to make the farm flourish, called upon Madame to repay Mr. Bull the thirty pounds he had advanced to keep the workmen from starving,—and reminded her that the poor gentleman was at his wit's ends for money himself,—that as to Madame's complaint that the overseers had employed more Bulls than Frogs to superintend the affairs of the farm, he assured her that Mr. Bull would in the future sanction no such proceeding; that although he could not deny that the farm belonged to the Bulls, no invidious distinctions were to be made; that for his own part, he always thought it was of the first importance for foremen to make themselves acceptable to the workmen they were appointed to superintend; and that no person was fit to be school-master who would not grant the boys a holiday whenever they desired it. Then turning round with a low and graceful bow to the Frogs: Do not fear, said he, that there is any design to disturb the form of society under which you have so

long been contented and prosperous.* However different you may be from Mr. Bull's other calves, he cannot
but admire the arrangements which have made you so
eminently virtuous, and which have secured to you

---

* "Do not fear that there is any design to disturb the form of
society under which you have so long been contented and prosperous."

It will perhaps occasion some little surprise in Old England when
they learn that the first thing that has struck the Chief Commissioner,
who has been sent out to enquire into causes of discontent and dis-
turbance which (according to the representations of Mr. Papineau
and his adherents) have so long disturbed Canada, is the peaceful
and happy state of the French Canadians.

Those who are acquainted with the real state of things in that
country will feel no astonishment at this. It would be difficult to
find in any part of the world a body of people more contented, gay,
and amiable, than the inhabitants of Lower Canada ; satisfied with
little, their small farms fully supply their wants ; although fond of
intercourse with each other, they wish not for any extension of their
social circle. That circle includes all that they love, respect, and
reverence ; and they seldom trouble themselves with aught beyond
it. Engrossed with their own harmless occupations, they leave all
their greater temporal cares to the Notary of the village, as they
unreservedly confide their spiritual concerns to their spiritual pas-
tors. Thus relieved from all serious anxiety respecting their political rights in this world, or their future happiness in another, they
pass their lives in as much serene enjoyment as can well fall to the
lot of man.

We cannot wonder that his Excellency the Governor-in-Chief has
expressed so much satisfaction at "the good conduct and tranquil
bliss" which he finds has been created, preserved, and handed down
from generation to generation among this people ; but we think his
Excellency must have wondered at finding this state of things when
he had been sent out to redress the grievances under which they
were stated to labour, and to allay the ferments which were supposed to prevail among them to an extent which endangered the
public peace.

That those in whom these amiable, uneducated people, confide,
have abused their confidence, is undoubted ; and that the influence
which has been acquired over them may be still more mischievously
exerted, is highly probable, particularly if his Majesty's ministers
continue to increase the consequence of the demagogues who deceive them by paying more attention to their statements than they
do to the King's Representative. But still, as the people are, in
point of fact, happy and contented,—as they do not practically feel
any oppression, it may be doubted whether they would leave their
peaceful homes to follow Mr. Papineau to the field, if he were disposed to lead them there, although they will doubtless continue to
sign any petition that he or his satellites prepare for them.

that happiness and tranquil bliss which your numerous
petitions of grievances, and the ninety-two resolutions of
your amiable mother, proclaim that you possess. Mr.
Bull will protect and foster the benevolent, active and
pious teachers, under whose care and guidance you have
been conducted to your present happy state. Your fens
shall be preserved to you; the pools in which you delight to recreate yourselves shall be handed down from
generation to generation. Let not the name of Bull
alarm you, for although the Bulls did once possess
themselves of the country, and their title has not yet
been formally extinguished, it is my desire to secure to
you the peaceful possession of this land, and no Bull
shall approach your happy dwellings, except the Rom-
ish Bulls, which you so much admire and reverence.
Then drawing himself up with great dignity, and wheel-
ing round to the Bulls, he exclaimed: Of the Bulls, and
especially those who require the draining of the fens
and marshes,* I would ask, is it possible you should
suppose there can be any design to sacrifice your interests, when it is clear to all the world that it was by
draining his marshes, fencing his fields, opening roads
to the market-town, and bringing his farms into their
present high state of cultivation, that Mr. Bull attained
the prosperity to which he has advanced himself. It
was for the express purpose of making his farms on this
side of the lake like those on the other, that he has settled and cultivated them at a vast expense. Rely upon
it that he will not abandon that purpose on Frogland
Farm, to which he has encouraged you to remove, but
with that constancy and good faith which has ever characterised him, he will not fail to sustain on this part of
his property that system which has so long been held
out as a boon to all his children, and as an inducement
to you to remove here, and here to embark your hopes
of wealth and happiness.

* The commercial classes. (See the Speech.)

Why, what the —— are we to make of all this blowing hot and cold? said the Bulls, as they passed out of the hall.

I know what I shall make of it, snuffed Madame, through her Papernose ; I shall take what I like of it, and toss what I don't like to the winds.

As soon as the beldame returned to her own room, she whipt off her mask and displayed her own hideous visage. She retained, however, her darling Papernose, which she had so long been accustomed to croak through that she could not part with it. She then plainly stated that it was all nonsense to talk of altering the marriage articles, of choosing their own trustees, or of any other of the long rigmarole hobgoblin tales, with which she had been accustomed to amuse, and sometimes half scare the children, while she wore her mask, that it was now high time to burn the marriage articles, kick the trustees off the farm, and plainly tell Mr. Bull that if he did not keep his overseers at home, she would tar and feather them. She added, however, that, as she had'nt yet matured all her plans upon this matter, it would be as well, for form's sake, to give Goose-Frog an answer to his speech, just to tell him that if he did everything she desired, perhaps she would'nt pull his house about his ears at present ; that she considered it a great impertinence in Mr. Bull to interfere between her and her workmen ; and that as to repaying the money she had advanced, she would take it into consideration with the same views and sentiments, with which she had always considered subjects of this kind. That as to the Bulls and Frogs dwelling together in peace and harmony, she assured him that she should conduct herself with the same impartiality towards them, that she *had heretofore done* (which was as much as to tell the Bulls to look out for squalls), that the farm would be a mighty pretty farm if managed to her mind, that she confidently expected to get the whole control over it herself, and hoped, from what she had seen of Goose-Frog, that he was the very man to help her do so.

Goose-Frog, in reply, thanked her for the kind and flattering manner in which she had spoken of him, and assured her that he should adhere faithfully to the line of conduct he had already intimated to her ; but which of the two opposite lines he meant, the Bull line or the Frog line, he did not explain.

Immediately after this denial to repay Mr. Bull the money he had advanced to the poor labourers, she applied to Goose-Frog for a round sum to defray the expense of bribing some of John's renegade sons, to aid her to ride rough shod over the Bulls. Goose-Frog opened both his eyes as wide as he could, raised the lids of them, and stared her full in the face, for he could scarcely believe she could seriously make such a request, when she had left the whole of John's servants without a farthing to bless themselves ; but perceiving that she urged it with all due gravity, he exclaimed, well —— me if I don't admire your impudence, tip us your daddle my old dame, I'll do it *cheerfully*.

Madame pocketed the money, gave three cheers for the three G's.* and walked off singing—

"Goosey, Goosey, Gander."

Indeed she now feels that she has a carte blanche, not only to walk up stairs and down stairs and in my lady's chamber, but to go wherever she chooses, to do whatever she likes and to say whatever she pleases ; but as neither her sayings nor doings will give much satisfaction to honest folks, we will pursue her history no further, but just wind up with a word or two of advice to old Mr. Bull.

And first, my good sir, you have brought all this trouble upon yourself.

After you obtained possession of Frogland, you publicly proclaimed to all your children that it was to become part of the Bull estate, and that the farm was to be managed according to the Bull system.† It is true

* G—f—d, G—y, G—ps.
† See the proclamation issued from St. James', 7th Oct., 1763.

17

that you agreed with old Mr. Frog, that the Frogs on
it might either hop off to him, or stay on it with you,
but saving their privilege of going to purgatory, which
was fully preserved to those who remained, they were,
in all respects, to conduct themselves like Bulls.* Now
before you let Master Bull-Frog out of leading strings,
you should have ascertained whether he could walk;
before you consented to give him a wife you should
have considered whether he was capable of managing
one : you should have drawn the marriage articles in
such a way as would have secured the cultivation of that
part of your property on your own system.   You should
have insisted upon it that the children should be brought
up to speak your own language,† and instead of any

---

* See the articles of capitulation, dated September 8, 1760, particularly the 41st: and the treaty of Paris, February 10th, 1763, article 4th.

† Never was a greater mistake made than in permitting the French
language to be used in the legislative debates in Canada. The French
inhabitants of that country had not a shadow of claim to this indulgence.
They were not entitled to a Representative Branch in the Legislature,
either under the articles of capitulation in 1760, or under the treaty of
Paris in 1763, by which Canada was ceded to the British Crown. It is
true that by the proclamation issued from St. James', on the 7th of Oct.,
1763, for the encouragement of the settlers of the British possessions
in America generally, his Majesty stated that so soon as the state and
circumstances of the Colonies therein mentioned, should admit of it,
the Governor with the consent of the respective Councils, should sum-
mon General Assemblies. But this was a proclamation from the King
of Great Britain to his subjects, announcing to them that they should
enjoy the rights of Englishmen wherever they settled, so soon as the
state of the Colonies in which they should settle would admit of it.
The King's subjects in Canada, whether of British or French origin,
had a right to expect that in due time this engagement would be fulfilled. But it was only as British subjects that they had a right to
expect it.
The Canadians had no right to claim a Representative Branch as
Frenchmen, nor to demand that the French language should become
the language of a British Legislature. It is not an honest fulfillment of
this proclamation to give a Colony to which Englishmen had been encouraged to remove, a Legislature in whose proceedings they can take no
part, unless they qualify themselves to do so by acquiring the use of a
foreign tongue. Surely if one or the other must submit to the inconvenience of learning a different language from that in which they had
first been taught to speak, it was more reasonable that in a country belonging to England, the French should qualify themselves to enjoy the

farago about liberality to the Frogs, you should have remembered that both justice and policy required that on every part of John Bull's property, John Bull's sons should have the predominance.* Had you done this

privilege of Englishmen by learning English, rather than that the English should be excluded from the se privileges unless they learned French. Intelligent men of French extraction would soon have learned to express themselves with sufficient facility in the language of the country to which they had transferred their allegiance, by remaining in Canada after it became a British Province, when they had the option of removing from it with their effects; and those whose incapacity disqualified them for this easy task would have been no loss to a Legislative Body.

Had the boon of an English constitution been accompanied with the reasonable condition, that all discussions respecting the privileges it conferred were to be conducted in English, no measure would have been more effectual in accelerating the introduction of English feelings among the Canadians. A knowledge of our language would have led to an acquaintance with our literature and laws among the upper classes, from which the happiest results would have followed. At present the inhabitants of British and French extractions are as much estranged from each other as they were at the period of the conquest. The French majority in the House of Assembly now claim as a right what was improvidently granted them as an indulgence. A large portion of them understand French only, and the few English who can find their way into that Body are reduced to the humiliating necessity of abandoning their mother tongue, in order to make themselves understood by their auditors. The privilege of using one language or the other at the will of the speaker is an utter absurdity. The devisers of such a scheme would, we may suppose, have recommended the builders of Babel to have persisted in their audacious attempt, after the confusion of tongues had been inflicted upon them. One language or the other must of necessity be exclusively used, and as the French party are so completely lords of the ascendant in the Canadian House of Assembly, Englishmen are compelled to forego the use of their own, in their fruitless attempts to stem the torrent of revolution, into which these *ingrates* are endeavouring to force the country.

* Little could the gallant Wolfe have supposed that the fruits of that conquest, which he purchased with his life, were to be enjoyed by the conquered, instead of the conquerors, — that the noble Province which his valour wrested from our ancient enemy, and added to the British dominions, was quietly to be surrendered to the vanquished French. For is it not a surrender of it to them, when, while they adhere most pertinaciously to their old prejudices, and continue to cherish French in preference to British feelings, they are told by the King's representative, " That in every country, to be acceptable to the great body of the people, *is one of the most essential elements of fitness for public station.*"

As they still form a large majority of the inhabitants of Canada, what is it but to tell them that Frenchmen ought to rule the country in

it would have been the ambition of every Frog to have
swelled himself into a Bull before this time. All that
were worth receiving, would have succeeded, and if a

future, for with the prejudices which are so carefully instilled and preserved among them by their leaders, none but Frenchmen will be
acceptable to them. The declaration means this or it means nothing.
If acted upon, Britons in a land that belongs to Britain are to be excluded from all authority. If not acted upon, the majority of the inhabitants of that land are told by their Governor that power is withheld
from those *who alone possess the most essential elements of fitness for
the exercise of it.*

Much is it to be regretted that the subject of national origin has been
introduced into the speech of the King's representative.

That the French party possessing all the power which the elective
branch can exercise, has long made it a subject of complaint that
Frenchmen are not selected for official situations, we know; and if, notwithstanding their own exclusive conduct, the government were aware of
any instance in which the just claim of a person of French origin had
been overlooked, and an Englishman of inferior qualifications preferred,
it was its duty to set that matter right; not on the ground of origin,
but on the ground of the superior fitness of the individual for the office.
But among these qualifications, an attachment to our institutions,
English feeling, and a preference of the British constitution over that of
any other country, should ever stand foremost. That man is not worthy
of the name, nor can he possess the feelings of a Briton, who could debar a fellow-subject from the fullest enjoyment of all his rights (and the
right to hold offices of trust and emolument, when duly qualified for
them, is a valuable one), merely because his origin could be traced to a
different source from his own. But if those of foreign descent choose to
preserve themselves as a distinct race, to cherish feelings that are not
British,—refuse to become our brethren, and avow their hostility to us,
our language, and our laws, then they never can be—I will not say so
well qualified as Britons—they never can be in any degree qualified to
hold offices of trust and confidence under a British government.

Shall Mr. Papineau, who, five years ago, publicly denounced the
House of Lords as a nuisance; who, within these few weeks, has professed his admiration of republican institutions, and called upon his colleagues in the Assembly to prepare the minds of the people for the introduction of them; shall he, with these hostile feelings in his heart,
and this treasonable language upon his tongue, be entrusted to serve a
Monarch whom he would dethrone; or selected to sustain a Constitution
that he would destroy? Surely, surely, neither Mr. Papineau nor his
adherents could ever be deemed worthy of the confidence of their
Sovereign, or qualified to hold any office under the British Crown.

Do I mean to denounce the whole French population of Lower Canada,
to hold them practically to be aliens, and to declare them unworthy of
the confidence of the Government under which they live? Far from it.
I have in a previous note expressed my opinion of the great body of the
Canadian inhabitants, and concurred in the admiration which their
orderly conduct has excited in the Governor-General.

few of them had burst in the attempt, no great harm would have been done. But by your neglecting these matters your own children have been sacrificed. The conquerors have been laid at the feet of the conquered. Your own system of cultivation has been prohibited, and a vicious one, under which the Bulls can never thrive, has been retained. The Frogs, instead of emulating the Bulls, presume to dictate to them ; instead of feeling it an honour to form part of your noble family, they disclaim you and boast that they are Frogs, and that Frogland is their own.* They tell the Bulls, that if they do not like to submit to their sway over the land, they may leave it, and instead of chastizing them for such insolence, you have truckled to them and have actually directed your overseers to prefer Frogs to Bulls in the selection of workmen. Instead of supporting the authority of your overseers, you have listened to every captious and unfounded complaint against them. After selecting men whose high character was a sufficient pledge for their good conduct ; men whose names were respected and whose services were gratefully appreciated by all who bore the name of Bull ; men who were incapable of any act of oppression or injustice—you have not only submitted to hear these men maligned and defamed in the most opprobrious manner, but you have encouraged the Frogs to persist in such conduct by re-

---

Contented with their lot, we should look in vain into their peaceful cottages, for the *aspirants* to office. No determination of ours will exclude them from what they will never dream of seeking. It is their leaders, who should be excluded.—men who possessing the confidence of this simple people (and who, for obvious reasons, will continue to possess it), use it only to deceive them,—vaulting through the means of this ill-deserved confidence into the Assembly, and carrying with them inveterate prejudices against the conquerors of the country. They can ill brook the sway of the descendants of those conquerors. They long to destroy their power and influence, and to regain by art what their ancestors lost by arms.

Shall the British Government lend itself to these views? Shall they bestow offices of trust and confidence with equal complacency upon those who would support, and upon those who would subvert the King's authority in the Country? Verily this is liberality with a vengeance.

* *La Nation Canadienne.*

calling them and sending one overseer after another merely to induce an increase of abuse, until vituperation has exhausted itself, and they now audaciously tell you that they mean to have nothing to say to you nor your overseers.

And now, Mr. Bull, what are you to do? In the first place, you and Mrs. Bull must decide whether it is worth your while to retain your property on this side of the lake or not—for depend upon it, if you lose Frog-land your other farms will soon follow.* If upon due consideration you should convince yourself that you may as well abandon them—then for heaven's sake say so. Do not set the tenants on this side of the water to cutting each other's throats, in a contention whether

---

* It is the consequences that must follow if the turbulent demagogues in the Canadian Assembly should succeed in severing that Province from the British Empire, that renders the dissensions there so interesting to the inhabitants of British America generally. It is true that difference of origin will not be the cause of discontent in the other Provinces, but there never was a country yet in which a few out of power did not wish to dispossess the few that were in it, and there are not wanting characters in each of the British Provinces, who would gladly follow the example of the Canadian Patriots. If the Government of Great Britain timidly surrender the prerogative of the Crown to the popular idols in Canada, they may depend upon it they must also bow the knee to Baal in every other Province.

I mean not to state that there is any discontent among the inhabitants of British America; on the contrary, I think that as there are few people who have more cause to be satisfied with their lot, so are there few more generally contented with it. But there are no faultless constitutions or Governments, any more than there are faultless individuals in this world, and if those who sigh for power in the other Provinces are encouraged by the success of the demagogues in Canada to attempt to wrest it from the hands in which the laws of the land have placed it, they will not fail to follow the example. Contented as the great body of the people may be, if every little defect which may be discovered or imagined in our institutions, or every trivial mismanagement or mistake in the administration of public affairs is dwelt upon and dinned into their ears by brawlers who see little prospect of success by other means,—and those who pursue this course, are not discountenanced by the Government at home, then that discontent so natural to man, will soon be generated, and the cause of that dissatisfaction, which every man more or less feels with his actual state, will be attributed to misgovernment, when in fact it is only the lot of humanity and proceeds from what—

"Neither Kings nor Laws can cure."

they shall continue your tenants or not, if you really do not desire to retain them. This would not be fair dealing with your best friends on this part of your property. Many here are most warmly attached to you, and would grieve to part with you; but if you wish to part with them, they would see that nothing was left for them, but to submit to your decision, and endeavour to make the best of their lot. There are a few young calves perhaps who are impatient of control, and would like to take a frisk with those with whom you quarrelled some years ago; but the greater number while they admit that those who scampered off when you attempted to milk them, have thriven wonderfully well since, think that there are some indications of their beginning to gore each other,* and therefore deem it would be just as prudent to stick to you until they see a little more clearly how the others get on by themselves.

---

* The neighbouring States are frequently alluded to by our patriots as models for our imitation. No man whose head or heart is rightly placed, will join in the senseless clamour against them, in which some of our ultras indulge. When the connexion between them and the mother country was severed, nothing remained for them but to create Republican institutions, and substitute the people for the Crown as the source of power; the state of society rendered any other course impracticable, and I envy not that man his feelings who does not wish them success in the attempt that they are making to regulate social intercourse and to advance social happiness with the least possible interference with the private conduct of the individuals composing the community. *It still, however, remains an experiment*, and some of the wisest men among them, staunch friends to freedom too, cannot at all times repress a fear that order cannot be preserved without a greater infusion of power into their system of Government, and that it will be difficult to induce the people to clothe their rulers with as much authority as the preservation of the public peace may require.

With the tumults which have arisen in many of their large cities, and the conflicting interests of the various states of the Union before our eyes with the angry contentions and menacing language of the slaveholding and non-slaveholding States ringing in our ears, surely mere prudence, independent of all higher feelings, should induce the inhabitants of British America to rejoice that they still form a part of the noble Empire of Great Britain, under whose powerful protection their rights and liberties are secured to them, without their being involved in that momentous experiment, on the result of which our neighbours have all that is valuable to man at stake.

Therefore Mr. Bull, if you desire to retain your farms on this side of the lake, you will have no great difficulty in doing it, but then you must plainly remind Mrs. Bull that a great estate cannot be rendered productive without continued outlays. Your milk seekers lost you a fine property before, take care that your milk savers don't lead you into the same scrape now. If you do not think that the advantages you derive from supplying your out-farms with what they do not raise and supplying yourself from them with what you cannot raise, compensate for the expense of providing overseers &c. &c., then give them up in peace and leave them to shift for themselves ; but if you wish to retain these advantages, you must not begrudge paying the cost of them.

While you fed the overseers, things went on pretty smoothly, their authority was recognized, and all their efforts for the improvement of the property were cheerfully forwarded. But when you began to suck the calves instead of feeding them, they began to kick up their heels and splash mud instead of milk into the mouths of your half-starved bailiffs.

Now depend upon it this notable scheme of yours will never answer.

If the overseers are to continue your servants to take care of your interests, and to see that the regulations you make to secure the benefit of supplying these farms to yourself are adhered to, then you must continue to bear the expense of maintaining them. If they are not worth it, say so, and have done with them.

But independent of the preservation of your own authority, Mr. Bull, you owe something to your children whom you have encouraged to settle in Frogland, and who, by your indiscretion, have been subjected to the tyrannous caprices of Mrs. Bull Frog.

That vixen not content with the power which she has already usurped over the Bulls, wishes to dispossess them of the little protection which the trustees may afford to them, and has required you to allow the Frogs to name trustees. Now, as the appointment of them was secured to you by the marriage articles, exercise that right then not as the beldame wishes but as justice requires. Reconsider and amend them so as to secure to your own children those rights to which they are entitled, on every part of your property; let them not while dwelling in your own land, be subjected to those who voluntarily continue foreigners. The task is not an easy one, perhaps, but let the performance of it be confided to honest, intelligent and diligent men, and it will no doubt be accomplished; let no invidious distinctions be made, let all your children, whether by descent or adoption be admitted to a full participation of your paternal care and affection, but let no spurious feeling of liberality induce you to sacrifice your own family to those who abhor both you and them.

Comply, then, with Mrs. Bull-Frog's request to alter the marriage articles, but do it in a spirit which will make her feel that, " She seeks for justice more than she deserves."

18

LOUISA COLLINS,

Who died at MARGARETVILLE. 16th of Oct., 1834, aged 1 year and 5 months.

———

Sweet babe, into the room where thy little corpse now lies, wert thou borne each morning in the arms of thy mother or thy nurse, and when wearied even with so lovely a burthen they asked, "who will take the Baby?" how many kind voices exclaimed " I will, bring her to me," how many kind arms were extended to fondle and caress thee, and when thou didst draw back, cling round thy .mother's neck, and lay thy dear little head upon her bosom, thy sweet expressive smiling countenance, looked not a refusal but only said—and oh how plainly did those eyes bespeak thy feelings—" I love to be here."

But the question " Who will take the Baby?" has been put by a Voice we heard not, and He who said " Suffer little children to come unto me and forbid them not," has said, " I will." Let His Will be ever done, let no murmuring voice arise to dispute it. Dare we wish to snatch her back from Him who even here took little children in His arms and blessed them.

Perhaps the sweet little Angel Anna, who when thy feeble voice first expressed its moans in this world of pain and sorrow, so sweetly soothed thee,—perhaps she who first so fondly drew thee to the arms of thy earthly father, hovered over thy death bed, soothed thy dying agonies, and accompanied thy blessed Spirit in its flight to the Throne of thy Heavenly Father, for

> The World so calmly did'st thou leave
> So quietly thy Spirit fled,
> We watched to see thy bosom heave,
> When thou wer't numbered with the dead.

Let thy mourning mother remember that she is now the mother of three Angels, who may perhaps be employed by her Almighty Father to minister more to her happiness even here, than they ever could have done had they remained in this world; but however it may please Him to dispose of or employ them, of this she may be assured—and let that assurance be her consolation—they are happy, eternally happy, with Him and only through Him who died to purchase happiness for them.

THE following lines were suggested to the writer by reading Goldsmith's beautiful Poem of "The Traveller." He has had a few copies printed for circulation among his friends, whose partiality will induce them to view it favourably as the production of an

OCTOGENARIAN.

REFLECTIONS ON PASSING EVENTS.

A Pilgrim, wandering through this world of woe,
Struggling with sin and sorrow as I go,
Where sinful passions in our bosoms reign,
And sinful pleasures ever lead to pain :—
Where can the soul find comfort or relief?
Where safely seek a solace for its grief?
Where gain that peace for which it vainly yearns ?—
Until from earth's delusive joys it turns,
Fixes its thoughts on Thee, Great God of Heaven,
And seeks the bliss by Thee so freely given
To all who fly for refuge to Thy Son,
And say, what e'er betide, "Thy will be done."
"Where'er I roam, whatever change I see,"
May my glad heart for ever turn to Thee :
Still to my Saviour turn, with ceaseless praise,
And seek Thy guidance thro' life's devious ways.
    Blessed be that Book, which guides me to my God,
And makes my soul submissive to Thy rod ;
That teaches me that blessings ever flow
From Thee, e'en when they come in guise of woe.
O ! let me not, with vain presumption, dare
To doubt the wondrous truths it does declare,
Nor bring Thy mysteries to reason's test—
On which proud man would fainly have them rest.
He asks why Power Supreme permitted ill ?
And vainly asks, for none his doubts can still,—
Yet ill abounds, where'er he turns his eyes,
Thro' every region underneath the skies.
He seeks a remedy ;—Thy Blessed Word
Would turn the sinner to his dying Lord,—
Bids him a remedy for sin to see
In Him who bled on the accursed tree.
But faith, alone, o'er humble hearts bears sway,—
And the proud sceptic turns in scorn away,
While humble sinners listen to the call,
And cast their cares on Him who cares for all.

Thus humbly trusting in Thy Blessed Word,
And fearing only Thee, I look abroad
On the dread scenes which now assail our race,
And from all bosoms peace and comfort chase,—
Save those, who feel Thy Providence can still
Surpassing good produce from passing ill.
Amazed, we see a Christian host arrayed
To save the Turk from Russia's threatening blade.
Well-meaning but short-sighted men deplore
That Britain's sons their precious blood should pour
In such a cause. " No! let the accursed power
Of the False Prophet sink for evermore !"
But He who seeth not as man doth see—
He, from whose eyes all mists forever flee—
May, and we trust He will, our fears becalm,
And guided on by His Almighty Arm,
Our Christian hosts his Blessed Word may spread,
Where'er His arm that Christian host may lead.
Then, not alone, shall Mahomet be hurled
From that fair portion of our fallen world,
Which by his ruthless sword th' Imposter gained.—
But those sad errors which pure truth hath stained,
And both the Greek and Roman Church defile.
Shall draw a cleansing stream from Britain's Isle,
Where pious men of God in bands unite
To spread His Word e'en 'mid the raging fight.
For not alone the Soldier with his sword
Rushes to battle,—but Thy Holy Word,
A precious burthen, in his pack he bears,
To rouse his courage and to calm his cares.
Well tutored by its sacred lore, he knows
No fears while struggling with his country's foes.
If from the field in triumph he returns,
With Britain's glorious deeds his bosom burns ;
If death o'ertake him in the fearful strife,
The foeman's steel but opes the Gate of Life.
Thus Vicars felt—Vicars, the Soldier's friend—
Who, with his comrades, oft his prayers did blend ;
Daily, with them, he pours his soul to God,
'Till, in his Country's cause, he pours his blood.
No lingering agony his course impedes,—
Soon, freed from mortal coil, he upward speeds,

From fields of carnage in this world of woe,
Where peace and joy around God's Throne e'er flow.
What wondrous change then meets his ravished sight,
To fill the Christian Hero with delight !
No longer listening to War's dread alarms,
He sinks in glory in his Saviour's arms.
But when before, in War's disastrous train,
Went forth that priceless cure for all our pain ?—
When did we see the Ministers of Peace—
And may their blessed number soon increase—
'Mid want and suffering, gather in the Camp,
To sick and wounded men to show the lamp
Of God's own Word,—their saddest wounds to heal,
And to their souls the blessed truth reveal,
That the keen pains their bodies now endure
May of immortal souls produce the cure,
And all their sufferings may but blessings prove,
If they will turn them to the God of Love.
Say, thro' what source did He, Who works by means,
Send forth such comforts to those dismal scenes?
Yes, 'twas the work of His Almighty hand,
Which, years long passed, stirred up a little band
Of Christian men, His blessed Word to spread,
Of Christian men, now numbered with the dead ;
But e'er the hand of death had closed their eyes,
They looked, with grateful wonder and surprise,
At the vast work that little band had wrought,
Thro' Him whose favor and support they sought.
Long may that work His blessed aid receive,
'Till all mankind his blessed Word believe.
No note or comment from the pen of man,
They sought, to explain the great Creator's plan ;
Trusting on Him, they sent His Word abroad.
Pure as it issued from the lips of God.
That little band, now grown a mighty mass,
Striving each year the former to surpass
In works of love to bless the race of man,
And cause them thro' God's Word his works to scan,
Now to the battle field that Word they speed,
To soothe the soldier in his hour of need.
Strange it may seem such messenger to send—
Where blood and carnage on its steps attend ;

19

But wist ye not the blessed Prince of Peace
Declares the Christian warfare ne'er shall cease ;
Nor must the Christian warrior ever yield,
Or in the tempting court, or tented field.—
For in the court, or in the camp, 'tis meet
The Word of God should guide our wandering feet.
O ! that that blessed Word may do its work,
And reach the feelings of the sensual Turk !
O ! that its piercing truths with power may seek
The subtle bosom of the wily Greek !
That crowds of Christian converts soon may come
Forth from the darkness of benighted Rome :
And Turk, and Greek, and Roman, seek the Cross,
And learn all other gain is only loss !

    If 'tis His will—such blessings may ensue
From deeds which every human heart must rue ;
But tho' His good assume the shape of ill,
We bow submissive to His Holy Will.

    See yonder stalwart form, his mother's pride,
With manly step towards the foe now stride,
Into the thickest of the fight to dash :—
Alas ! he falls ! oh ! what a fearful gash !
The majesty of manhood now lies prone.—
One dreadful blow has brought that warrior down :
His comrades lift him from among the slain,
And bear him senseless to his tent again.
Say, does the sleep of death those eyelids close ?
Nay—he's but sinking in a fitful dose.—
For soon he lifts again his throbbing head,
And sees an angel kneeling at his bed.
What gentle hand is that which smoothes his brow,
And bathes his temple,—"Florence, is it thou ?
" Is it thy gentle step, which softly glides
" From couch to couch where misery resides.—
" Where mangled limbs and gaping wounds abound,
" And death, in direst form, is hovering round ?
" Thou ! born to wealth, to luxury and ease,
" How camest thou 'mid scenes of woe like these ?
" 'Twere fitter far thy menials should bestow
" Such toilsome care." Sweet Florence answers—" No—
" Tho' born to wealth, to luxury and ease,
" I feel my duty lies in scenes like these.

" Did not my Saviour quit the realms of Bliss
" To wander through a world of woe like this,
" To seek the wretched,—and has made us know,
" We please Him best, when we are soothing woe ?
" Does not my Sovereign, 'mid the cares of State,
" Feel deepest interest in the Soldier's fate,—
" Haste to the shore, to welcome his return ?
" And while with pain his fevered frame may burn.
" Her woman's heart pants to bestow relief,
" And sweetly sympathises in his grief ;
" And early was my youthful heart embued
" With the sweet 'luxury of doing good.' "
E'en so, fair Florence ;—yes, thy gentle heart
Has wisely fix'd upon that better part
Which Mary chose—which Jesus most approves—
And which should be the choice of all He loves.
Sweet Christian maid—devoted to His Cause—
Guiding thy steps by His most holy laws—
In that dread day, when all shall hear their doom,
Thy Saviour's smile from thee shall chase all gloom.
    But while on earth the Christian draws his breath,
Familiarised to scenes of war and death,
· He looks to Him, who good from evil draws,
And to His care confides his country's cause.
    Yes ! look to Him, and hush each murm'ring sound,
Nor fear no fitting leader can be found
To guide thy gallant sons against the foe,
And Britain's conquering standard once more shew.
He of a hundred fights has left the stage,
Mourned by his country, in a green old age,
By no long sickness to his couch confined.—
No powers impaired of body or of mind,
Ever intent on duty to the last,—
A few short hours—and all life's pains were past.
Who now shall lead our soldiers in the field ?
Who now the sword of Wellington shall wield ?
We hear exclaimed by some, with faltering voice :
The Christian answers, " Leave to God the choice."
Perish the thought that Britain's race is run,
And all her mighty deeds in arms are done !
No murm'ring voice, Britannia shouldst thou raise ;
Naught from thy lips should issue, but the praise

Of Him, who forced thy stubborn foes to flee,
And yield Sebastopol to France and thee.
'Tis true, before they fled, they made thee feel
That they were " foemen worthy of thy steel ;"
The more thy breast with gratitude should glow,
For such a triumph over such a foe.
Thy sons have shewn how Britons can endure
Both cold and hunger,—and of this be sure—
If further lesson must thy foe receive—
They soon shall learn what Britons can achieve.
When from the trenches to the open field—
Where boldest hearts to wisest heads oft yield—
They there shall learn, tho' Well ngton be dead,
His mantle o'er some British Chieftain spread
Shall proudly flow, each gallant heart to cheer,
And lead them on in Victory's career,—
Where future Wellingtons fresh laurels gain,
While future Nelsons triumph on the main.
Preserve the Faith for which thy martyrs died,
Nor fear that God a leader will provide ;
No lust of conquest does this hope inspire—
We fear not War, but Peace is our desire.
  Monarch of Russia ! clothed with such vast power—
Think, I beseech thee, of thy dying hour ;
Think of the agonising woe and pain
Which ever follow in War's dreadful train ;
And answer now, as answer then thou must,
If thou art fighting in a cause that's just.
Were but thy hapless country once relieved
From that sad legacy thy Sire bequeathed,
Of ruthless War,—and gentle Peace once more
Shed its soft influence from shore to shore,
No longer listening to ambition's voice,
But well directed to a better choice.
Thy savage hordes now striving to improve,
And teaching them both God and man to love :
Say, were not that a far more glorious plan
Than that long cherished by that wondrous man—
Half savage and half sage—his country's pride—
(O let him not remain his country's guide).
Let not his lust of conquest still prevail,
Which leads thee every neighbour to assail.

Thy power extending o'er a world so wide,
From Neva's banks to Amoor's mighty tide,
Might well suffice.   Then be it thy desire,
With love of peace and knowledge to inspire
The millions who are placed beneath thy sway,
Nor add to those who now thy will obey.
But mildly strive to soften each rude heart—
To spread and cultivate each peaceful art ;
Teach them their savage passions to subdue,)
And the bright path of science to pursue,   }
This were a God-like work for man to do.   )
    Oh ! that War's trumpet its sad blasts might cease,
And Europe's sons once more might rest in peace :
But let not British blood be spilt in vain,
Nor heroes fall, a treacherous truce to gain.
If Muscovy does really rue the hour
When she defied both France and England's power ;
If her brave sons at length have learnt to feel
That vainly they contend against their steel,—
And real Peace again its head uprear,
Blessing alike the Peasant and the Peer,—
Then welcome, oh ! how welcome were the voice
Of smiling Peace,—then should all hearts rejoice ;—
Princes and People, then their thanks should raise,
And to the King of Kings give all the praise.
    But what dark cloud is that we now descry,
Casting its shadow o'er the western sky,
And lowering as it points to Britain's shore,
As if the trump of war might blow once more ;
Calling Britannia's and Columbia's sons,
Against each others breasts to point their guns ?
O ! can it be, Columbia, that thy sword
To Russia's Despot now will aid afford ?
Why do thy freeborn sons, alas ! appear
Inclined to aid a tyrant's mad career ?
Is it that tyrants in thine own loved soil,
Afric's dark sons of freedom still despoil ?
'Twas a sad legacy that did remain,
When valiantly thou didst thy freedom gain
From British rule, which Britain to thee left,
Of men, whom she of freedom had bereft ;
But she has long wiped off the shameful stain.

Whilst thou art lengthening the dreadful chain
To regions where the freeborn red man's race
Then sought support and pleasure in the chase.
That hapless race, yielding to His decree,
Which dooms the savage from the sage to flee,
Hath left that fertile region in thy hand
That thou mightst there fulfil the great command—
Increase and multiply man's race on earth—
But let not that fair land to slaves give birth.
If, in the sickly South, fair freedom pine,
And the poor slave must there all hope resign
Of his chain loosening 'till he sink in death—
Taint not the western breeze with slavery's breath.
    Sons of the North, whose earliest breath was drawn
Where first your country's freedom had its dawn.
Be ye united in one gallant band,
From slavery's curse to save Nebraska's land.
Will not your pilgrim sires start from their graves.
If ye shall people such a land with slaves?
Oh! would those men, who this sad course pursue,
Think of the day when they that course may rue!
When looking up from that dire gulf below,
Which parts them from the sainted soul of Stowe,
How will they then lament, her thrilling tale
Of misery (which ever must prevail
Where slavery uprears its cursed head),
Did not on their hard hearts its influence shed,
Ere they were doomed for evermore to dwell,
The slaves of Satan, in the realms of Hell.
But think not, friends of freedom, I would urge,
(Much as I may deplore this cruel scourge
Still stains your land), that ye the sword should draw
Against your brethren;—may that blessed law,
Which binds thy States in one confederate band,
The rudest shock of discord still withstand.   (1)
Let not thy fields be stained by civil war,
The direst ill which man on man can draw ;
Still strive in peace that evil to remove,
And leave the issue to the God of Love.
    Farewell, Columbia ! This my parting prayer—
That all whose hearts the Saxon blood may share,
May live in peace, and harmony, and love,

And only strive each other to improve.
"And now my humble muse would spread her wing,
"Softly where Britain courts the eastern spring,
"Where every peasant boasts his rights to scan,
"And learns to venerate himself as man."
Land of the Free, where floats on every gale
An air too pure for slavery to inhale,—
The darkest slave that e'er left Afric's shore,
Once touch thy soil and he's a slave no more,—
Spurning alike his master and his chain,
And praising God, he stands erect again.
True he may feel the doom of man, for there
Of thorns and thistles earth must have its share ;
And he, alas ! may daily learn to know
Man's bread is bought by labour of his brow :
But still, however scanty be his fare,
He proudly feels no lordly master dare
Against the freeman raise his cruel hand,
Nor threat the lash shall fall at his command.
"True, he may see some palace raise its head,
"To shame the meanness of his humble shed,—
"And costly lords the sumptuous banquet deal,
"To make him loathe his vegetable meal ;"
Yet even then, the soothing thought delights,
That all around are bless'd with equal rights,—
The proud man's castle, and the poor man's cot—
However different may be their lot,
This consolation may the owners draw
That both may claim the care of England's Law.
And tho' the brawling demagogue declare—
All are entitled to an equal share
Of this world's goods—he knows the task were vain
To strive such dangerous doctrine to maintain.
Enough for him, that on fair freedom's soil
Each may enjoy the fruit of his own toil ;
This England's boast—her equal laws secure
Alike the property of rich and poor,—
Altho', as erst her sweetest bard confessed—
"Some are, and must be, greater than the rest."
In that blest land, may order long prevail,
And vainly may the demagogue assail
That glorious fabric, which, from age to age,

Has been improved by statesman and by sage ;
Still vainly strive to part the Church and State
And from their stations drive the good and great :
Long may all orders in the realm be seen
To join in prayer for our beloved Queen.
May every virtue which adorns a throne,
Victoria's royal bosom ever own,
And all that could an humbler station grace.
Glow in her breast and beam upon her face.
Her God to honour and Her people bless,
Be the first wishes which her heart possess !
May She of those insidious wiles beware,
And guard her subjects from the dangerous snare,
With whioh Rome strives the heedless to entrap.
And once more seat them in its dangerous lap.
May those fair Isles which own her gentle sway,
Never again the Papal power obey.
Could Erin's gallant sons be once released
From the debasing tyranny of priests,
And stand erect in Erin's fertile Isle,
Then peace and plenty round each cot would smile ;
No longer bowing down to Priest or Pope,
But on the Saviour placing all their hope,—
Learning His will from His most Holy Word,
From which, alas ! they've been so long debarred.
Then Celt and Saxon kneeling at one shrine,
Would offer up joint prayers for thee and thine.
And the deluders and deluded share
The supplication of that earnest prayer.   (2).

        Be it the love of power, or love of pelf,
That prompts the priest to turn upon himself
That reverence which to God alone is due,
Oh ! may that gracious God his heart renew !
Reclaim him from the error of his ways,
To teach his flock their God alone to praise.
Nor longer pour the ill-directed prayer
To Saints, who once were fellow-sinners here !
Would their warm hearts to that pure Church were led,
Which owns Victoria as its temporal head,
Whose beauteous liturgy a prayer provides
For all the ills which human life betides,
In that plain language which all understand,

Throughout the length and breadth of Britain's land!
Over that Church may Sumner long preside,
His precepts teach, and his example guide
Prelate and priest God's Sacred Word to search,
Nor for the Saviour substitute the Church.

    Daughter of Edward! such the warm desire
Of one who knew and loved thy Royal Sire!
What tho' his martial discipline was stern
Himself submitted to each rule in turn,—
But when from his stern duties he sought rest,
No kinder heart ere beat in human breast,—
No tale of woe was poured in Edward's ear,
But ever found a ready listener there :—
Witness, when down his manly cheek the tear
Flowed freely, Thomas, on thy mournful bier ;   (3).
Witness, when that sad catalogue of grief,
Which overpowered thee, Goldsmith sought relief,
How readily he did relief extend,
And to thy dying hour remained thy friend.
Long were the tale to tell of all the good,
Which from that royal hand so freely flowed.

    Tho' fourscore years have cooled my youthful blood,
Thanks to the gracious Giver of all good
I still, in age, His mercies can enjoy,—
Still, in His service, would my hours employ.
With friends, and family, and plenty, blest,
And waiting calmly, till I sink to rest
In those kind arms, where sinners seek repose
When all life's anxious cares in death shall close.
Oft on my early years does memory dwell,
Reminding me of one I loved so well,—
Thy faults, thy virtues, rising to my mind,
Nor to the one nor to the other blind,—
I bring this tribute from the shrine of truth,—
To Thee, the Friend and Patron of my youth.
   20

NOTES.

(1.)

ALTHOUGH I infinitely prefer the construction of society in England to that which prevails in America, and think that respect for those who are born to high station quite consistent with manly self-respect in those who pay it, while it generally stimulates those who receive it to cultivate the high and honorable feelings which dignify our race and extend their influence to all classes of society, I am not so blinded by my attachment to the noble institutions of my own country, as to be insensible to what is admirable and praiseworthy elsewhere.

The circumstances under which civilized succeeded to savage life in America, precluded the establishment of an order of nobility there; and any attempt to introduce one, either at the termination of the Revolutionary War, or at any time before or since, would have been impracticable and absurd.

If America were cut off from all communication with the rest of the civilized world, she would feel the want of such an order very sensibly, and would probably find that she had purchased her plethoric liberty at the expense of the loss of most of the refinements of life :—but that communication has ever subsisted. The ocean, so far from dividing mankind from each other, now rapidly facilitates their intercourse; and though separate governments will probably long continue to exist, man is daily becoming more familiarised with man and each country may borrow from the other much of good, and alas! much of evil too.

Viewing, then, the American Confederation, without reference to my predilections as a British subject, and considering the circumstances under which it was formed, I cannot but entertain great respect for those who framed it. It was a noble attempt to regulate social intercourse and to increase social happiness, with the slightest possible interference with individual liberty, and I heartily wish them success in the great experiment which they are trying—to preserve and diffuse the principles of self-government throughout the extensive region over which they now exercise some authority. Difficulties, great difficulties, they unquestionably have to encounter, and as their numbers increase, these difficulties, it may be feared, will increase with them; the turbulent and the lawless may require a stronger force than law to control them, and that force may clothe the ambitious with power to violate liberty. But let them not despond,—they are growing up under their institutions, and may learn to enlarge or contract the power of those who govern as circumstances may require. Much, oh! how much, is involved in the preservation of that Confederation. While it subsists, the conflicting interests of the different States will continue to be the subject of discussion in the national and state Councils, and the dread appeal to the sword will not desolate the fertile fields of North America, and spread misery there, as it has lately done among the families of Europe. I envy not that man his feelings, who can look upon the result of this experiment of self-government, which so many millions of our Saxon brethren are making, without wishing them success. Would that Europe could secure its inhabitants against the recurrence of the horrors of war, by some institution similar to that of the American Confederation. But of that, alas! there is little prospect. America has my best wishes for the perservation of her Congress,—not for the good that it has done, but for the evil that it may prevent.

Independent of those generous feelings which human beings should feel for the welfare of the human race, Britons may contemplate the prosperity and unexampled progress of America with some glow of pride. From us they have inherited their love of freedom and their spirit of enterprise,—from us they learnt to reconcile the preservation of order with the preservation of liberty,—and though with them, as with the manly race from whom they are descended, order is sometimes endangered,

> " And by the bonds of nature feebly held,
> Minds combat minds, repelling and repelled,
> Ferments arise, contending factions roar,
> Repressed ambition struggles round the shore,
> 'Till overwrought, the general system feels
> Its motions stop—or phrenzy fire the wheels."*

Yet, when the danger appears imminent, the friends of order, in both countries, somehow regain their influence and preserve their institutions. To what is this owing, but to that combination of the love of freedom and order, which pervades both countries to a greater extent than it can be found elsewhere? Prior to the revolution, each of the thirteen Colonies possessed a constitution, as similar as circumstances would permit, to that of the Mother Country,—and the Colonies were accustomed to self-government. Subsequent to the Revolution, they retained the same forms, though the source of power was transferred from the Crown to the People, Yet, notwithstanding this important change, the love of freedom, that it in some measure rendered exorbitant, did not annihilate the love of order, which had previously co-existed with it, although the latter occasionally received some rude shocks. It still, however, exists, and exercises much influence throughout the Continent of North America. A remarkable instance of this occurred in the recent settlement of California—where the gold mines attracted a crowd of lawless, reckless men, whose atrocities soon astounded all who heard of them. It was generally supposed that nothing but a military force could have reduced such a set of miscreants to any approach to order,—but in much less time than could have been supposed possible, civil tribunals were established, and gradually extended protection to life and property, without the intervention of military power.

---

* Goldsmith's Traveller.

While every attempt that foreigners have made in Europe and South America to imitate our Institutions, has hitherto proved abortive, we see our descendants in North America extending our language and our laws from the Atlantic to the Pacific. Ought not, then, the parent to be proud of the child—and the child to be proud of the parent? May the demon of discord fail in every effort to tempt the Anglo-Saxon race to draw their swords upon each other.

(2.)

Yes? Let our prayers, our earnest prayers be offered up for our deluded fellow subjects who still profess the Religion of the Church of Rome. There are some who think that Religion is not a term that should be applied to that Church—but I am not of that number. Amongst its members have ever been found men whose doctrines and whose deeds evinced that they were real Christians; and I trust there are many, at this hour, who look through the mummery of its forms, and the multitude of its Saints, to that Saviour through whom alone cometh salvation. But this is not the general tendency of the teaching of the Church of Rome; the truths of the Gospel have been gradually overlaid with so many forms and ceremonies, some harmless and some hurtful, and it accords so much more with the feelings of our fallen nature, to prefer superstitious rites to pure, spiritual worship, that the great mass of her members, particularly the lower classes, rest in these forms alone. To them vital religion is a stranger; they place the safety of their souls in the safe keeping of the Priest, and deem that a rigid compliance with the dictates of the Church may be substituted for that purity of heart and practice which Christianity enjoins. The power of the Priest over those who labor under this delusion is unlimited, and greatly endangers civil as well as religious liberty.

Let us not lay the flattering unction to our souls that, in these enlightened days, there is no risk of our becoming again subject to the tyranny and torture of the dark ages. Rome still grasps eagerly at power. Witness the daring act by which England was divided into Papal Sees? Look at the Concordat between the Pope and the Emperor of Austria, which places the Protestant subjects of the Emperor at the mercy of Papal tribunals! And suppose not that we are secure because we have our own Representatives to protect us from such an outrage. It was asserted, many years ago, in the *Quarterly Review*, that the power of Popes and Priests might become more dangerous under a Representative Government, than it had ever yet been; that, while Kings and Princes were the depositaries of civil power, Rome courted them, and ruled through them. But Kings and Princes were not all equally submissive, and sometimes contended successfully for the preservation of their rights. But, when authority emanated from the masses, the Priests would no longer court, but command; and it would remain for them to dictate to their deluded followers who should be selected for our lawgivers, and what laws such lawgivers should make. Do we not see symptoms of a realization of this prediction on both sides of the Atlantic ?

These observations are made with no spirit of hostility to my Roman Catholic fellow-subjects; for their sakes as well as our own, I wish they were liberated from the thraldom which endangers both. They do not appear aware of the immunity they enjoy where the civil power is in the hands of Protestants. They may slavishly submit, if they choose, to the dictation of their Priests, in all matters civil and religious, but they cannot be *compelled* to do so. Should the spirit of enquiry be raised in them, they may open a Bible without being consigned to a dungeon for so doing; or, if they think the candidate for whom the Priest orders them to vote not so well qualified as his opponent, they may exercise their franchise as they may judge best. Whether they or we may be allowed either privilege, if the Priests directly or indirectly unite all civil and religious power in themselves, admits of little doubt. Dungeons, as dark and deep as those in which the Madai were incarcerated, can be sunk whenever priestly power prevails. They have been emancipated by Protestant Legislatures from all civil disabilities, and never again may Protestants attempt to secure their own religious liberty by violating that of others. Never more may recourse be had to penal statutes, which can have no other effect upon high-minded men than to raise a spirit of resistance, and make them cling closer to a cause which, while so assailed, they would deem it dishonorable to desert. But should not all the friends of vital Christianity, however they may differ upon minor points, unite to aid the efforts that are now making to enlighten our Roman Catholic brethren, and convince them of the dangerous errors of the Church of Rome, by circulating the Scriptures among them in the language they understand? The Priests will doubtless use every art to counteract this pious effort, for their own power must fall before an open Bible. But let us trust that prayer and perseverance will overcome all difficulties, and that the blessing of God will finally rest upon those who give and those who take His holy Word.

(3.)

Lieutenant Thomas was the son of a respectable loyalist, who, by the recommendation of His Royal Highness the late Duke of Kent, obtained a commission in the Royal Fusiliers. He possessed much of His Royal Highness's confidence and esteem, and was well worthy of it. While in command of a party in search of deserters, the accidental discharge of a brother Officer's pistol gave him a wound which occasioned his death. His Royal Highness was affected even to tears, when informed of the melancholy event.

Poor Goldsmith,—nephew of Oliver, and son of Henry,—to whom "The Traveller" was addressed, had served with credit, during the American Revolution, in the 54th regiment. He was a warm-hearted Irishman, and had formed an inconsiderate marriage with a lady of great beauty but no money, and, on the termination of the war, felt it necessary to sell his commission, and devoted what remained of the money it produced, after payment of his debts, to the erection of mills in New Brunswick, which, with his energy and perseverance would have afforded a comfortable maintenance for himself and family; but, just as he had completed an expensive dam, he unfortunately fell upon a broad axe, and received a desperate wound, which confined him to his bed for weeks. In the absence of the master's eye the work was neglected, and the autumnal rains swept away the dam before it was completed and rendered secure, as it would have been but for this untimely accident. Upon his recovery he set to work with great energy to rebuild the dam. Scarcely was it completed when the mill took fire, it was reduced to ashes, and he was reduced to ruin.

When these accumulated misfortunes reached the Duke's ear, although the sufferer was a stranger to him, the tale went to his heart. He sent for him to Halifax—found him ready and willing to exert himself to the utmost in any honest way—appointed him, first, an assistant Engineer in the works then going on here, and, subsequently, procured for him an appointment in the Commissariat which gave him a comfortable subsistence, and befriended him throughout his life.

Indeed, it was an admirable trait in His Royal Highness's character, that, unless compelled by their misconduct, he never forsook any whom he had befriended. He was lenient even to their faults, unless they involved a breach of military discipline—there he was ever strict.